THE FINEST LIES

David J. Naiman

ISBN: 978-1-7375036-1-3

First Edition Empire Old Line Media 2021

www.empireolm.wordpress.com

For my children, Andrew and Maddie, siblings extraordinaire

and my dear sisters, Beverly and Heidi

PART ONE

NICOLE: MORNING

CHAPTER 1

"What could possibly be wrong?"

Nicole was so done with her brother it wasn't even funny. She stomped up the stairs, hitting every step with the maximum force to express how annoyed she was. If her mom hadn't already left for work, she would have called Nicole dramatic—and said it *dramatically*, bathing in that classic parental brew of irony and hypocrisy.

But Nicole didn't think she was dramatic so much as rightfully expressing the unfairness of it all. Why should she be the one to go upstairs? Yes, she'd been watching her videos on the downstairs TV since she'd rolled out of bed to walk the dog, but did Jay need the TV now, right now, right when she was so obviously still using it?

After flopping onto the comfy chair

upstairs, Nicole rolled her eyes at the boxy TV facing her. She wondered why they even bothered to plug it in, seeing as how nobody used it. The upstairs TV was a relic compared with the downstairs flat-screen TV. That was the theme in this house. A few nice things they got back when her parents actually made new purchases surrounded by ancient things from the last decade, patched together by duct tape and admonitions to *please be careful!*

Nicole pulled out her phone, but before she could cue up her videos, the TV sputtered and a fuzzy image of a peculiar man appeared on the screen. His eyes widened and sparkled. "Would you like a brand new brother?" a voice-over boomed. "Call now!" Above his head, the words CALL NOW flashed in golden lettering. At the bottom of the screen, a phone number scrolled.

Nicole located the remote and mashed her thumb into it, but she couldn't turn off the TV. The same image and phone number persisted on every station. Nicole hadn't the slightest doubt this was all, somehow, her brother's doing. An impressive trick, she had to admit, but she was not going to tolerate his messing with her.

Leaning forward, Nicole prepared to race downstairs, to tell Jay a thing or two, to let him have it as she should have done yesterday. But when her fingers brushed against her phone, a thought popped into her head. It expanded into an idea, frightful and thrilling, displacing her anger with vindication, intensifying the more she mulled it over.

Maybe I should call, Nicole thought. *A brand new brother sounds perfect.*

"That's it. New and improved! Call now."

Nicole smiled, sensing a personal connection as though this commercial spoke directly to her. She cradled her phone in her hands. A fingertip flicked across the screen without her even needing to concentrate. Her phone had long ago become an appendage, as integral as a foot or a kidney.

After Nicole entered the number, her finger hovered above the dial icon. Something held her back, but she couldn't imagine what it could be. She might have guessed self-preservation had she any means to gauge the lurking danger. Had she any inkling her impetuous nature would fix her on a chaotic course beyond her control.

She did want a new brother. As long as he wasn't like Jay, who always said things to upset her and never did what she wanted him to do. She thrust aside her unease and tapped the icon. Instead of a ring, Nicole heard more of a choking sound, a gasp as if someone strangled.

"Hello, Nicole. Are you ready to change your life?"

The voice on her phone was identical to the voice-over in the commercial. Nicole figured this guy must own the company or something. "Maybe," she said. The man on the TV screen stared at her while she spoke. Nicole leaned to the left and right, and the man's face tracked her each time. She hesitated. "How much does it cost?"

"Do you mean money? Oh, no. It won't cost you any money. Not one cent. But there is a cost."

"What is it?"

"Nothing for you to worry about, my dear. Nothing at all. Your satisfaction is guaranteed or your money back."

"That seems fair. Wait, I thought you said —"

"Now, now. Don't worry about a thing. We'll simply replace your brother with a better one. This offer doesn't come around every day. It is, to be candid, a once-in-a-lifetime opportunity." The man on the TV winked but not subtly. His head dipped so low that his oversized hat nearly slid off. "Decide quickly. Supplies are running out."

The words CALL NOW lit up in a sickly yellow, casting a jaundiced glow across the face of the eccentric man with the whimsical hat and sparkling eyes.

"Then yes! What do I have to do?"

The man lifted his head. His lips gave a twitch. The voice answered, "Nothing more, nothing more. You've done it! Congratulations, my dear. Call the same number if your new brother malfunctions, and I'll send an attendant straight away." When he disconnected, the TV flicked itself off and Nicole heard her father's voice.

"Nic, come downstairs, please. Jay has something he wishes to say."

When Nicole arrived, she sagged with disappointment. Her brother looked the same. Same broad chest. Same confident grin. Stupid, worthless commercial. At least it didn't cost her any money.

"I'm sorry, Nic," Jay said. "I only wanted to use the TV to kick you out. That was wrong of me. Please take the remote and accept my apology."

Nicole stared open-mouthed. Jay appeared the same, his voice sounded the same, but this was not her brother. Sweet.

"Thanks," she said.

He handed her the remote, flashed the kindest smile she had seen from him in years, and left the room. Nicole watched her videos in utter bliss. Once she was caught up, she decided to check on this new brother of hers. If he was going to be awesome, she might as well be friendlier. As she made her way upstairs, she thought about the number on her phone and doubted she would ever need to call it again.

Her brother's door was ajar. Walking closer, she heard him chewing on something, maybe granola given all the crunching. She pushed the door open and stepped inside. Robot Jay took another bite of his phone and looked up at her. Metal and plastic bits ground together. He chewed slowly, savoring every morsel.

"Everything all right, my wonderful sister?" When she didn't answer, he popped the rest of the device in his mouth and licked his fingers clean.

"Sure," Nicole said, backing out of his room. "What could possibly be wrong?"

CHAPTER 2

*"Deference produces
quite an appetite."*

Nicole darted into her room and pressed her back against the closed door. Her fingers trembled as she brought up her Recents and tapped the number.

"Customer service, the honorable Phineas Lindencroft presiding." Nicole recognized the same flighty voice from the commercial. Except now she detected an edge to it she hadn't noticed before, a baleful glint scraping the polished surface. "To whom shall I direct your compliments?"

"Compliments? I think you mean complaints."

"My *dear* Nicole," he said, emphasizing the word *dear* as though jamming the thing with his heel to squash a pesky insect. "I am as sure of my words as I am standing in the mirror next to you."

Nicole pivoted to face the same man from the commercial, who now appeared crisp, awash in vivid color. She lowered her phone as she scrutinized him, unsure what to make of his wobbly frame or his bright blue suit, which shimmered as though saturated with the infant stars of a nebula. His baggy garment hung over his shoulders yet contracted puzzlingly at the elbows and waist. Topping all this was a sleek felted hat with a wide brim. Tufts of hair extruded above each ear like an overgrown thicket. He held his head with majestic authority, but she didn't think much of his bulbous nose or scraggly face.

The man was an oddball all right. But when Nicole met his gaze, he held her rapt. His eyes twinkled with every twitch as though each pupil had captured an unsuspecting galaxy within. All at once, she imagined billions of souls howling from billions of lightyears away. She drew back, unsettled by staggering anguish and despair. Phin blinked and the sensation passed. Nicole shook it off.

"Nothing delights me more than to serve you," he said and tipped his hat.

"Um. What was your name again?"

"Phineas Lindencroft, but you may call me Phin. I find the moniker conveys a warm glow, like that of a benevolent uncle."

"Maybe I should call you Uncle Phin."

Phin stiffened. "Don't be daft! Uncle Phin was my grandfather."

"Riiiight," she said, stretching the syllable as one tends to do while wondering if they are speaking with a crazy person. "You told me to call back if my new brother malfunctions?"

"A malfunction!" Phin expelled a hearty laugh. "Improbable. He's a BroBot 3000. Top of the line, I'll have you know. Was he rude? Surly? Did he try to get his way?"

"No."

"Did he make fun of your hair?"

"No. Wait, what's wrong with my hair?"

"I don't understand." Phin thrust his palms in the air with such gusto, his suit jacket bulged at his shoulders, eclipsing his ears. "In what way did he malfunction?"

"I caught him eating electronics," she said, waving her phone at him.

Phin lowered his arms. He dragged a nail across the scratchy part of his neck. Finally, he nodded, and his previous grin returned. "And."

"And? And nothing. He was eating electronics."

"My dear girl. A BroBot's got to eat. Deference produces quite an appetite."

Nicole gripped her phone, sensing the danger. "But he's going to eat up all the electronics in the house."

"Don't worry." Phin flicked his wrist,

shooing away her concern. "He eats other things. He won't starve."

"No, I'm—I'm not worried about him *starving*. I'm worried about him eating up all the electronics in the house!"

A lopsided smile wriggled across Phin's face the way a three-legged dog might cross an icy pond. "Ah. Looking out for number one. Excellent. That will make the last part of today so much easier."

"What's the last part?"

"All in due time, my dear Nicole. These things mustn't be rushed. Now, let us focus on your current predicament. I shall send an attendant straight away. The first order of business is to intensify BroBot's enthusiasm for complimenting your hair."

Nicole placed her hands squarely on her hips. This ridiculous man would not get the better of her. "Has anyone ever called you frustrating?"

"No, but I've been called the Baron of Balderdash."

"I'll bet you have."

"And the Comptroller of Claptrap. And the Dean of Drivel."

"Ugh. You're going to be the death of me."

Phin raised an eyebrow. "What tipped you off?"

"Huh?"

"Relax. You worry too much. Your

problems will all be solved by the day's end. Have I ever steered you wrong?"

Nicole considered this. "I'm starting to think so."

"Oh. Then perhaps you shouldn't listen to me." Phin tapped his chin. "That is quite a conundrum."

"Yeah, you're the Captain of Conundrums."

"Am I?" Phin beamed. "Thank you, Nicole. I shall add it to my archive of appellations."

Nicole backed up a step and veered from one leg to the other before settling back where she started. Phin observed her frustrated shifting with the curious detachment of a spectator at a flea circus. Finally, she spoke. "I did not mean it as a compliment."

"Perhaps not, but I took it as one. And now it's mine." Phin's wicked smile broadened. He tilted forward until his forehead pressed against the glass. "It's mine forever, and you may not have it back."

CHAPTER 3

*"I know your handwriting
well, dear sister."*

Phin's image dissolved with a spark, leaving Nicole to stare at her horrified expression reflected in the mirror. "What is wrong with you?" she bellowed. Nicole yanked open her door only to find her father staring at her with a patient, worried expression.

"Nothing is wrong with you, Nic. You're great just the way you are."

"No, I, uh—thanks, Dad."

Her father forced a smile. "I have news you'll enjoy. The two-hour delay has officially become a snow day."

"It's finally snowing?"

"Barely, but they're predicting six to eight inches," Dad said. "I'll believe that when I see it. You know how things work around here. The mere threat of snow is enough to create mass panic across the state of Maryland."

Nicole groaned. "Yes, Dad. Not like when you were a kid in Maine, where they expected you to tunnel home through three feet of snow."

"Ha! We would close for blizzards. This is a dusting. There isn't even an inch out there." Dad stretched his back. "Anyway, have you walked Scruffy yet?"

"First thing this morning."

"Excellent. Do you have any homework?"

Nicole froze. Homework on a snow day? The mere proposal assailed the laws of nature. She half expected lightning to strike him down. "I have a math packet. That's it."

"Please get it done. I'm not sure when Mom is coming home. Her shift at the hospital ends in the afternoon, but she may need to stay late if the snow picks up. As for me, you'll be happy to know that a new client contacted me, so I'll be working downstairs in my office today. We'll break for lunch. Maybe later, we can throw snowballs?"

An awkward silence followed.

"Come on, Nic. Don't tell me you're too old to play in the snow with your dad because you're in high school. We're going to be cooped up in the house all day. What do you say?" He opened his arms wide.

"I'll think about it. See you at lunch?"

"Right, got it." His arms fell to his sides.

"See you then."

Dad left, and his voice bellowed down the hallway. "Jay. The snow day is official. Do you have any homework?"

"Doing it now."

"Really? Wow, you are on the ball today."

Nicole huffed the huff of the perennially put out. Reliably on the ball was more her thing than Jay's. Stupid BroBot. She pulled out her math packet, but her phone dinged before she could start, and she got caught up in a group text. Maintaining a sustained cheerfulness with her friends exhausted her, especially when she had algebra to do. She didn't mind the math. Math was her best subject, the academic area where she most excelled. Not that her parents made a big deal about it considering Jay did well in every subject.

Oh, right, she remembered. *The BroBot 3000.*

Nicole brought her packet to Jay's room and knocked on the door.

"Please come in, my wonderful sister."

She entered and found the bot sitting on the floor, a pen in each hand, writing two essays simultaneously. The handwriting resembled Jay's but neater. He wrote at a steady pace, not even pausing when he spoke.

"You'll be pleased to know that the attendant has brought me up to code per your specifications. Your hair shimmers pleasingly in the light."

"Um, thanks, I guess." Nicole instinctively fluffed her hair until she realized what she was doing. "Can you help me with this?"

The robot stopped writing one of the essays and took the packet from her. "Absolutely. I'll have it done in a few minutes."

"No! Don't write on it."

"No need to worry. I know your handwriting well, dear sister."

Nicole's phone dinged, and she looked down. She had gotten behind on the group text. As usual, all the girls were competing for attention from Brandi. The more Nicole scrolled, the more her anxiety flushed. She was still well-positioned but needed to focus if she wished to stay on top.

"Yeah, sure," she said, punctuating her brush-off by fluttering her fingers. "Go ahead." Nicole concentrated on the group text. She had entered high school as Brandi's bestie and would not allow these upstarts from the other middle school to take advantage of her recent humiliation to knock her off her BFF status. Her thumbs tapped furiously while Robot Jay wrote his essay with one hand and completed her math packet with the other.

After a few minutes, he told her he had finished. Nicole put her phone down and flipped through the packet. She had to admit that he had done a fantastic job: all problems solved, all work shown, and all completed in her handwriting as promised. He had saved her at least a half-hour. Her new brother was impressive. Although she wished he would chew more quietly. It sounded as if he was eating granola again.

She looked up with a start and shrieked. The BroBot stopped chewing. They both stared at her phone, which had a bite-sized piece missing from a corner. He raised an eyebrow while Nicole hyperventilated. Finally, the bot came to an understanding and, snapping her phone in two, offered her the longer piece.

"Where are my manners? I am pleased to share." He popped his portion in his mouth while presenting hers on his palm as though displaying it on a silver platter.

Nicole grabbed the remainder of her phone and pressed it with her thumb in a futile attempt to turn it on. Instead, a single plume of smoke rose from the top.

Robot Jay spoke between crunches. "Is something the matter?"

"Stay here," Nicole commanded.

"Certainly, dear sister." The bot smiled warmly, exposing bright metal and plastic slivers between his teeth.

CHAPTER 4

"Prepare to be dazzled!"

Nicole stormed back to her room and stared at her reflection in the full-length mirror. Her hair sure was tangled this morning. *No, stop that, stay focused.* She tried to dial the number on her half phone and yelped with frustration.

"How am I supposed to contact you now?" The mirror had no response. "Phin!"

Phin appeared before her in profile. He fixed his hat and shifted to face her. "Ah, you have arrived with another compliment."

"Complaint. It's pronounced—skip it. Look what BroBot did to my phone." Nicole lifted the piece for him to see, shaking it furiously as if her severed phone was a rolled-up magazine and Phin was a naughty dog. Not that she would ever strike Scruffy.

From deep within his pocket, Phin

produced a monocle attached to a chain. "How curious," he said, squinting through the monocle at her phone. "What an odd shape for a bite."

"He didn't bite it. He snapped it in half."

Phin let the lens slip from his fingers. "In anger?"

"Well, no. He was splitting it with me."

"Ah." Phin lifted the monocle by its chain and dropped it into his pocket. "That was generous of him, wouldn't you say?"

Nicole seethed. "No, I would not say. I would say he took a bite out of my phone. And snapped my phone in half. He *destroyed my phone*!"

"So he has," Phin agreed. "Although if you had desired a different outcome, you might not have left your phone within reach of a hungry robot."

"You—" Nicole jerked her fist in the air until she regained her composure. She took a deep breath and started again, deliberate and determined. "You sent an attendant. He said he was up to code."

"Did he forget to compliment your hair?"

"Enough about my hair! We didn't have school today and my hair's a mess!" Nicole stamped her foot. "I am losing my patience."

"I'd be happy to help you find it. Where did you see it last?"

Nicole glared at Phin. She could not understand how he could be so dense, how he could fail to grasp the magnitude of the havoc he had unleashed. She would have to sound it out for him. "I. Need. My. Phone."

"Of course you do," Phin said, sprouting his slippery half-grin. "How else can you text Brandi about how stunning and fantastic she is or how any boy would be fortunate to have a fleeting flash of her attention? My dear Nicole, I am mystified by your need to be friends with someone who requires constant ego-stroking. Brandi strikes me as an emotional tyrant and a most disagreeable person."

"You—you don't understand," she sputtered. "It's not like that."

"Isn't it?"

"Ugh!" Nicole glared at his grin, now fully formed and widening by the second. "You're one to talk about disagreeable people. I think you are the most disagreeable person in the entire world."

"Preposterous!" Phin said. "I doubt I'm even in the top ten."

Nicole let the remnant of her phone drop to the floor. She stumbled backward until she landed on her bed, cradling her head in her hands.

"Please. Let's not quarrel," Phin said. "Something else is required to satisfy, and I believe I have the solution. I can activate a setting on the BroBot 3000 that will provide external sustenance so he will not need to eat while in your house."

Nicole looked up with a start. "Then turn it on!"

"Certainly. But do understand, this is a premium setting, so I will need to levy a cost."

With a heavy sigh, Nicole stood up and walked over to the mirror. "I thought you said there would be no charge."

"Do you mean money? Oh, no. I'm not interested in money. What I desire has a much greater value. An irreplaceable value. One which will be mine before the day is through."

His grin took her breath away. "Wait, what is that supposed to mean?"

Phin twirled his hand, each long finger fanning out in a hypnotic wave-like pattern. "It was but a trivial remark. Pay it no heed." Nicole remained skeptical. She considered then resisted a faint but distressing sensation that a more sinister motive lurked beneath Phin's flaky charisma. "I am merely the Harbinger of Hogwash, my dear. You know that. Come, come, let's move our discussion forward. In exchange for activating the external sustenance setting on your BroBot 3000, I will add one of two hazards to your day. You may choose which. Are you ready?"

"So I can choose."

"Of course. None of this works without free will."

"None of *what* works?"

"My dear Nicole, I only serve to give you what you most desire." He bowed with a cultured grace. "Now, to demonstrate the first hazard, I will need you to stand on your chair. Go on, bring your chair over to the mirror and climb up. I'll wait until you're ready."

Nicole dragged her desk chair to the mirror and stepped up.

"Excellent. Oh, you are so going to enjoy this. Prepare to be dazzled! Do you know the game children love to play where they pretend the floor is lava? For option one, I will make the floor actual lava."

The floor liquefied into a flaming crimson causing an intense heat to saturate the room. Molten lava bubbled, discharging arcs of fire into the air.

"You can move about the house by jumping —please, Nicole. If you scream, you won't be able to hear me—from furniture to furniture. Won't that be fun?"

"Turn it off! Turn it off!"

The lava sucked into the carpet with the velocity of a gas burner being extinguished.

"Did you find the lava unsatisfactory or are you eager to hear option two?"

Sweat trickled down Nicole's cheeks. Singed hair framed her expression of absolute terror. "Are you insane? I could have burned to death!"

"Naturally. Lava is upwards of a thousand

degrees Centigrade. Direct contact would cause you to burst into flame. Kids love this game."

"Not with real lava," Nicole said. "They *pretend*."

Phin tapped his lips. "That can't be right. I don't see how the game would be any fun if there are no real consequences."

"It's an excuse to jump on furniture," she said, waggling her hands. "No one uses actual lava!"

Phin straightened his suit while he chewed over her words, literally moving his jaw with cow-like kinetics. "How curious. Times sure have changed since I was a lad. Although, upon further consideration, I was always sad when I lost my less athletic playmates."

Nicole's hands settled firmly upon her hips. "You don't seriously expect me to believe you."

"I expect nothing. That is why I am never disappointed."

"Right, well, I don't think your story is true."

"It is entirely and unequivocally true," Phin said, "excepting those portions I may have exaggerated or fabricated to suit my needs."

Nicole scrunched her face. "What are you, a lawyer?"

"No. I am the Titan of Tautology."

"Of course you are." Nicole groaned. "Why do I keep setting you up?"

"An intriguing question, but alas, no time

to ponder. May I present option two: birds with razor-sharp talons." Two birds appeared on Nicole's dresser. Their plumage shimmered blue-black with each agitated twitch. "Aren't they extraordinary specimens? I see you are speechless. Are you amazed? Enthralled? I'm sensing you may, in fact, be terrified. No need. No need! I assure you, their disposition is most amiable."

"Amiable?" Nicole's grip on the chair blanched her fingers. "So, the birds are friendly?"

"Absolutely! To other birds, that is. To young girls, not so much."

The birds spied Nicole, and their eyes bulged. A piercing cry erupted from their open mouths, reverberating through Nicole's eardrums and down to the pit of her stomach. Nicole dove behind the chair. "Take them away! Take them away!" she screamed.

The birds disappeared with the flip of Phin's wrist. "You fancy the lava then? Excellent choice. I knew you'd come around."

"No, neither. Both are terrible! The deal is off."

Phin fell back a step. "If you insist." He recovered his footing and shifted his ill-fitting suit a tad to the left. "I had been fully prepared to offer you a third option. But no matter. I wonder if BroBot will fancy the flat screen for lunch."

"Fine." Nicole stood up to face him. "What's the third option?"

"A hole."

She stared at him and wrinkled her nose. "That's it? A hole? Wait, like a black hole that tears apart the house?"

"My dear Nicole, you are *so* dramatic. No, just a couple of holes. Lacking gravitational fields, I promise."

She waited for more horrors. When none came, she said, "I guess that's not so bad."

"Not bad at all. A few holes off the side— hardly a bother! They're even portable. Envision, if you will, several holes gliding with elegance and grace."

"Hold up. How many holes are we talking about?"

Phin tapped his thumb to each finger in sequence, counting silently with his lips. "Perhaps a dozen. A baker's dozen. A score or more. It's easier not to keep count."

"Why do they keep increasing?"

"A marvelous property of holes, wouldn't you agree? Normal math rules do not apply. While splitting a whole in half gives you two halves, splitting a *hole* in half gives you two holes."

"Hang on. How are you spelling that?"

"Pish posh," Phin said, twirling his hand to create more finger waves. "Let's leave spelling to the roustabouts. Do we have a deal? I can always summon the birds if you'd rather."

"No! I don't want the birds. No one wants

the birds. No one wants the birds *ever*." Nicole dragged her chair back to her desk. She returned with a determined expression. "I'll take the holes. But you have to promise to fix my phone."

"All will be resolved by the day's end," Phin assured her. "On this, you have my word."

"Then we have a deal."

Phin bowed his head. "Until we speak again."

"Wait. What's going to happen?"

Phin poked a crooked finger under his hat and scratched. "The future holds so many delightful potentialities. Why skip to the end? Besides, I expect we'll find out soon enough."

CHAPTER 5

"Who's that scruffy runt?"

Phin vanished with a spark leaving Nicole to wince at her reflection. The lava heat had frizzed her hair worse than she'd ever seen. She smoothed her curls with her hands while she contemplated the holes. Odd for holes to move at all, even gracefully. And how could holes be portable? She wished she had asked a few more questions before Phin had zapped out of her mirror. Should she be concerned? She figured her dad would be all right in his office, and she hardly had to worry about her robot brother.

Oh, no, she thought. *Scruffy!*

Nicole hurried downstairs. When she reached the foyer, Scruffy lifted her ears and bounced to her feet. The dog dashed towards Nicole, zipped right by her, and spun around. Nicole scooped her up and stepped carefully, leery for stray holes, until settling on the blue couch in the family room.

Nicole stroked Scruffy's raggedy fur. Nicole might be having a bad hair day, but Scruffy had a bad hair life. Since the moment Nicole had met her at the farm, Scruffy had fit her name. Nicole had been the one to name her, although not intentionally. Nicole closed her eyes. Her memory of the event remained vivid as though the events unfolded around her.

"Who's that scruffy runt?" young Nic asked soon after they'd unloaded the car on yet another sweltering summer day. Her parents exchanged glances, but Grandpa didn't miss a beat.

"She's the runt like you said, and I suppose she is scruffy, but she's got more personality than all the other pups put together."

When Nic realized this was the puppy they had picked for her, the puppy she had been so excited to meet she had scarcely been able to concentrate for the last month of second grade, the puppy she hadn't stopped talking about for the entire three-hour drive to Virginia, she collapsed into a puddle of tears right by the knobby oak tree in the front yard.

Nic had been going to school long enough by then to know *personality* was the way you described something unattractive. Of course that runt had more personality than all the other pups put together. No doubt.

Her parents tried many times to get her to reconsider. Nic would have none of it. She sat with the pretty puppies and pet their silky fur. Grandpa assured her that she could pick whatever pup she wanted but stressed that he was certain she would want Scruffy if she gave her half a chance.

"Scruffy? Her name is actually Scruffy?"

When Grandpa smiled, the creases deepened in his sunburned face. "You named her, Nic."

"Doesn't mean I want her," she said, and the battle of wills began in earnest. Nic vowed not to give Scruffy half a chance. Or one-third of a chance. Or two-thirteenths of a chance. She had been keen on fractions that year.

She nearly made it to the end of the month, but everything changed the day she heard Grandpa whooping it up in the front yard.

"She almost got General Scott! She almost got General Scott!"

Nic drifted outside to find Grandpa and Jay by the oak tree laughing so hard they leaned into each other to keep from falling over. In front of them, Scruffy chased a gray squirrel with a bedraggled tail around the tree. Now and again, the squirrel climbed the trunk, Scruffy barked, and the squirrel scampered back down only to race around the tree once more.

"In all my years, I've never seen this."

"Dogs chase squirrels all the time,

Grandpa," Jay said.

"Sure, but not like this. General Scott always scoots up the tree and stays put. He doesn't come back down until he is sure the dogs are gone. Why does he keep coming back?"

Jay's mouth hung open, deep in thought. Nicole recalled how sincerely Jay contemplated things back when he was eleven. He had been thin and sensitive, always gentle and considerate with her. Unlike her puberty-riddled brother nowadays, surly and buff, hanging out with his lacrosse buddies, ganging up to jeer at the freshmen.

"I don't know why he keeps coming back, Grandpa," Jay said.

"General Scott and Scruffy are playing. No two ways about it. Never met a squirrel who *wanted* to play with a dog."

By then, Nic had joined them and she slid her tender hand into her grandfather's huge calloused one.

"You named the squirrel General Scott?" she asked.

"Sure. He reminds me of Old Fuss and Feathers. That was General Scott's nickname back in the day. General Scott was a Virginian who chose to stay loyal to the Union. Didn't make him too popular 'round these parts, but folks are changing. Anyhow, the squirrel and Old Fuss and Feathers have the same pinched face."

"No feathers, though," Nic said. "Squirrels

don't have feathers."

"True, but to be fair, General Scott didn't have any feathers either." Grandpa winked, making Nic giggle.

When Jay ran to the tree, General Scott scurried up the trunk for good. Jay and Nic played with Scruffy until dinnertime, and from then on, no one wondered any more about which dog she wanted.

After packing up the car and their new pup for the trip home, Nic's parents planned their visit for the next summer. They would bring Scruffy with them, and she and General Scott could race around the trunk once more.

They never had the chance. Grandpa died later that year, and Grandma sold the farm so she could afford to move into an assisted living development. The tragedy had been one of many times Nicole learned about disappointment. Another time was when Jay stopped playing with her. Or when he started greeting her with nasty jibes. Or when he insulted her friends. Or all the times he mocked things that were important to her as if he was so great or the things he enjoyed were all that.

And the most recent time was two days ago when Jay did something so unforgivable that Nicole had no choice—*no choice*—but to do something equally unforgivable to him.

CHAPTER 6

"That's freaky."

Nicole held her dog's face in her hands and scratched behind her ears while Scruffy thumped her tail against the couch cushion. Her blotchy fur hadn't aged well, but Scruffy never lost her lovable puppy eyes or her earnest expressions that telegraphed every emotion for all the world to see. So when Scruffy's ears pricked forward, Nicole looked to see what her dog had spotted.

A hole glided across the family room, drifting like an oversized air hockey puck. Nicole gasped and pulled Scruffy close. Nicole tried to gauge the hole's depth, but the center was as inky black as a starless night. The broad edge contained dark, splotchy shades, creating a dappled circumference. While smaller than Nicole had imagined, the hole's diameter was a smidgen longer than an adult shoe, large enough to drop a leg but not wide enough to swallow her whole.

Nicole tucked her feet beneath her, taking no chances. The hole lingered in front of the couch. Nicole couldn't explain it but she had the creepy sensation that the hole was sizing her up. Scruffy growled, in tune with this new threat.

The hole backed away, gliding towards a pen lying on the carpet. In a flash, the hole dilated, tripling in size while thinning its edge. The pen plummeted silently. Nicole listened for a thud at the bottom, but it never came. Was there no bottom?

"That's freaky," Nicole said. Scruffy raised the pitch of her growl.

The hole snapped back to its original size. Its edges reformed and vibrated. The pulsations intensified then focused on two opposite points of the circle, which clenched toward each other until they connected, dividing the hole. When the holes separated, the sound resembled the noise made by a stone tossed into a pond.

Bloop!

The two holes glided off in opposite directions. Nicole had the distinct impression that they were pleased with themselves. Nicole, however, wasn't pleased at all. She had not bargained for this. Phin must have tricked her. She couldn't specify in what way but she was certain that he had.

Scruffy leaped off the couch and chased the nearest hole. Reaching the perimeter, she assaulted the hole with furious barks. The hole quit gliding and rotated instead, as though to face her. By then, Nicole had also given chase, calling for her dog to get away. The hole expanded, startling Scruffy with the sudden lack of carpet. Nicole dove forward and looped a hand under her dog just in time.

In her awkward position, Nicole slid into the hole. She tried to grip the inner walls with her free hand, but the sides were impossibly smooth. Instead, she swung her dog out of the hole and reached up with both hands. Finding the edge with her left, Nicole pushed with enough force to flip herself over and roll away from the hole.

Scruffy bounded onto the couch and cowered between two cushions. Nicole backed a safe distance away, dizzy but relieved. She didn't want to think about what might have happened if she'd fallen in, what sick nightmare Phin had in store. Maybe she'd boil in lava or have her eyes pecked out. Some snow day this turned out to be.

The hole dilated and contracted, and at the moment of maximal size, a pen shot out, looped in the air, and fell harmlessly on the carpet. Nicole knelt down and snatched it up. Most of the pens in the house looked the same, but she was sure this was the same pen that had been swallowed up. The pen appeared intact, no worse for its travels. No burns or peck marks, anyhow.

Nicole placed the pen on the table by the couch, circling around the hole to maintain a safe distance. The holes frightened her, but she couldn't look away. *Exciting and dangerous, just like Gavin.* For a moment, Nicole wondered how this past week might have been different had she also kept her distance from Gavin.

Scruffy emerged from her cushion fort and growled. Her fur asunder, Scruffy's body and tail straightened into a line.

"What is it, girl? What do you see?"

What she saw was what Nicole had forgotten: the second hole, gliding ever closer behind her. Nicole spun around but a beat too late. The hole expanded, and Nicole plummeted straight down, her scream extinguished in an instant.

CHAPTER 7

"It wasn't my fault!"

The absence of light and sound confounded her. The closest she'd experienced to this was the moonless night at her grandparents' farm, but at least then she could enjoy the stars. At least then she could listen to a soothing wind that rustled the leaves. Now, her cry dissipated into the void. After one more futile attempt, she gave up. Not much payback to yelling if you can't hear it.

Nicole noted a falling sensation but different from the Freefall ride at Rehoboth Beach, where her stomach would rise into her throat and gag her. Her descent through the hole remained constant, even gentle once she got used to it.

But just as her tension began to fade, Nicole found herself standing motionless in a cavernous room surrounded by chatter. She recognized the location as the Park Hollow High School lobby. The stuffy aroma of bustling teenagers filled the air, and the sun's rays extended through the glass doorway, warming her skin. Why would anybody be here on a snow day? Or, for that matter, why would she be here?

Hello?

No one responded. Or noticed her at all. She recognized Hannah and Keiko leaning against a table, affecting a cool if somewhat dorky vibe. Hannah could almost pull it off, anyway. She used to be cool. Hannah was part of Nicole's clique back at Pine Woods Middle School before she had her meltdown and Brandi thought it best to box her out.

Cool was not in Keiko's nature. Her body language radiated introvert, arms rigid at her side, head down and tilted towards Hannah. Wearing the same outfit as last week didn't help her case. Although now that Nicole thought about it, so did Hannah. That was odd. With Brandi's guidance, Hannah had honed her fashion sense in middle school just like Nicole. Certainly, she knew better.

Unless…

Nicole experienced a rush of déjà vu, all woozy and pink. Math Club was a week ago. That would explain it, but if this was them waiting in the lobby a week ago, then she should be nearby. Nicole turned and gasped. There Nic stood, texting on her phone while also wearing the same outfit from a week ago.

Nicole tried to walk, but the hole had penned her inside a cramped enclosure surrounded by smooth invisible walls. Unable to flee, she knew what she would soon be forced to witness. This day was never far from her thoughts. And soon to come, the moment when she was meant to begin the most spectacular romance of her teenage life.

As expected, Gavin rounded the corner, shadowed by his lacrosse buddies. Gavin strode forward, the sweat glistening off his thick arm muscles, head held high. Nicole hadn't seen him coming a week ago because she was texting on her phone. Just as well. No way would she have had the audacity to do what she did next. Not if she saw him like that. Even now, knowing how badly this would end, Nicole's heart fluttered at the sight of him.

Traveling with Paulo and Devin as usual, Gavin motioned with his head. "Math Club geeks," he told them. "Check it." Gavin stopped in front of Keiko. His posse followed suit.

Keiko recoiled at the attention. Hannah tensed, ready to rumble.

"Math Club girls." Gavin's words dripped with contempt. "I can barely tell you apart from the boys."

"Who cares what you think?" Hannah spat back.

"Everybody." Gavin turned to his friends,

and Paulo and Devin confirmed his conceit. Gesturing toward Keiko, Gavin continued, "You could at least try to dress nice. What are you even wearing? It's like a sack of potatoes."

Nicole watched Nic shove her phone partway into her pocket and storm over there. Nicole admired her determined expression, her confidence. She wished she could always be like that. But she knew this was a spontaneous reaction to his slight, the consequence of Nic's accumulated experience standing up to her brother directed squarely at Gavin. This wasn't bravery so much as instinct.

"Hey! I think she looks cute in that outfit," Nic said, "and since when did the lacrosse team become the fashion police?"

The boys howled, and Paulo slapped Gavin on the back. "She got you, man!" But just as Nicole remembered, Gavin didn't get upset or lash out. No need to act threatened when you're king of the pack. Instead, he stepped into Nic's personal space and held out his hand.

"I'm Gavin."

Nic took his hand and shifted her lips. "Yeah, I know who you are. We've met before. I'm Nic." She waited for recognition but received only a blank stare. "Jay's sister."

Gavin's mouth went wide when he laughed. He continued to hold her hand and lifted it to the side to check her out. "Oh, yeah. Nic. Well, you sure have grown up nicely."

This was the moment, Nicole remembered. The moment when she fell for him hard. Her fury extinguished, Nic could hardly focus on anything except how he still held her hand, or how his gaze brushed across her body, hungry, lighting tiny sparks in deep places.

The next bit had been a blur, so Nicole watched as though for the first time. Gavin spinning her around as though they were dancing. Gavin plucking her phone from her pocket and typing in his info. Gavin suggestively inserting her phone back into her pocket to the salacious cheers of his posse. Gavin throwing shade at Hannah with a contemptuous side glare as he strode away. Gavin, the most popular boy in the school—a senior!—had flirted with her in front of everybody.

Keiko thanked Nic after Gavin and his buddies left, but Nic hadn't noticed because already she had her phone out, texting excitedly as she drifted away.

"Don't bother," Hannah said. "Once her phone is out, she's in her own private world. I'll bet she's texting Brandi with, like, a hundred emojis."

Nicole frowned. She wasn't wrong. In fact, she was exactly right. It only sounded bad when Hannah said it.

"That was nice of her to stick up for me."

Hannah curled her lip. "You think so because you don't know her."

Hey! Nicole hadn't meant to speak out loud and braced for Hannah to argue back. She didn't, of course. Clearly, no one could see or hear her.

"No, but I should. We're the only three freshman girls in Math Club," Keiko said. "We should be friends."

"Friends with Nic? Lol. I gave our friendship chance after chance in middle school, and the same thing always happened. She betrayed my trust. Like it was nothing. She'll do the same to you. That's what she does. See, she forgot about you the second that boy flirted with her."

Keiko smiled. "Some girls get like that with boys."

Hannah bumped Keiko's shoulder with hers, and Keiko bumped her back. "Shut up, you know what I mean." Hannah brushed her hair back. "Nic isn't worth it. She'll throw you under the bus the moment it's convenient for her."

No, I won't.

"That's too bad." Keiko jammed her hands into her pants, which did not look like a sack of potatoes but were a tad on the baggy side. "She's smart and stands up for herself. I'd be friends with her."

I'd be friends with you too.

"If she wanted to be friends, she'd talk to us. Not walk away the second Gavin leaves."

"Yes," Keiko agreed, "but it was nice of her to defend me."

"Don't be fooled. Nic was defending herself. She's the only person she cares about. Well, her and Brandi."

That's so not true!

"We were all a little immature back in middle school." Keiko's tone was hopeful, almost pleading. "Maybe she's changed."

Hannah scoffed. "She'll never change."

Why are you so mean?

Keiko tented her eyebrows and spoke softly. "She might."

Hannah altered her stance as though preparing to box. This was not an argument she intended to lose. "Like all the times she blabbed about private stuff just to get closer to Brandi?"

It wasn't my fault!

"Or when she trusted Brandi over me at my Bat Mitzvah?"

It wasn't my fault!

"Yeah, sure, she *might* change," Hannah said, her cynicism particularly rank on the word *might*. "But she won't. And do you know why? Because nothing is ever her fault."

Nicole recoiled. Fresh tears streaked down her cheeks. Keiko nodded, conceding the point. This pleased Hannah but only briefly. She peeked over at Nic, still bent over her phone, and a profound sadness softened Hannah's features. Nicole knew that look. She recognized it as the same expression Hannah had at her Bat Mitzvah after Nicole had called her out. Heartbroken.

I miss you too.

Instinctively, she reached out to Hannah. As a captive observer, Nicole did not expect the wall to stretch, allowing her to connect with a warm shoulder. Hannah turned to meet her gaze, both girls equally startled. But their eyes never met. The wall snapped back, the floor opened up, and Nicole plunged.

Darkness and silence engulfed her. This time, Nicole welcomed it.

CHAPTER 8

*"Have you lost your
robot mind?"*

Nicole flew out of the hole feet first, hovered in the air for a moment, and landed hard on her side. She flailed her arms and legs on the carpet like an upended turtle until she could get her bearings. Anxious yet another hole would swallow her up, Nicole leaped to her feet and sprinted into the kitchen. She dove onto the table, grasping both edges and resting her face against the synthetic wood.

Thinking about all the horrible things Hannah had said made Nicole fume. How could she? After all the years they'd been friends. Sure, they were no longer close, but Nicole never talked trash about Hannah. She would tell off Hannah first thing tomorrow, Nicole promised herself. Until then, she decided to take a few deep breaths and maybe stop hugging the furniture.

When she sat up, Nicole saw Dad standing by the cabinets with a concerned expression. Her shriek startled her father, who spilled coffee out of his mug. They stared at each other while Nicole straightened up.

"Everything all right?"

"Yep," Nicole answered. She dangled her feet over the table's edge, real casual, as though this was a thing she did all the time, as if sitting on the kitchen table embodied perfectly normal behavior, nothing to see here.

"Are you coming down?"

"Yes."

Bloop!

"Or no." Nicole scanned the floor. The hole she had popped out of meandered down the hallway with its twin. Her father also looked down, but from his vantage point, all he could find amiss was his spill. He placed his mug on the counter and reached for the paper towels. Nicole watched him wipe his spill and prepared to tackle him away from any stray holes if necessary. None materialized.

Dad tossed the wet towels and turned back to Nicole. "Are you and Jay getting along?"

"Sure. No problem. We're great. Thanks. Everything's fine."

Bloop!

Nicole gripped the table tighter.

"Sounds like Jay's playing a new video

game."

"Huh? Oh, yeah, that would explain the sound. A new video game."

Dad picked up his coffee and sipped. In recent years, his presence made Nicole awkward, yet the safe feeling she experienced with her dad since she was a little girl had never left. After what she'd been through, Nicole drew on it, absorbed it, let it seep into her and calm her breathing.

Nicole must have left all the uncomfortable for her father because he shifted his mug from hand to hand until he chuckled to himself. "I guess this conversation isn't going anywhere. Lunch at noon?"

"I'll be here."

He moved to leave but hesitated. "Here, as in still on the table?"

"No."

Bloop!

"Maybe. See you at noon." Nicole swung her legs again, all nonchalant, totes chill, her focus never once leaving the floor.

After a deep sigh, Dad walked back to his office. Nicole, exercising caution, snuck after him so she could monitor for holes. Dad closed the door just as Robot Jay came down the stairs. Nicole motioned to get his attention, shushed him before he could speak, and gestured for him to follow her. In short order, she was back on the kitchen table with the bot by her side.

"May I speak now, dear sister?"

"We have holes."

The BroBot shifted his head, his expression glazed over as if he was computing something. He blinked and straightened. "What type of holes?"

"The nightmarish type. Holes that ambush you, that shoot you into your past to torment you."

"Ah, you mean interdimensional portals." When Nicole didn't respond, he pointed at one gliding across the kitchen. "Like that one." Nicole nodded. "Are they a gift from Phin?"

"A gift? Are you insane? No. Phin put them there in exchange for your external sustenance thing."

"Of which I am profoundly grateful. Being properly sated is an enormous relief." Her robot brother smiled. Nicole still found this creepy. The only smiles her brother pointed at her these days were tainted with arrogance. "Your kindness never ceases to impress. Jay is most lucky to have you as his sister."

Nicole scoffed. "Tell him that."

"I am unable to comply with your request. Is there anything else I may do for you?"

Bloop!

"Yeah, keep me from falling into those stupid holes!"

The BroBot froze once more, his expression blank. After a few seconds, he blinked, and his movements resumed. "To protect you most effectively, I'll need the stick in Jay's room. I shall return presently, dear sister."

Nicole swung her legs while she waited. She tried to concentrate on the holes, but her thoughts circled back to Hannah. The spite Nicole had witnessed overwhelmed her. She could not imagine why Hannah would say such horrible things about her. She and Hannah had been inseparable in elementary school. Hannah used to come over all the time to practice dance moves. They loved running around the backyard with Scruffy.

Soon after starting middle school, Hannah was the one to suggest they hang out with Brandi and Maya. That worked out great, at least for a while. Brandi helped them with their hair and clothes, and soon the four girls got noticed wherever they went. Everyone rushed to talk to them, invited them to hang out. Really, everyone wanted to be seen with them. Especially the boys. To be that popular right when boys became interesting gave Nicole a constant stream of intoxicating pleasure. No way would she give that up just because Hannah had second thoughts.

Yes, Brandi hogged the spotlight. And yes, Brandi expected the other girls to follow her, Nicole admitted as much to Hannah privately, but they all knew Brandi was the prettiest. A pecking order always develops within a group, and Brandi seized the top spot for herself. All Nicole did was claim the second spot. And everything would have been fine if Hannah and Maya had accepted that. They were the ones who got competitive. They were the ones who got all conniving and devious. Typical of Hannah to deflect the blame on her. Like it was her fault.

Nicole noticed the robot striding toward her using the butt end of Jay's lacrosse stick to drag a hole. To Nicole's horror, he brought the hole into the kitchen and, standing a safe distance away, used the stick to position the hole directly under Nicole's feet.

"Would you like to jump into this one, dear sister?"

Dumbfounded, Nicole let her gaping mouth do the talking until her anger coalesced into words. "Have you lost your robot mind? I'm not jumping in there!"

Nicole and the bot stared at each other, Nicole with the fiery rage of a thousand exploding suns, and the bot with the confusion of a BroBot 3000 programmed with facial expressions to replicate confusion.

"I have cross-referenced Jay's aggregate knowledge on interdimensional portals with my standard database and concluded the odds of your atoms being ripped apart is far lower than you might expect. Some people enjoy these as a mental pleasure vacation. They direct where they wish to travel using their thoughts."

Nicole couldn't remember thinking about anything during her descent, consumed as she was with blind terror. It didn't matter. She could not conceive of an alternate universe where she would voluntarily jump into the holes. "Take it away."

"Certainly, my wonderful sister." Flicking his wrist, the robot launched the hole out of the kitchen. He banked it against the wall in the hallway, causing it to ricochet out of harm's way in the foyer. "I've gathered all the holes I could find in the library."

"We have a library?"

"The room with all the books."

Nicole chuckled to herself. She always regarded that room as the play area. Piles of toys had once cluttered the shelves and the floor. She and Jay had spent hours there many years ago. Nowadays, neither did much more than walk through the room. "Right, the library."

"Come, let me show you what I've done."

Nicole followed him back through the hallway into the foyer, where her robot brother used the butt end of the lacrosse stick to guide the stray hole into the library with the others. The carpet in the library resembled Swiss cheese. Nicole estimated at least twelve holes, colliding around. One by one, the holes ceased their motion when the bot came near, like naughty kindergarteners who'd noticed their teacher had entered the classroom.

"I don't think they enjoy it when I move them around." Robot Jay held up the lacrosse stick, and the holes backed away.

Good, she thought. *Serves them right.* "I need you to pick everything off the floor. I don't want to breed these things. And keep them in this room while I talk to Phin."

Nicole climbed only a few steps before the bot called out. As he did, the stairs gave way. She reached out and caught the step above. Her dangling feet failed to get any traction as they brushed against the smooth walls. Her fingertips chafed from rug burn, slipping ever lower from her weight.

"Grab the stick. I'll pull you out."

Nicole reached for it with one hand and lost her grip with the other, slipping into familiar, smothering darkness.

CHAPTER 9

"I know how to properly accessorize!"

Nicole didn't scream. She'd already done this ride. Much like at Rehoboth Beach, the second time at the adventure park was always pretty chill. So instead of panicking, she took her new brother's advice and tried to direct where the hole should take her. *Bring me to the next day when Gavin flirts with me and everything is perfect.* She thought it a few more times for good measure, but a queasy unease told her she was too late. Before Nicole dropped, she was thinking about something else, a question that nagged her since her last hole excursion: when had Hannah first doubted their friendship? Eighth grade, she figured, and if the robot was right about thoughts directing the hole, this would be where, or at least when, she was headed.

The falling ceased, and Nicole stood before a class of students. Excited murmurs and adolescent stank assaulted her senses. She brightened as she recognized her crew in the back. They all looked so young! Maya still had a bow in her hair, so this couldn't be any later than seventh grade. Her brother must be wrong. Stupid robot! She had fallen into some random scene, or maybe not so random. Most likely, Phin had chosen it for his tormenting pleasure. She sure would let Phin have it, presuming she made it upstairs without falling through any more holes or having her atoms ripped apart.

A jangling sound broke her train of thought, and Nicole turned to see Mrs. Vespa, her former science teacher, notorious for wearing huge metal bracelets that clanged together whenever she moved her arms. Nic had never particularly connected with Mrs. Vespa's fashion sense but kept her opinion to herself once Brandi expressed her view.

"She is our only teacher who knows how to properly accessorize."

This became a private joke between Nic and Hannah. One time at the mall, Hannah donned every metal bracelet on display and flailed her arms as though tottering across an ice patch. She sang, "I know how to properly accessorize / Brandi said it, so it's legitimized." Nic laughed so hard, she snorted. They sang and twirled together until the saleswoman kicked them out.

Totally worth it.

Nicole noticed a short kid rise from his seat, his face taut with a steely determination. He looked prepared to forge deep into the Amazon basin, damn the piranhas. Nicole gasped. *Is that Jake?*

He also looked young. And cute, in retrospect. Jake had always been intense, a turnoff for her back in middle school, but now Nicole found him alluringly mysterious and wondered what he looked like. The thought intrigued her. Too bad he went to one of those magnet high schools. She'd have to remember to do a deep dive on social media tomorrow or whenever Phin recovered her phone, presuming he kept his word.

Standing before Mrs. Vespa's class brought back memories of her middle school crush. Instinctively, Nicole turned to check out Aiden. She gasped again. He was nearly unrecognizable. Puberty had scarcely begun to mold him: a few whips of hair and a splattering of acne marred his otherwise cherubic face. He was early in the muddled process of becoming handsome, a feat he would accomplish before the end of eighth grade. But Nicole remembered liking him even back then, even before he wasn't much to look at, even before she admitted it to anyone besides Hannah.

Aiden's main attraction at the time was that he always said hi to her. Only to her. She could be with her friends—heck, she could be standing *right next to Brandi*—but Aiden would always stare directly at Nic when he said hi. She found nothing sexier than a boy who made it clear he liked her best. Nic wanted to respond, to let him know she noticed or even reciprocated if she was honest, but she never did. Because more than wanting this, Nic wanted to be like Brandi. So, like Brandi, she played it coy.

"Give them just enough attention to string them along but never show you care one way or another," Brandi had said after yet another gaggle of boys flirted with her and, more times than not, ignored Nic's existence. "It never fails to make them want you more."

She wasn't wrong exactly. Brandi's endless stream of boys did respond by making more of an effort or a pleading request or a grand gesture, never failing to swell with desperation, always on the verge of bursting. Yes, this worked fine for Brandi but not so much for Nic. Not with Aiden anyway. Although maybe it would have if she'd had more time or if Hannah hadn't swept in to steal her guy. True, Aiden was never officially her guy, but she had called dibs. Quite clearly. And Hannah knew it despite twisting it all around, acting as though the debacle at her Bat Mitzvah was somehow Nic's fault.

She saw Jake talking to her group in the back and knew immediately what day this was. This was not the day Hannah had first doubted their friendship. If anything, Nicole remembered it the other way around: the opening salvo of Hannah's betrayal. Nicole couldn't hear the conversation from across the room, but that hardly mattered. Jake only ever spoke to them once, and she remembered. This was the day they had to pick teams for their class projects. The four girls had to separate into two groups. This day was a nightmare.

Brandi marched to the front of the room, followed by Nic, Maya, and Hannah. They surrounded that nerdy kid whose name Nicole couldn't remember and asked him to let them join his group. You would think the nerdy kid would react to his good fortune with relief or even joy, given how he had unwittingly won the popular lottery. But as Nicole recalled, the kid went in a different direction.

"Please, girls, one at a time," the boy said. "I am limited to two choices. You may each make your case as to why I should choose you, and then I'll make my decision."

Nicole laughed. She knew her younger self hadn't found it funny at the time, but watching his conceit two years later amused her. She knew it wouldn't last. Not after Brandi cast her spell.

"Oh, Norman. You are so adorable." Brandi touched him gently on his shoulder, and the game was over. "Would you mind if I chose for you?" Her tone bespoke a soft generosity, but her slick grin belied this fiction. She knew her touch, her compliment, her searing confidence would tame him. A dumbfounded Norman could hardly do more than dip his head. Firmly back in control, Brandi addressed her friends. "Nic."

Nic smiled brightly.

No, don't smile. She's about to be horrible.

"I would have chosen you, but a little birdy told me you don't like Maya's hair bows. Why do you hate cute so much? OMG! And you never accessorize. It's like you've learned nothing from me. So I choose Hannah."

"What!" Maya said. "Why Hannah? Why not me?"

"Oh, Maya. You've had those same hair bows since fifth grade. Maybe it's time to get a new look? Just saying."

A dejected Maya fought tears. She reached for her bow while Brandi pulled Hannah closer. Nicole remembered having changed Brandi's mind but couldn't quite remember how she'd pulled this off. The simmering rage that swelled in her younger eyes alarmed Nicole, flooding her brain with memories. She tried to back away, but the hole limited her mobility.

I don't want to watch this part. Phin? Phin!

"You know, Brandi, if you want to talk about someone who hates accessorizing, you should talk to Hannah." Nic spoke with an insidious calm as when the air pressure sinks, and you can sense the impending hurricane with each quivering hair follicle. Hannah pleaded with her eyes, but her younger self either didn't see it or chose to ignore it. She had Brandi's full attention. "We were at the mall the other day, and Hannah put on a whole bunch of clunky bracelets saying, *I know how to properly accessorize!* She was so funny, dancing around, saying how it must be true because Brandi said so. It's too bad you missed it."

Brandi shot Hannah a dirty look. Hannah wilted. She took Maya's arm, and they slunk away. Brandi turned back to Norman. "See how easy that was? Here's our group of three."

Nicole drew back as Hannah and Maya passed by. She hoped they would move further away, but they stopped immediately to her left.

"I told you she was like that," Maya said.

"I know Brandi is like that, but Nic? Not Nic. She's my best friend."

Maya grunted. "Not anymore. Not if you get between her and Brandi. I think Nic made it clear who is most important to her."

"I don't want to believe it." Hannah spun her finger around the bottom of her shirt, entangling her fingertip. "But she betrayed me like it was nothing. Like I was nothing, in her way to be shoved aside." She gripped her knotted shirt in a fist. "I can't trust her anymore."

Don't twist this around. You told Brandi what I said about Maya's hair bows, so you started it. I was getting you back. I was getting even.

Hannah freed her finger with a yank. "How

did she know what Nic said about your hair bows?"

Right. Pretend like you don't know.

Maya reached for her bow again. She tugged it aggressively, nearly undoing the whole thing. "I overheard her talking to you about it. It's not like I told Brandi to get Nic in trouble. I asked Brandi if she still liked it, and she's all, *Yeah, it's cute. Why, who doesn't like it?* So I told her." Maya tugged at her bow again. "Do you think I should keep it?"

Hannah reached up and guided Maya's hand away from her bow. "I think you should keep it for today. Don't give Brandi the satisfaction by taking it out now. Maybe you can come over this weekend? We can try out new styles."

That's smart.

"Yeah, thanks," Maya said. "That's smart."

I said it first. Nicole shook her head. *No, I said it two years later. Two years too late, and you didn't even hear me.*

"We'd better find a group before we have to split up," Hannah said.

"Ugh, this is going to be so demeaning."

Aiden cleared his throat, startling Maya and Hannah. Even Nicole had forgotten he was there. "I need two for my group." Aiden sat with his arms folded on his lap, overtly casual.

"Were you listening to our conversation?" Maya charged.

Aiden grimaced. "I tried really hard not to, but you are standing right in front of my desk." His voice cracked on the word *desk*, but he maintained his composure even under the withering glare of two pretty girls with absolutely no patience. He pressed on. "You should grab this great offer while you can. My topic is the death of coral reefs and how it will lead to the destruction of ecosystems in the sea and, I don't know, spiral horribly out of control? It's another cheery reminder of how our generation has no future and we're all doomed. What do you say?"

"Wow," Hannah said. "How could we say no when you make it sound so inspiring?"

"I know, right?"

Maya exhaled the weary sigh of a popular girl letting you know she was slumming it by merely acknowledging your existence. "Fine, whatever."

"Great. So we have our group."

Hannah glanced over to where Nic stood with Brandi and looked back at Aiden. She extended her hand. "I'm Nic's friend."

Aiden blushed and awkwardly shook her hand. "Hannah, I know. Nice to finally meet you."

"Finally," she agreed, grinning at him.

What are you doing? Stop flirting with him!

Nicole sprang forward, trying to reach out to Hannah, but dropped through the floor before she could make contact. Nicole screamed into the darkness, her voice muted but her rage unquenched. Her silent yell extended throughout her descent until she shot out of the hole and crumpled into a ball beside the BroBot.

He speared the hole with his lacrosse stick and guided it into the library with the others. Nicole stumbled to her feet. "Did you get them both?"

"Yes, dear sister."

Brushing back her wild hair, Nicole scoured the floor, primed to attack. "Because they split into two after they swallow something."

"I am aware."

She shot her robot brother a look, thinking he might be mocking her, but detected no trace of ridicule in his forthright expression. Satisfied, Nicole advanced to the stairs, ever vigilant, and called back to the bot as she climbed, step by careful step. "Keep watch over the holes. Phin and I are going to have some words."

CHAPTER 10

*"I do so enjoy reliving
my worst ordeals in
excruciating detail."*

Nicole took a few minutes to inspect her room, kneeling and stretching her hands across the length of the carpet, including under her bed and in the closet. Once satisfied that her floor was secure from stray holes, Nicole stood before her full-length mirror and, for once, enjoyed her reflection. She felt at peace with her decision to forgo the primping expected of her on a regular school day, no longer so bothered by her tousled hair.

Nicole rotated her body in profile and tugged the bottom of her shirt to accentuate her breasts. She had recently advanced to a B cup, not that she wore one today. After loathing her figure for years, Nicole relished her successful progression to perky. But her pleasure ceased the moment she thought about Brandi, whose precocious curves dominated the attention of anyone who passed. Next to her, Nicole blended into the background, perky or no.

Although she *had* attracted Gavin. Briefly, yes, but for several glorious days, she allowed herself to feel valued. At least until that boy got distracted as they always do. Thinking about Gavin both aroused and irritated her. She pushed the sentiment aside and called out for Phin.

Phin appeared in the mirror, as urbane and chaotic as ever. "Greetings and salutations, Nicole. To whom shall I direct your compliments?"

Nicole held her tongue, not wishing to fall into that old trap again. Instead, she put on airs and affected Phin's tone. "My compliments, yes. Thank you ever so much for delivering holes that drop me into life's most traumatic moments. I do so enjoy reliving my worst ordeals in excruciating detail."

"Excellent! Far be it for me to nitpick, but that strikes me as more gratitude than a compliment. Nevertheless—and always the more—I remain your humble and obedient servant." Phin bowed, tipping his hat.

"Yeah. I was being sarcastic."

Phin straightened to his full height and peered at her, one eyebrow raised. "Ah, sarcasm.

The favorite garment to cloak those who feel most exposed. You wear it well, my dear. Like a straightjacket. Or cement blocks bound to your feet."

Nicole twisted her lips. "Now *you're* being sarcastic."

"Not at all. I mean each word precisely as I say it. But you must understand, as much as I yearn to take credit for your illuminating excursions into the past, I cannot. You are directing the holes, not I."

"Me? No, I don't think so." Nicole scoffed at the notion. "The holes torture me by bringing me to horrible, stressful moments in my life."

"Perhaps, but this is not their intent." Phin scratched a fingernail up his neck. When it reached his chin, his finger snapped into the air, pointing skyward. "Think of them as highly focused mirrors. They bring you to the moments that define you as a person."

"You think I'm defined by stress?"

"Aren't we all?" The gleam in his eye glowed brighter the more excited he became. "It is easy to pretend to be someone you are not when everything is going well. Stressful circumstances provide the best measure of your mettle. They are the fertile soil of truth. If you are troubled by what grows, plant better seeds."

Nicole took a step back, regarding him suspiciously. "I know there's an insult in there somewhere."

"On the contrary. I am filled with benevolence and public spirit. How may I assist you today?"

Nicole frowned. "You can start by not saying things like that."

"Doubtful, my dear. I am the Grand Poobah of Grandiose Pontifications." Phin jutted his chin in three-quarter profile as though posing for a postage stamp.

"Right, right. Of course you are," Nicole grumbled, already regretting what she had said. Complaining never got her anywhere with Phin. What she needed was information. "Getting back to the holes. Robot Jay thinks they are interdimensional portals."

"Interdimensional portals," Phin repeated and added a dismissive chuckle. "Jay reads too much science fiction; he has confused the robot. No, my dear. They're not portals but cylinders of space-time, each containing an infinite array of hyperbolic disks representing the nature of the universe at a given time and place. But all that technical gobbledygook lacks the suitable poetry befitting such a romantic entity. So I call them portable holes."

"Why portable?"

"The only way to travel! You've seen how leisurely the holes move. They wouldn't be practical without that handy convenience. Can you imagine me herding them from house to house? Absurd. We'd never get anywhere in time for dinner. And I'm sure you've observed how they are self-replicating?" Phin winked again in slow motion as though worried she might miss it. "Saves me scads of money on my nuclear fission budget." Before Nicole could respond, Phin lobbed an arm in the air. "Yes, I know what you're thinking. I've heard it all before. Wouldn't self-replication disrupt the geodesic coordination of the curved manifolds?"

"I was not thinking that."

"And how does time dilation factor into this?" Phin shrugged like a naughty boy caught with his hand in a cosmic cookie jar. "Paradoxes are so inconvenient. Rather than niggle any further, I created a view-only version. No editing! I mean, you *can* edit, but don't do that lest you introduce a cataclysm that rips the fabric of space-time. Oh, what a hassle that creates. You couldn't comprehend the mass of the sewing machine required to mend that tear."

Nicole squinted at him. "I can't tell if you're serious."

"Certainly you can tell me. I can keep a secret. I have many secrets." Phin's dastardly grin grew from ear to ear. "But first, tell me one of yours. Why do you keep jumping into the holes if you don't direct them? That sounds wildly random, and you don't strike me as the wildly random type."

"I didn't go into the holes intentionally."

"You didn't?" He recoiled, aghast. "How

could this be? They move so slowly. Certainly you can outrun them."

"I can outrun one. The others keep sneaking up on me."

"You need to keep track of them."

Nicole sneered. "There is no possible way to keep track of every hole."

"No possible way," Phin repeated and clucked his tongue. "If you would allow the indulgence, my dear Nicole, I suggest you name them."

The discordance between his helpful expression and his unhelpful advice left her sputtering for words. "Name them?"

"That's it."

"Name them!"

"Now you've got it!"

Nicole lifted her hand the way a traffic cop halted commuters by sheer will. "Let me get this straight. Cylinders of space-time are self-replicating all over my house, sneaking up on me, shooting me off to the most stressful moments of my life, and your great idea is to name them."

"Precisely! Imagine you're stranded in a room full of children. Before you know their names, you are in dire peril. But once you do, a quick scan tells you everything you need to know. Simply give each hole a name."

While she hated to encourage him, she conceded his logic was sound, even if impracticable. "How would that even work? I can't tell the holes apart. They all look exactly the same."

"As do many twins, yet their parents manage."

"Still not helpful," Nicole told him. "I can't tell twins apart, either."

Phin folded his arms, causing his suit to bulge to new heights above his shoulders. "Yes, yes. I understand how that would be difficult for you. You focus too much on appearance, a most distracting idiosyncrasy. To succeed, you must combat your very nature." He unfolded his arms and beckoned her closer. When she complied, he bent forward and spoke in a conspiratorial tone. "The trick to telling twins apart is to discount appearance and focus on personality instead."

She brushed him off. "That makes no sense. You can't see personality."

"But you most certainly can! Think less about how they look and more about how they look at you. You can catch it in the first twinkling and never be wrong, even when they do freaky twin things like swap clothing."

That is absurd, Nicole thought, until she remembered how the first hole glided and rotated in a way that seemed to size her up. One could consider it a personality of sorts. Against her better judgment, Nicole considered the possibility that Phin was actually on to something. "The first hole kept giving me the stink eye."

"Ah! You've met Tess."

"Tess?"

"Short for tesseract. I call her Tess. She and I go way back." Phin chuckled to himself. "She's an old wag. I knew you two would hit it off. Please relay my kind regards."

"I will not be doing that."

"But first! We must think up a topic before your next excursion. All this willy-nilly hole jumping simply will not do. I suggest you focus your attention on the root problem. You do realize where it lies?"

Nicole glared at him. "I think you're my root problem."

"No, my dear. I am referring to the time before we blessed each other with our companionship."

"Then I don't know. Right now, I'm mad at Hannah. And Gavin. And Brandi, if I'm honest with myself."

"And what a pleasant surprise that would be. No, think deeper. These things you focus on are the familiar trials and tribulations of teens. Always with their unique problems in all the usual, mundane ways. But you are special, Nicole. I choose my subjects carefully, of that you can be certain." Phin's deepening grin crinkled his cheeks. "A particular familial interaction yesterday caught my attention."

"Jay!" The anger induced by this memory

caused Nicole to squeeze her eyes shut. Had she not done so, she might have noticed Phin peek at the carpet where a nimble hole slipped beneath the door and glided in her direction.

Phin continued when Nicole looked back at him. "Why, yes, your brother. Remember him? The person you so blithely replaced this morning. Certainly he factors into all this. In my infinite generosity, I have gifted you a new and improved brother, along with the means to explore the rot that has loosened your bonds."

"Yes. You are so kind."

Phin raised an eyebrow. "More sarcasm, I presume? Your gratitude notwithstanding, you may wish to explore the root cause. Think back to a wee pup with scruffy hair."

"What, do you mean that day on the farm?" Nicole brushed him off. "I remember everything perfectly."

"No, my dear. This is quite unlikely. The past contains as many reflections as the future holds possibilities."

As Nicole considered what Phin said, a growing dread sent prickling shivers cascading to her toes. She preferred to keep that particular memory intact. Her dread soon progressed to fear and settled into an abject panic. "I don't want to play this game anymore."

"Yet play you must. Have a lovely trip." Phin peered down.

Nicole scanned the carpet a moment

too late. Her yelp rang into the air before extinguishing the instant she plummeted through the hole.

CHAPTER 11

"We'll be in different worlds."

The sweltering Virginia summer enveloped Nicole upon her arrival, making her skin clammy. A tepid breeze teased her before tapering to nothing. Memories seeped through the stagnant air. Nicole loved it so much she could burst. Everything, even the dank aroma of hay and manure, reminded her of Grandpa.

Nicole never thought she could go back, certainly not like this. Her mother had last been to the farm a few years ago and told the family how the developers had razed the stables and planted an array of cookie-cutter homes in two sprawling loops across the property. The former farmstead had become unrecognizable. Grandpa would have hated it, but it had long since been up to him. The horse industry had been declining for decades, and creditors found little value in nostalgic pastures.

Faint voices drifted through the air, followed by boisterous laughter. The porch creaked. Nicole spun around to come face-to-face with her eight-year-old doppelgänger. The girl shifted from leg to leg, her internal conflict evident in the creases of her nose. Nicole crouched down for a better view.

You're so cute. Why didn't I think it at the time?

Little Nic puckered her lips, balled her hands into fists, and strode onto the lawn. She marched toward the old oak tree where Scruffy and General Scott circled while Grandpa and Jay cheered them on.

You go, girl. Claim your dog.

Louder porch creeks alerted Nicole to a new presence, one she had not expected: her parents. They looked younger, of course. Thinner, too, especially her dad, who had to be at least eighty pounds lighter. But Nicole was most astonished by how they stood together so comfortably, deep within each other's personal space. They even held hands. Nicole couldn't remember the last time she had seen that.

"Do you think it will work?" her mom asked.

"Maybe," her dad answered. "Your father can be very persuasive. Although not always. As I recall, he couldn't convince you not to marry me."

"Oh, stop." She smiled at him, her eyes soft. "You need to get over it, George. He's learned to like you."

George cringed but in a way that still conveyed amusement. "Like? I don't know, Lynn. *Like* may be too strong a word."

"Tolerate?"

George pursed his lips and nodded. "I'll accept *tolerate*. I would have also accepted *at least he gave me grandchildren*."

"You are too kind." Lynn hugged his arm.

"I learned from the best."

She rested her head on his shoulder briefly before pulling back. "Oh! I meant to tell you. I spoke with Donna earlier. We're a go for the carnival by the mall next week. She and Hannah will be at the slides around noon."

"This is the Donna you know from wine club?"

She dropped his arm. "*Book* club."

George chuckled. "It's odd you ladies call it book club when wine is clearly the main attraction."

"What do you care what we call it?" Lynn eased into him. "I'm always frisky when I get home."

George pulled her closer. "That is true."

Who are these people?

"I hope this works and things turn around for Nic," Lynn continued. "I think if she can make even one friend at school, she won't be so lonely and sad."

What? Nicole tried to remember who she was friends with in second grade but drew a blank. Was she really lonely and sad back then? All she could remember about elementary school was hanging out with Hannah. That must have started this summer.

"So Hannah's the daughter?"

"Yes, George. Obviously, Hannah's the daughter."

"I mean, you didn't say. I was making sure."

Lynn rolled her eyes. "I shouldn't *have* to say. You can figure it out from context clues."

"I did! That's what I—that is exactly what I did. I did the thing you said."

"Good job, George." A budding smile formed at the corners of her mouth, tempering her annoyed tone.

George reached for her hand. Their fingers tangled. "I did a good job. I pay attention when my wife speaks to me."

"Uh, huh." Lynn rested her hand on her husband's chest as he pulled her closer.

"I've got the plan now," George said, his eyebrows triumphant. "Donna and Hannah will be at the slides, where we will casually bump into them, act all surprised, and hang out with them for the rest of the afternoon."

"Uh, huh."

"And Hannah's the daughter."

Lynn tapped his chest. "If you say so. I wasn't paying close attention."

"Oh, that's big a mistake," George said, tut-tutting like a disapproving headmaster. "You need to listen to context clues. There's going to be a quiz later."

"Oh, no!" They pressed their faces together, their noses touching. "Will you help me study?" Lynn asked.

What is happening? You two used to be cute?

"I might. What's in it for me?"

They shifted towards Nicole as they kissed. Nicole pressed back as far as she could. Lynn drew away, stood on tiptoes, and brought her lips to his ear. "Bring over a box of condoms, and you'll find out."

Ew, Mom!

They made out again. Nicole cringed, yet she couldn't look away. She couldn't remember her parents ever being so passionate. About anything, let alone each other. All three were so caught up in the moment, none saw Grandpa step onto the porch. A hand landed on George's shoulder. After a firm shove, he stumbled off her.

"That's my daughter," Grandpa said, and without breaking his stride, he entered the house. Lynn covered her grin while George tensed.

"Relax, George. He's kidding."

"He knows we're married, right?"

Lynn shrugged. "I may have told him after I

pushed out the first baby."

"Great. Can you tell him again? I bring it up only because I'm worried he might murder me in my sleep."

She thwacked his arm. "Don't worry, big boy. You sleep with me."

"Exactly. What if he finds out?"

Lynn laughed again. Nicole had never seen her parents enjoy each other's company so much. *This is so weird.*

Grandpa poked his head back outside and gestured to the lawn, where Scruffy and the children ran around the oak tree. "Mission accomplished, by the way. Looks like you'll be taking home the one pup."

"Thanks, Daddy."

Grandpa stepped outside. He put an arm around his daughter and kissed her head. "Anything for my baby girl." George started to thank him, but Grandpa brushed by him and reentered the house.

George looked sideways at his wife. "Why do you always act like you're six around your father?"

"I don't know, George. Why do you always act like you're a teenager around me?"

He nodded. "Fair enough."

Lynn threaded her arm around his waist. She rested her head on his shoulder while they watched their children play. Nicole watched them. She still couldn't get over her parents.

When did these two become so affectionate, so dynamic? No, she asked the wrong question. When did they stop?

All three were lost in thought until Grandma's walker rattled against the doorway. Her shaky voice called out, "Lynn, I need help setting the table."

"Of course, Mom. George, call the children."

"Dinner! Come inside and wash up." He waved to Nic and Jay.

Nicole pivoted to watch the two kids run with Scruffy nipping at their feet. Nic stopped to lift the dog after nearly tripping over her. She walked the last bit with Scruffy in her arms. "Daddy! Daddy! Can we take Scruffy home?"

"Sure, baby girl. Whatever you want."

"Yay!"

She ran inside with the dog. Jay lingered on the porch, waiting until his sister was gone before he spoke. "Nic knows the dog is for both of us, right?"

"Scruffy will be the family dog."

"Yeah, *I* know, but does Nic? 'Cause she keeps saying how Scruffy is her dog, but that's not fair. I wanted her first. She was going to pick one of those boring pups, and I was getting Scruffy. Mom said."

Did not.

"It's better if we take the one dog home."

"Yeah, that's fine. One dog is fine. But make sure Nic knows Scruffy is *our* dog."

Dad motioned Jay over to the chairs on the porch. They sat down, and Dad placed his hand on Jay's back. "Listen, bud. Nic is going through a rough time at school. She still hasn't made any friends."

"So I can't—"

"Hold up. Let me finish. Scruffy will be the family dog. No one is taking her from you. But, well, Nic needs a companion more than you do. Do you understand what I'm saying?"

Jay hesitated. "I guess so."

"Let her have this," Dad said. Jay turned away. From where Nicole stood, he stared right through her, deep in thought. "We're a family," Dad continued. "Families take care of one another. Not only the parents, all four of us."

"But I'm a kid." Jay crinkled his forehead. "How can I take care of anybody?"

"Don't worry. You don't always have to do things. Being there for someone when they need you is often enough. Or letting them get their way when you know it's really important to them."

Jay nodded, slowly at first, then more assuredly. "I understand. She can say Scruffy is her dog if it's really important to her."

"Thanks, Jay. I'm proud of you. You're getting so grown up." Dad moved his arm around Jay and pulled him close.

Jay didn't react, his gaze still fixed into the distance. Finally, he turned back to his father.

"Was it weird being an only child?"

"No. Quieter, yes. But Mom, you know, she has four older brothers, and they always look out for her."

"Didn't two of them threaten to beat you up back when you guys were dating?"

"Yes, Mom has a scary family, but that's a whole different conversation." Dad trembled as if locked in a walk-in freezer, amusing Jay. "When you love someone, you do whatever it takes. That's how families are. Each of us looks out for the others."

Jay cocked his head in surprise. "Does that mean Nic looks out for me?"

"Of course. You're her brother. She loves you like crazy."

Jay turned back to the lawn. Nicole gazed into his kind eyes, mesmerized by his intensity. "That's good. It's getting harder to tell."

"What do you mean?"

"It's just—we don't do as much together anymore. And I'll be starting middle school soon." He looked back at his father. "We'll be in different worlds."

"That happens when you get older. It's totally normal. I think the main problem for Nic is she's been unhappy. But now she has a new dog. And she might make a new friend this summer. We'll see. Things may turn around for her soon."

Jay's tone mirrored his father. "I hope so. I

hope Scruffy—" He winced and started over with a sincerity that took Nicole's breath away. "I hope Nic's new dog makes her happy."

Dad smiled at Jay.

"Let's go, guys," Mom called out from the doorway. "Men can set the table too."

"Coming!"

Nicole watched Dad and Jay go inside. She wiped her eyes and rubbed her tears on her shirt. She looked back at the knobby oak tree. Shadows from the porch and tree stretched together across the lawn. A squirrel scampered midway down the trunk. They regarded each other until the ground opened up and swallowed Nicole. She enjoyed her descent, comforted by the inky blackness, the absolute silence. It gave her time to think.

When she shot into the air, Nicole used the momentum to flip and land on her feet. She spied the hole and lunged for it, catching its edge. The hole vibrated, but she held on. It tried to glide away, knocking her to her knees. She tugged it back.

"How are you portable?" she asked the hole. The hole responded by dilating. Nicole stiffened her arm to keep herself away from danger. The hole contracted back to its regular size. It vibrated again. "If dividing makes you multiply, how do I subtract?" The hole tugged but could not free itself from Nicole's grip. "Addition?" In the mirror's reflection, she detected a second hole lurking behind her. She lifted the first hole, peeling it off the floor, and slammed it on top of the second hole.

Nicole gasped at the single hole before her. It tried to glide away, but she snatched the edge and stripped it off the floor. When Nicole stood, the hole kept its shape but did not move or vibrate. Twisting the hole, Nicole noted that it disappeared while in profile. "Are you two-dimensional?" She rotated the hole until it lined up perpendicular, and again it vanished.

Carefully, she stuck her free hand into the hole. Nothing came out the other side. "Freaky," Nicole said. She swung the hole until it faced her, and watched her hand disappear into the cool darkness within. She extended her arm inside to the elbow. Much to her relief, nothing tried to drag her in.

Nicole withdrew her arm from the hole and spun the hole the other way so she could observe the back of the hole when she entered the front. The reverse side appeared as shadowy as the front. She hadn't understood much of Phin's explanation about the holes. Should she be messing around with them? Then again, reacting to Phin had gotten her nowhere. All he did was toy with her. She was prey to him, a plaything. She needed to learn how to work the holes so she could shift the dynamic.

With a renewed confidence, Nicole pressed her arm back inside. Within the hole's murky blackness, a cross section of her arm appeared with two bones surrounded by fleshy parts and pulsating blood vessels. Nicole leaped back and screamed.

CHAPTER 12

*"Is something wrong,
dear sister?"*

The hole popped out of her hand and slid down her forearm. Nicole snagged it right before it reached the floor. Hyperventilating, she examined her forearm, relieved to find it intact where it had appeared severed. As her breathing slowed, her relief transitioned into determination. Nicole flung her door open and hurried down the stairs, clutching the hole in front of her. She had devised a plan and would not be delayed.

At least, not until her father opened his office door. "Is everything all right?"

Nicole came to an abrupt halt at the bottom of the stairway. "Yep." She righted the angle to keep the hole in profile. While her father squinted, Nicole rested her elbow against her side, but couldn't hide the awkward way she extended her hand, as though she were offering him invisible candy.

"Right, that's good," Dad said. "I ask only because you screamed like you were being attacked."

"Yeah, I, um, I was trying out a new dance move, and I tripped." She twisted her arm behind her head and shimmied.

"Huh. I have not seen that dance before. Are you getting into country music?"

Nicole was as confused as her father. "Why country music?"

"You look like you did when you rode horses on the farm: holding the reins with one hand and waving the other." Dad mimicked her dance, elbow against his side, hand gripping an invisible reign, the other arm flapping in the breeze. "Hee-haw!"

While pleased that he believed, or at least accepted, her explanation, Nicole couldn't shake her alarm as she recognized the troubling contrast between her current father and his vibrant, younger self. She wasn't affected so much by his extra girth and thinning hair—she was used to that, jarring as it was. No, there was something else, a sadness she hadn't noticed until now. One that must have always been there, a constant hiding in plain sight. After having spent time with her father's former self, Nicole could no longer ignore the disparity evident in every motion, every feature. Even as he smiled at her, Nicole could sense an underlying melancholy, sequestered but substantial.

Dad stopped dancing, sensing the moment had passed. "I'll make lunch in a half hour. I need to finish one more thing." She didn't respond, so he continued, "The snow is picking up a bit. I'm going to shovel before Mom comes home. We can throw snowballs after lunch if you want. We don't have to. You probably have other things you'd rather do."

"Oh. Oh, yeah! We should totally throw snowballs."

He blinked at her unexpected enthusiasm. "Really?"

"Sure. Daddy-daughter time. That'll be great."

Dad gaped at her. His eyes glistened. "Daddy-daughter time. Great. See you in a bit." He twisted away and shut the door.

Nicole continued down to the foyer where the BroBot stood, lacrosse stick in hand, guarding the holes.

"Greetings, dear sister. I see you've brought me two more holes."

"How—" Nicole glanced between the bot and the hole to check if something had changed. It had not. "How can you tell that I have two holes?"

"By the thickness."

"The—they're two-dimensional! There is

no thickness."

After pausing to reassess her human limitations, the robot blinked. "To clarify, I am observing the energy signature thickness, not the geometric thickness."

"Of course you are."

"And may I add, your hair has gained a lovely robustness."

"Of course it has. Virginia humidity will do that. I should bottle it up so I can sell it to absolutely no one."

The bot attempted to process this new information. "I do not believe that would be a viable business if no one would purchase it."

"Good point. Listen, I need you to help me capture the holes. I'm going around to the other side to stack them. You stay here and do not let any holes escape the library."

"I shall endeavor to do so, my wonderful sister."

Nicole grinned as she walked away. Even meaningless compliments held a certain shine after enough repetition. Upon entering the kitchen, Nicole turned to meet the soft patter of dog paws scurrying toward her. She squatted to pet an excited Scruffy.

"Hey, girl!"

Scruffy leaped into the air, bouncing off the floor with giddy excitement. Normally, Nicole would catch her in midair and pull her in for a hug, but with only one hand available, Nicole sort of dribbled her, as though Scruffy was a playground ball fallen off the roof, except furry with adoring eyes that emanated unconditional affection. But in a flash, Scruffy shifted into wolf mode. She backed away, tummy to the floor, tail pitched upward, and emitted a low growl. Engaging with Scruffy's alarm, Nicole searched the floor for holes until she recognized the obvious.

"Oh, don't worry, Scruffy. I've got this one, see?" Nicole held up the hole, posing like a boxer before the cameras. Scruffy lowered her tail a degree. Nicole shook the hole with her fist. "I've got the hole, not the other way around," she explained. Scruffy bobbed her head and spun in a circle. "Good, girl! You stay here while I stack the holes." Nicole backed away, prepared to repeat the *stay* command if needed. Scruffy remained in the kitchen, thumping her tail.

Nicole advanced to the carpeted area where the holes congregated. The BroBot stood on the other side in the foyer, lacrosse stick in hand like a wizard with his staff. The holes bunched in groups, a few playfully lurching into the others. One by one, they spotted Nicole and responded by rotating and gliding closer. She kneeled down and slammed the hole onto the closest one. After peeling it off the carpet, she repeated the process. She had dispensed with only a few holes this way before the other holes recognized what she was doing and reacted with pandemonium.

The holes scattered in all directions, careening against other holes, the brown couch, the walls, the bookshelves. Robot Jay worked his lacrosse stick to keep the holes from fleeing into the foyer. Nicole wondered if he had intrinsic robot skills or Jay's well-honed goalie skills. Either way, he kept his area secure.

For her part, Nicole snagged a hole with her other hand and used both holes as a defense to deflect the incoming holes so none could outflank her. For a time, she didn't even try to stack any. Keeping them contained in the library consumed all her effort. Worried the holes would overwhelm her, Nicole devised a new strategy. With a captured hole in each hand, she deflected the wild holes to her left until she had isolated a single hole on her right and stacked it. After several minutes, Nicole had reduced the hole population to three, including the two she held. She released one hole, stacked it, chased down the last wild hole until capturing it, and stood in the center of the room, exhausted but victorious, the final hole dormant in her grasp.

"Well done, dear sister."

Nicole wiped the sweat from her forehead. Her triumph gave way to the realization that she didn't know what to do next. "How do I keep this last one in check?" she wondered, lifting the hole.

"Place it on the carpet, and I shall guard it for as long as you wish."

"No, that's not going to work. Dad is making lunch soon, and you have to come. Oh, no! Can you eat people food?"

"Certainly."

Nicole flashed him a side-eye. "I thought you ate electronics only?"

"I subsist on electronics, but I can eat people food in the sense of ingesting, not digesting. The food goes through my system and comes out the same as for you, except in bulkier chunks. Do you want me to describe the process in more detail? There are lubricants involved."

"Nope. Already sorry I asked." Nicole shook it off the way Scruffy did after a dash through the rain. "I've noticed that the holes are passive when I've got my hand in them. Is that true when you use your stick?"

"Yes. Once I've speared them, they no longer resist."

"Good. I wish I could use the stick to hold them, but it would fall through. Oh, wait! Sure I can." Nicole motioned for the stick and the robot complied. She moved to the far wall of the library where the bookshelf ended and the stairwell began. After gauging the triangular area to confirm there would be enough space, she slammed the hole against the wall and shoved in the stick.

The stick slammed into something, surprising Nicole. There had never been anything within a hole before. She withdrew the stick and reintroduced it, carefully this time, until she had inserted half the length. Nicole sat by the hole, waiting to see if the hole moved, or expelled the stick, or did some other crazy, unexpected thing. Scruffy trotted over, and Nicole pet her.

"I think we're safe now." Nicole pointed to the hole. Scruffy looked at her, at the hole, back at her, and dashed where she pointed, into the blackness. Nicole gasped. "No! Scruffy, come back!"

"Don't worry, I've got her," her brother said from inside the hole.

Nicole froze. How did Robot Jay get inside the hole? And how was she going to get him out? She turned to the foyer and found the bot standing exactly where she had last seen him.

"Is something wrong, dear sister?" he asked.

Nicole turned back at the hole. "Jay, is that you?"

After a prolonged silence, the same voice responded. "Nic? Actual Nic? Ha! I was wondering where you were. How did you get in there?"

"In where?"

"The hole Scruffy ran out of."

Nicole sputtered like a short-circuiting robot. "How? What the—" She took a deep breath and tried again. "Where are you right now?"

"I'm in the library. Where are you?"

"I'm also in the library. A room neither of us has ever called the library before today."

"Seriously, right?" Jay laughed. "NicBot came up with it."

Nicole flushed. "NicBot?" Panic constricted her airway. *Oh, no,* she thought. *No, no, no.* "Jay? Did you replace me with a robot?"

Silence filled the air. She could hear Jay breathe on the other side of the hole. "Wow," he said. "This is awkward."

PART TWO

JAY: MORNING

CHAPTER 13

*"You have made a wise
and prudent decision."*

With a potential snow day looming, I plan to start gaming as soon as possible and break only for lunch. I have a late start when Nic beats me to the TV. This is what I get for hitting the snooze button to celebrate the two-hour delay. Don't ask me why my little sister can't watch her videos on her phone like a normal person. Sure, the TV screen is bigger but seriously—stick your phone closer to your face! The perspective is the same. This is not complicated.

Eventually, I boot Nic upstairs, the least I can do after my sister made it painfully clear yesterday that she would stop at nothing to destroy my life. I'd rather not get into the details but trust me, she deserves so much worse.

Frustrating my gaming plans further, a

freaky guy appears on the screen. A voice-over offers me a brand new sister. He says *new and improved* as though he's a castaway from a schmaltzy late-night infomercial. A phone number appears at the bottom of the screen with the directive CALL NOW flashing above his head. Pressing various buttons on the remote has no effect. His eyes lock on mine. The odd thing is, I can't look away. I wonder if I should call the number if only to get rid of him.

"That's it. Go on. Call now."

You know, maybe I should. My sister and I don't have much in common anymore besides our parents. I don't know if we never did. It didn't matter when we were young. I mean, my Dad always says that when I was little I could play with a box for five hours. So it figures I would play with that other kid who hung around the house all day. I remember my sister and I used to joke around all the time, but now Nic takes everything way too seriously. She's become moody ever since she started middle school. Ever since Brandi came into the picture. And especially ever since Brandi inspired Nic's toxic obsession with popularity.

Yeah, my sister and I got on fine when we were little, but everything became complicated when we grew up. I suppose that's the recurring theme of being a teenager: everything becomes complicated.

Now that I think about it, a brand new

sister sounds pretty good. I search for my phone and locate it under a controller. After punching in the number, I hover over the green button. I'm not hesitating so much as messing with him. Part of me wonders why I bother. I mean, it's a commercial, right? But I do it anyway. I want to see if I can get a reaction.

As impossible as it sounds, I do. The freaky guy squints and juts his head like a turtle. He extends one hand, cupped as though holding a phone, and points to it with the other hand, motioning over and over for me to press the button.

"What, like this? You mean like this?" I say, each time moving my finger towards the phone only to veer off the last moment. He drops his hands and the voice-over sighs long and hard, the way my dad does when he tells me dinner is ready and how long until my game is over and I say five minutes and he knows I'm lying because it's always at least ten and probably closer to twenty.

All right, enough teasing. I press the button. The voice on the phone sounds the same as the voice-over from the commercial. And he is disturbingly cheerful.

"Hello, Jay! Are you ready to change your life?"

"Um, I think you're overselling this."

"My dear sir. This is a once-in-a-lifetime opportunity." The freaky guy on the TV winks as if he learned by watching a YouTube winking tutorial with the playback set at quarter speed. "I'm waiting for an answer."

"To what?"

Now he sighs the way my Spanish teacher sighs when I say *Hola* with a hard *H*. Like I'm supposed to sound like a native speaker because I have an A in the class. I'm from Maryland, not Mexico. If you don't want to hear cringy Spanish, talk to Paulo. Of course, his parents are from Guatemala, not Mexico, but you get the idea.

While the freaky guy stares me down, I think more about my annoying little sister because I know she must have done something, *something*, to the TV before she passed me the remote. Although the more I think about it, and the more I can't shake the freaky guy, the more I admit a grudging respect for Nic. She's not technologically advanced, to put it kindly. I have no idea how she pulled it off. Well played, Nic.

"Sure," I say, "I'll take a brand new sister." You know, to get rid of him already. "But I also want a ham sandwich to-go and don't be stingy with the mustard."

Now he sighs as though the full mass of the universe weighs upon his puffy shoulders. This guy sure does sigh a lot. "I'm a tad light on ham sandwiches this morning," he says. "How about I replace your annoying little sister with a brand new and improved sister that meets or exceeds your specifications, and later you procure your own lunch?"

As I consider his offer, I notice his eyes sparkle. Were they always this bright? The freaky guy is freaking me out, but I don't want to let on. If there's one thing I've learned in high school, it's always act like you've got it together.

"How about this," I say, still chill about the whole thing. "If you also promise to get off the TV so I can play my video games, you've got yourself a deal."

He grins wide, crazy wide—I'm talking Chesapeake Bay-wide—and bows his head so low, his Abe Lincoln retro hipster hat nearly slides off his dome.

"Congratulations, dear sir. You have made a wise and prudent decision. Nothing delights me more than giving virtuous teens exactly what they deserve. Call the same number if your new sister malfunctions, and I'll send an attendant straight away."

The TV clicks off. Just as I suspect a whiff of malice lurking beneath his polite manners, my dad's voice breaks my train of thought.

"Jay. Before you start another game, Nic has something she wishes to say." Footsteps thump down the stairs, and I stand, anxious to meet this brand-new (and improved) sister of mine. When she appears, I'm frankly surprised by my disappointment. Other than having brushed her hair, Nic looks no different from ten minutes ago. Then again, maybe not. Her smile is natural rather than guarded. As if she actually means it! In a way, that is freakier than the freaky guy.

"I'm sorry, Jay. I was hogging the TV even when I knew you wanted to use it. Please accept my apology."

"Um, sure."

Dad beams before leaving the family room, clearly crediting his parenting skills for our unusually positive interaction. I motion for Nic to join me. What I do next can best be described as effing insane, but it's the only way I can be certain. I lift two controllers. "Do you want to play?"

"Of course, dear brother."

Yeah, she's a robot. There is literally no other possible explanation.

CHAPTER 14

"Get good."

My actual sister's disgust for video games is matched by my contempt for her phony friend Brandi. Or, for that matter, the conniving Brandi clone Nic has become. Contrast that to my robot sister, who gleefully takes the controller and cradles the thing in her hands as if she's holding a baby rabbit. Much like my actual sister, she has no clue. This should prove interesting.

"I'm going to call you NicBot," I tell her.

"You may call me Nic if you wish."

"No, too weird. Not that this isn't already weird but, you know, weirder. Let's try a fighting game." I set it up and proceed to thrash her mercilessly. It's almost not even fun, like picking off newbs from the internet. In other words, exactly what would happen if Nic ever played me, except without any bickering, quitting in a huff, or bitching to Mom and Dad. This battle will be brief. I need maybe another ten seconds to finish her off. "Yo," I say. "Get good."

NicBot tilts her head, devoid of expression, and blinks. "Download complete," she says, and from then on, she's invincible. Aerials with twists and flips. Crazy moves I've never seen before, and I've watched most "best of" compilations out there. None of my counter plays do any damage. Before long, she has destroyed me.

My jaw drops. "What happened?"

"I got good, as you requested. That was most enjoyable, dear brother. Would you like to play again?"

"Hold up." I dump the controller on the couch. I'm not touching the thing until I figure this out. "So if I tell you to do something, you'll do it?"

"Within the confines of my programming, yes. I am a SisBot 4000 and my purpose is to be the best possible sister pursuant to your specifications."

"Sweet." I consider the thousands of options this unlocks and know immediately which one to choose. "Let's try a multiplayer game. Here." I borrow her controller to cue her up and pass it back to her when I'm done. "Give yourself a handle while I check if Paulo is online."

I put on my headset. This is going to be sweet. If anyone is due comeuppance, that would be Paulo.

Before we begin, Dad pops into the family room, bursting with excitement. "I have news you'll both enjoy. The two-hour delay has officially become a snow day."

I high-five NicBot. Her enthusiasm is sluggish, then dialed up to eleven. She'll need to download a modulator. We'll address that later.

Dad looks at NicBot and asks, "Have you walked Scruffy yet?" After a clunky pause, she answers, "This morning."

Where is Scruffy? I scan the carpet, realize what I'm doing, and stop. Dad's eyebrows are already deepening. I worry he has sensed the bend in reality, and I'd rather not encourage his suspicions. Maybe he'd find all this as interesting as I do but it's not as if I understand how it works. I'm going to keep it to myself for now. The last thing I want to do is rile Dad up before I can explain what's going on.

"Do you two have any homework?"

"No," I say, and NicBot follows suit.

Dad squints at me. "Don't you have an English essay?"

"Not due until Monday."

"But didn't you say—"

"It's fine," I say. "I'll do it this weekend."

"Right." Dad stretches his back. "I guess I'm the only one with work today. A new client contacted me so I'll be in my office. We'll break for lunch. Maybe later we can throw snowballs?"

He eagerly awaits a response.

"I've got a lot of gaming to do. We'll see how it goes."

"Got it. See you at lunch." Dad brushes it off, but disappointment warbles his tone. I feel bad about it but, you know, gaming.

After Dad leaves, NicBot turns to me. "I have a math packet due tomorrow. It should take me only a few minutes."

"Lucky you. I actually have two essays to write, and the other one is due tomorrow. Maybe the snow will be heavy. Do you think we'll have off again tomorrow?"

NicBot doesn't answer. I consider having her add a meteorology function, but those predictions are wrong half the time anyway. I contact Paulo instead. Not surprisingly, he's online and responds straight away. "Wassup, Jay!"

"Hello, gamer. Are you ready to get destroyed again?"

Paulo's taunting laughter comes through loud and clear on my headset. "If by *again* you mean for the first time by some team you put together, then yeah." Paulo is hardcore but never tires of beating me. I'm the only one on the lacrosse team who gives him a challenge unlike Devin, a casual gamer with no skills, and Gavin who doesn't play at all. "You sound hungry for abuse, and I am ready to serve."

"Sure, Paulo, but I should warn you. I have a

good feeling this morning."

Paulo trash-talks while we wait for other gamers to fill out our teams. "Get good," I whisper to NicBot, and she does her robot seizure thing. Download complete. Man, I wish I could do that. Must be nice to be a walking cheat code.

Once we start, the game goes as expected with NicBot leading the team on a brilliant campaign, the likes of which have not been seen since the march of Napoleon. Hold up, I'm going switch that to Genghis Khan because we slaughter them. Paulo is the last man standing. We light him up.

"Oh, wow. It just be like that."

"Told ya," I say. "We crushed you, man."

Paulo scoffs. "*You* didn't crush me. *She* did. Who the heck is SisBot 4000?"

I freeze, gripped by a panicky sensation. How does he know about the SisBot 4000? I eke out a lame "Who?"

"SisBot 4000. The handle of the supergamer with the sick moves."

"Oh, right, yeah, her. She's some internet rando."

"Really?" he says, stretching the word as if it's a rubber band he's about to snap in my face. "Cause when she talks I can hear her on your headset."

Busted. I am such a crappy liar.

"So the internet rando is sitting right next to you," he continues, clarifying further for the morons in the audience.

"Right, yeah. I'm messing around. She's, uh, she's my cousin."

"No kidding. Is she hot?"

"Shut up, Paulo. She can hear you."

Paulo laughs. He obviously already knows. "Hey, SisBot 4000. Have you heard the rumors? Jay's got a really small peen."

I disconnect. "And we're done," I say, tossing the headphones on the couch. "Ignore him."

"What's a peen?"

I cringe. "You seriously don't know."

"I am equipped with a standard database required to cover anticipated parameters. Beyond that, I know everything Nic knows. No more, no less."

So not a whole lot, at least when it comes to anything sexual. Some people assume Nic is experienced because she hangs out with Brandi, but Nic is jarringly naive. Middle-grade-level cussing makes her wince. Who knows how she's handling high school. She's the reason I got into the habit of saying *effing*. You drop an F-bomb on Nic, and she will lose her shit.

"I don't have time to explain all this to you," I say, and flippantly add, "download Urban Dictionary or something."

NicBot tilts her head and her expression goes blank. Then she blinks. "Download complete."

"What! Oh, no. Please tell me you did *not* download Urban Dictionary."

"I did, as requested."

Great. For fifteen years, I've managed not to rattle Nic's fragile innocence, yet in less than an hour, I have already corrupted the robot version. "How do you feel?"

"As a robot, I have no feelings, so I feel the same."

"Lucky for you. After ten minutes on the site, I want to take a shower."

"I understand. If I had to describe the sensation, the closest approximation would be dirty. Dirty as in balls deep in a vat of splooge." She smiles warmly, an unnatural expression that would have been disturbing even if my little sister hadn't said *balls deep in a vat of splooge*. Despite the download, my robot sister maintains Nic's innocent demeanor. "You and Paulo must share a locker room."

"Huh? I mean, yeah. We're on the same lacrosse team."

"So that is how he's familiar with your small peen?"

"What? No! He's kidding. Ugh." I bury my head in my hands. She may be friendlier than Nic, but NicBot is equally frustrating. "I do not have a—wait, why do I care what you think? You're a freaking robot. And why does it sound like there's a cow in the family room? What are you eating?" I lift my head and watch NicBot take another bite of the game controller.

I have no words for this situation. We stare at each other. I'm floored while she grazes on electronics. She slurps up the last bit, leaving only the cord with a couple of splayed wires.

NicBot eyeballs the controller on my lap. I would think one controller would be enough food, but what do I know about feeding robots? I offer it to her. She flashes another of those unsettling Nic smiles and devours the controller to the cord like the ravenous robot that is my new and improved sister.

So much for my plan to play video games all morning. And now I'm going to have to find more clients to tutor so I can buy new controllers. Even worse, she's still hungry. NicBot plucks her phone out of her pocket and her smile lights up. I've seen Nic do this a thousand times—it's her usual reaction to looking at her phone. Stuffing the device into her mouth on the other hand, not so much. NicBot scarfs the thing the way Scruffy devours table scraps.

"I'd offer you my phone, but I'm expecting a text from my girlfriend," I say and immediately feel compelled to correct that lame-ass lie. "Well, not expecting so much as hoping. And not girlfriend so much as former girlfriend who no longer wants anything more to do with me. Even that's charitable considering what she said."

"What did she say?" NicBot asks as she

licks her fingers clean.

"I don't want to talk about it. Especially not with you." I cringe at the absurdity of getting irritated by a program. "Sorry. I know you're not Nic. But you look like her and that is setting me off. Hey, didn't you say you know everything Nic knows?"

"Yes. I understand that you're talking about Jenna."

"Right. Then I don't need to explain this, do I?"

NicBot smiles in such a kind way, I get flashbacks to when we were kids. "We don't need to talk about anything you don't want to, dear brother."

Now I feel extra dumb for snapping at a robot. I'm about to vow never to do it again when I notice NicBot drooling at the TV as though it's a pizza with all the toppings.

"Don't even go there," I say. "The TV is off-limits. We can't afford to replace it. Not since Dad lost his job, anyway."

NicBot settles into a striking facsimile of surprise and concern. Her head position and brow furrowing are impeccable. Props to the coders tasked with emotive facial expressions. I doubt human Nic could have conveyed her emotions with such finesse. "Nic is unaware of financial concerns."

"Yeah, our parents don't like to discuss money. I know because they had to talk to me about paying for college. As in, they couldn't. My options are community college with a job or a full-ride scholarship somewhere."

"Good thing you're smart."

I brush away her comment. "Smart is rarely enough to get you a full ride. The package the University of Maryland offered me was mostly athletic with enough merit tossed in to cover the remainder. And it's annually renewable so there's no guarantee I'll make it through all four years. When I told this to Paulo, he was like, *Easy, don't get injured.* He gives such helpful advice."

"That certainly is helpful. If your injury affects your ability to play, you might lose your scholarship."

"Yeah, that was—forget it. Right, so the plan is not to get injured," I say. "Good thing I don't play a violent sport."

"I believe lacrosse is in fact—"

"Stop. Let's focus on your issue." I tug my phone out of my pocket and hold it a safe distance from NicBot. "I'll contact the freaky guy. This counts as a malfunction, I think." As soon as I press the button, the freaky guy appears on the TV screen. He's staring off to the side as if I've walked in on him at a private moment. He shifts to face me, the glint in his eyes as beguiling as ever.

"Customer service, the honorable Phineas Lindencroft presiding. To whom shall I direct your compliments?"

I don't even have to think about it. "Definitely to the coders of NicBot. She is one kick-ass gamer." As I speak, I stuff my phone into the relative safety of my pocket. "I'd show you what I mean but I'm down two controllers at the moment, um, honorable Phineas Lindencroft."

"Please, call me Phin."

"Sure, why not? Listen, Phin. The robot's great, but she has a critical design flaw. She needs to consume electronics. At what appears to be an unsustainable rate."

"Understood. Please allow me to assist you. I can activate a setting on the SisBot 4000 that will provide external sustenance so she will not need to eat while in your house."

I know this is good news, but the ease with which he offers a solution gives me pause. "How convenient. You know, Phin. That seems like a pretty obvious bug."

"Bug?"

"Bug, yeah. A flaw. And check you out, all set with a fix. Makes me wonder, Phin. If you knew about the issue and had a solution handy, why hadn't you corrected it in advance? What's your angle?"

"Patience, my good fellow. All will be resolved by the day's end."

"And that's intentionally vague. Resolved in what way? That could be good *or* bad." I hit him with my most determined stare. "You need to tell me what the hell is going on before this goes any farther."

Phin shifts his suit, nonplussed as ever. "My dear boy, the world does work that way."

"Says who, you?"

A grin flashes across his face as though a lightning strike before being dispersed by his thunderous guffaw. "You exalt me! But no, I cannot take the credit. I am a mere passenger on the cosmic supercollider." Phin flips his wrist as though to shoo away all concerns. "Like embryos and oligarchs, all will come together in time. I suggest you remain patient."

"Patients are for doctors, I want to know now."

Phin puckers his face as though I replaced his morning constitutional with a shot of lemon juice. "You have a singular humor," he says.

"And you have a strange charm," I counter.

Phin brightens immediately. "Hip, hip, hurray. Three quays for Master Jay." He tips his hat in a courteous way that also comes off as intentionally snobbish. "My dear boy, I acknowledge your haste, but let's take a moment for perspective. The celestial dance has endured for some fourteen billion years. And that's merely the last bit. If we allow ourselves to embrace the grand scheme of things, I believe you will find yourself more than capable of patience, at least until later this afternoon. Even without a medical degree."

"Fine."

Phin stretches his arms. "Your graciousness dazzles. I shall inscribe your peerless sacrifice into the annals of time." His patronizing elegance annoys me, but that's not even the half of it. "Returning to the matter at hand, if I may. To activate this premium setting, I will need to levy a cost."

"I knew it! NicBot is a free app."

Phin blinks at me. "I am unfamiliar with your reference."

"In-app purchases. That's how they get you."

"Indeed they do. Shall I continue?" I motion for him to go ahead given that he is obviously going to anyway. "In exchange for activating the external sustenance setting on your SisBot 4000, I will add one of two hazards to your day. You may choose which. Are you ready?"

I look over at NicBot. "I'm ready for this day to get a whole lot weirder," I say, and wince as I belatedly recognize the absurdity of predicting *weirder* to my robot sister. I turn back to the freaky guy on the TV. "Sure, Phin. Knock yourself out."

CHAPTER 15

"Don't let anything by you."

When I was younger, I wanted nothing more than to play baseball like my dad. My quick reflexes snagging line drives made me a Little League sensation at shortstop. Nothing got by me. Except when I was at-bat. Then practically everything got by me. By middle school, my fielding ability could no longer offset my poor hitting, and I was demoted to bench warmer. I tried out for soccer instead.

I hoped my quick reflexes would help me at soccer, but two minor obstacles popped up. The first was controlling the soccer ball while running. I could do either without a problem but both at the same time, not so much. At least, not without serious risk of face planting.

The second issue posed a more serious and less humorous problem. If something launches into my face, I grab it. I don't think that's a bad instinct. Why should I let something slam into my head when I have two functional hands to protect me? Letting them flop at my sides while in imminent danger runs counter to every impulse.

Around the umpteenth time I touched the ball in practice, Coach Scudder blew his whistle with a long, exasperated blare as if I had cut him off in traffic. I expected him to cut me in turn, but instead, he shifted me to goalie. I took to it right away and became a starter by eighth grade.

We did well that year, advancing to the county finals. The Park Hollow soccer coach had high hopes for me, but the transition to the high school level did not go well. The best players' kicking range expanded to the far corners of the net, well beyond my diving ability. I stuck it out as a backup on the jayvee squad for the year but bailed early into sophomore year. I'd already played benchwarmer. Not a position I planned to recap in yet another sport.

And that would have been the end of my spotty sports career if it hadn't been for drugs and alcohol. And by this I mean, if it hadn't been for the two varsity lacrosse goalies tearing around town fueled by drugs and alcohol until four in the morning. Their night ended when they wrapped their car around a pole. Besides the tangled front bumper, the damage included two broken headlights and two broken bones, a femur and a clavicle, if I remember correctly.

What follows, I remember vividly: Coach Coup looming before me as I leave our mandatory Good Choices student assembly, whose subtitle might have well been How Many Effing Times Do We Have to Tell You Not to Drink and Drive! He informs me that I will be trying out for lacrosse goalie. I laugh. That hulking middle-aged mass of muscle glowers, shutting me up quick. Nobody laughs at Coach Coup.

I try a gentler tack. "I played goalie in *soccer*. I've never even played lacrosse."

"Same concept," he says. "Don't let anything by you."

"Right." I make the executive decision to hold back further amusement. His marble-etched expression tells me I chose correctly. When I get to know him better, I learn he isn't mean. He simply never jokes about anything. Ever.

"I'm told you had trouble with the far corners." Coach Coup says it the same way a priest might say, *I'm told you enjoy fornicating with woodland creatures*. I am appropriately mortified. "That won't be a problem in lacrosse," he continues. "The goal is much smaller."

You can't argue the obvious. The goal is definitely smaller. But so is the ball. And the speed it comes at you is insane. Playing goalie in lacrosse is basically volunteering to get beat up for 48 minutes, even with the padding. Only a crazy person would do this. The odd thing is, I like it. I think I like it for the same reason my dad liked being a pitcher. I'm good at it. When you're good at something, you want to get better. And when you get better, you want to be the best. Coach Coup promoted me to starting goalie by junior year. Lacrosse is crazy fun. The downside? Gavin and Devin.

From a lacrosse perspective, I can't complain about those guys. Gavin and Devin are our star attackmen. They're the reason we're the highest-scoring team in our division. And, to be fair, the initial reason college recruiters swing by to check us out, a thing I care about ever since my depressing financial talk with Mom and Dad.

Gavin is a piece of work. I sense something is off about him soon after we meet. On the surface, Gavin's a superstar. Confidence oozes out of him. He's the flesh-and-blood version of the terrifying caricature on every lacrosse poster. Sinewy thighs sprouting from shorts. Blazing eyes sandwiched between helmet and square jaw. Hulking arms gripping the stick as though he's more inclined to pummel you with it than he is to catch the ball.

And it's not just the look. Gavin's a natural leader with the talent to back it up, at least in lacrosse. But there's a dark side with him, always an angle he's working to hurt someone.

With the team, he's always pulling practical jokes, which is no problem if everyone can have a laugh after. But no, the laughs are for him and him alone. His cruelty is as ever-present as a green streak on a fake tan. Couch Coup thinks Gavin leads the team in slashing penalties because of flawed stick handling, but I'm not convinced. I think there's another reason.

Gavin is an effing psycho.

I'm not the only one to notice. To the guys on the team, Gavin incites as much terror as entertainment. He gets away with it partly out of respect but mostly because no one wants to cross him. As captain, Gavin dominates the team with his charismatic pull, and we all revolve around him.

Among Gavin's many satellites, Devin is for sure the biggest, dumbest rock of us all. The guy has the build of a monster truck and the shagginess of a lowland gorilla. Devin could make it work for him but he's too awkward and, frankly, terrifying. Girls avoid him unless they're sloppy drunk at a party, and the inevitable after-party vomiting isn't solely due to a hangover. Devin is destined to become one of those older guys who roll up in a white van asking random girls on the street if they want to come inside to check out his speaker system and mini-fridge.

That about sums up Devin. Hairy and creepy. I think his spirit animal is a tarantula.

Given all this, you can understand why I don't think much of Paulo when I meet him. He's always hanging with Gavin and Devin. I know

I shouldn't assume guilt by association, but I suffer the same prejudices like everyone else. At least until Paulo and I meet up gaming and become fast friends over our headsets. We don't interact much in real life, but that suits me fine. If Gavin doesn't know, Paulo and I don't have to deal with him.

Mostly, Paulo and I talk about gaming, the thing we have in common. But he tends to open up about personal stuff during first-person shooter firefights. I think it's like therapy for him. Over the last few firefights, I've pieced together his backstory. Here's the basic gist.

Paulo moves to the area the summer before sixth grade. This is for sure the worst possible timing. You do not want to start middle school with zero friends. What happens next is exactly what anyone would predict: the bullying, bigotry, and basic harassment we've all come to expect from middle school.

But all that comes to a screeching halt the day Paulo and Gavin happen to be assigned to the same pickleball team in gym class. Those two pair up and crush all comers. From then on, Paulo is Gavin's boy. No one can pick on Paulo without risking Gavin's savage fury. So basically, no one picks on Paulo. Problem solved.

Gavin and Devin are already tight and now the three of them do everything together, including join lacrosse. I don't meet them until sophomore year when I join the team. By then, they are thick as thieves. Not knowing the backstory, I lump those three together until I met this sick gamer with the handle DontCrosseTheGatorBitch.

A crosse is another name for a lacrosse stick and my high school mascot is a gator, so I use my advanced deductive skills to conclude that the handle probably belongs to someone on the team. Soon after, I overhear Paulo go off on Devin about how his gaming skills are trash, and I start to think DontCrosseTheGatorBitch might be Paulo. I decide to solve this mystery by going all cloak and dagger. Don't ask me why. That's how I roll.

So one day at practice, Paulo's catching his breath on the bench while we're running drills. Coach Coup is letting the other goalies get beat up for a while, lucky me. I plop down next to Paulo, but I don't look at him. Instead, I act as though we're characters in one of those black-and-white film noir movies my dad loves so much. I say to no one in particular, "Don't cross the Gator, bitch."

I sense Paulo staring right at me, hard enough to confirm I got it right. Finally, he says, "NotADouche27?"

I nod, impressed that he guessed my handle straight away. I figure there are at least twenty-six other gamers who also claim not to be a douche.

"Cool," Paulo says. "Buy a headset. I hate

typing." And with that, he runs back on the field.

That's the approximate length of most conversations Paulo and I have in real life, but we talk every weekend, sometimes for hours. Paulo may be buds with Gavin and Devin but he's not like those two jackoffs. Never is this clearer than when Paulo tells me what really happened between Gavin and Jenna. Jenna with silky brown hair. Jenna with piercing eyes. Jenna, my girlfriend.

Briefly my girlfriend.

How many days can I claim Jenna was my girlfriend? A week at most, if I'm being generous. Don't scoff. It was an intense week. Against all reason, I'm optimistic she might still consider us together despite the awful stunt my sister pulled. I should probably text Jenna to find out where we stand, but the downside is then I would find out where we stand. Right now I prefer not knowing to knowing. I suppose this makes me a pessimist, not an optimist. Yeah, let's split the difference and say I'm a realist. As in, I really don't want to think about it.

I also really figured if anyone came between Jenna and me, it would be Gavin, not my sister. Gavin dumped Jenna months ago, but that's never stopped him from being possessive. It's rough for Jenna to have any association with Gavin, but at least those two hooking up had nothing to do with me. Unlike Amaya. That disaster is on me. Like an idiot, I introduced the two of them.

Amaya and I go way back; we practically grew up together. We met in preschool where she and I were praised for being the two children in the group who knew all our letters. We've been king and queen of the geeks ever since then, although neither of us properly fit the geek stereotype. I've got sports and Amaya's got style.

Amaya presents as the most cosmopolitan person in the world. Well, Baltimore County, anyway. She's a jet setter, a trendsetter, all spun around a bewildering secret. The farthest she's traveled is Orlando, Florida. Blame her grandparents for the misdirection. Amaya speaks fluent French thanks to her Haitian grandmother, dances a stirring tango thanks to her Brazilian grandfather, and dresses chic thanks to her other grandparents, who were famous back in the day for putting Milan on the fashion map. Amaya always dresses as if she stepped off the runway from Paris or Rio and is on her way to a photo spread for, well, Cosmo.

Incidentally, her parents are tragically dull. Passion must skip a generation.

As geek king and queen, Amaya and I unintentionally confuse people into thinking we're a couple. We aren't and never have been. But we've always been friends, latching together since preschool like binary planets, soaring through life a fair distance from the crowd. I don't know if Pluto and Charon have a sexual spark, but Amaya and I never did.

And yes, dwarf planets are planets. Don't even start. Are dwarf people, people? Of course they are. Don't be an astrological bigot.

The point is, I've always gotten a sisterly vibe from Amaya. Like she'd ride stallions with me any time but never ride me like a stallion. By the way, this is a less bizarre reference than you might think. Until my grandfather died, I spent part of every summer at a horse farm. Riding stallions with my sister is an actual thing I've done. Actually, the horses may not have been stallions. More likely they were geldings.

A quick aside on my aside—if you ever want to induce castration anxiety in a young boy, spend an afternoon teaching him the difference between a stallion and a gelding. Worked for me. Thanks, Grandpa.

My point is Amaya and I made a good couple in theory and good friends in practice. She remains one of the most understanding people I've ever known, generous in ways my male friends have never been. Like how she forgave me for introducing her to Gavin. Considering how Gavin mistreated Amaya, I've apologized several times, but she always brushes it off.

"I make my own decisions," she says.

Wow, right? She's a rare soul who takes responsibility for her actions rather than deflects the moment things go sour. If you've never met someone like that and have trouble imagining it, think of Nic and picture the opposite.

Although I haven't had that problem with NicBot. This is hard to explain, considering her programming is supposedly based on Nic. Hanging with NicBot this morning hasn't resulted in any of Nic's usual pitfalls. In fact, it's been pretty entertaining.

Anyway, all this is to say that when Phin offered paintball as an alternative hazard in exchange for the external sustenance thing, I leaped at the option. If I'm to be stuck in the house all day with no game controllers, I might as well find another way to have fun.

CHAPTER 16

*"You know I support you
in all your life choices."*

NicBot and I hunker down behind the blue couch in the family room, paintball guns in hand. The nervous energy displayed by the robot version of my little sister brings out my protective nature, although I suspect she was programmed with this goal in mind.

"Stay down," I whisper. "I'll take a peek." I poke my head above the couch and yank it back when I hear a click. Turbulent air ruffles my hair followed by a sharp splat behind me.

"How many?" she asks.

"Didn't get a good look. Or any, really."

NicBot slides the barrel over the couch while she peers around the side. She fires a single ball and stands. "Got him."

I leap to my feet, waving the gun by the

foregrip in case she's mistaken. She is not, and I feel silly. "Where did he go?"

"He disappeared when I hit him."

"Disappeared?" I swing around to check the wall behind me for the expected paint splotch. There is none. I turn back to NicBot. "I don't know what ammo we're using," I say, tapping the loader, "but it isn't paint."

"No. Maybe that's a good thing. We won't have to clean up after."

"True, that is a plus, but what happens if we get hit?"

NicBot raises an eyebrow. "Don't get hit?"

"Great advice," I say, and NicBot beams with pride. I don't understand why she doesn't get sarcasm. Nic is a master, a natural savant in the obnoxious arts. She would never fail to recognize a response dripping with it. "Anyway," I continue. "Impressive shot. I never even told you to get good."

"I do not believe that will be necessary. Nic has skills."

Skills? Nic? I think the most athletic thing I've seen Nic do is dance. Whatever, not worth arguing. We've got more urgent issues. "How many of them are there?" I wonder aloud. "And where are they coming from?" Footsteps scurry across the foyer, answering my question. NicBot and I drop behind the couch.

"Sounds like a troop," she says. In confirmation, a blistering volley of paintballs—

or whatever they are—spray over us. I press my back against the couch. Blue paint splatters the wall only to vanish in an instant.

We return fire over the couch. I don't know if our balls find their mark because I'm shooting over my head, but it does prompt a retreat. I catch a glimpse of one as he escapes around the corner. He's dressed in a soldier's uniform from the nineteenth century, but it's his headgear that makes me groan.

"I think we've been invaded by Prussia," I say. NicBot tilts her head in a manner to effectively simulate curiosity. "The spiked metal helmet tipped me off," I continue. "Also, my essay due tomorrow is on the Franco-Prussian War. And no, I don't think that's a coincidence."

"Phin may be having fun," NicBot says.

"That's what I figured." I motion for her to follow as I move around the couch. We don't get far before the advance guard charges. The pointy helmet formation is somehow both goofy and chilling. I clip the first guy, but not before he fires off a shot. A searing pain stabs my inner thigh followed by a compression that wraps around my entire body as though I've been transported to the ocean depths. I can neither breathe nor hold myself upright.

I fall in slow motion. Time decelerates around me while paintballs glide through the air in both directions. One impacts the wall behind the soldiers. Red paint explodes in an arc that bends the wall before it slaps back into place intact. A second ball with a sharper trajectory finds its mark. Red paint detonates against the Prussian and a similar arc lifts him off his feet. A moment later, the air snaps around him and he is gone. NicBot dives over me as she fires, picking off the entire row of soldiers, one after the other.

This triggers a memory, buried until now but so dynamic I can smell the pungent horse pasture sweetened by dogwood trees. Nic and I stand with Grandpa at a distant corner of his property where a sloping rise contains a row of stumps. We hold BB guns and take aim at cans perched on the stumps. My shots rattle but do not overturn the cans. *I nearly got the last one*, I say with unearned pride, my prepubescent voice grating to my ears. *Your turn, Nic*, Grandpa says. Nic knocks off four cans with four precision shots. Grandpa and I exchange glances. *Did I do it right, Grandpa?* Nic asks. *Yep*, he says. Grandpa's hand rests on her shoulder while she beams up at him. I toss my gun into the dirt.

All at once, the pressure releases. I gasp for air. NicBot looms above me, a warrior robot princess, her arm outstretched. For a moment, a familiar shame returns, but I brush it off. Who cares if Nic's a better shot than I am? Good for her. I can't remember the last time I've been impressed with Nic. It's cool that she's kick-ass.

"Are you hurt?" NicBot asks, helping me to my feet.

Once upright, I examine my pants. While the blue paint has vanished, a burning sensation lingers on my inner thigh. "That shot was way too close," I say, measuring the distance to my crotch with one fingertip. "I need to get my cup."

"Are you thirsty?"

"Not that kind of cup. A cup to protect my junk." Now she's confused by the word *junk*. "Look it up in your new dictionary."

"Junk. Ah, male genitalia."

"You got it."

"Curious how the other two definitions are *useless rubbish* and *something of little to no value*. Did women come up with the idea to include male genitalia?"

"I don't—" I cut myself off when I notice NicBot is smiling. I am the unwitting patsy of robot humor. "Nice. How about less commentary, more shooting Prussians."

"Of course, dear brother." She chuckles when she catches me smile. I was trying to hold it in so she wouldn't have the satisfaction, but she makes an amusing observation.

"Anyway," I say, "my cup is upstairs with my lacrosse gear. Let's try to cut a path to the stairs."

We advance, fingers hovering over triggers, barrels shifting to cover multiple angles as we round the kitchen and press through the hallway into the foyer. When we reach the stairwell, we spot a column of soldiers in spiked helmets positioned against the railing. A man in the center wears a feathery plume and the grandest handlebar mustache of them all. We flee under their opening salvo, blue paint bursting behind us.

"I do not believe a full-frontal attack is advisable," NicBot says after we reach the kitchen.

"No, forget that idea. I'll make my own cup," I say. "To get back to the ammo question. When I was hit, gravity got intense and time slowed."

NicBot's expression goes blank for a moment, presumably to access her database. And she's back. "The paintballs must contain supermassive energy to have a gravitational effect and warp time-space."

"That makes sense. I mean, as much as any of this does. I think we're blasting the Prussians back to their timeline. And one other thing, the hit on me warped time and gravity but also stimulated a repressed memory."

"Interesting. That may be a coincidence. I do not believe repressed memories are included in general relativity."

"No, Einstein must have missed it."

"Or it's unrelated."

I shrug. "I mean, he might have missed it."

"I see." NicBot speaks with the gentle prodding of a kindergarten teacher. "And which do you think is more likely?"

Ignoring her, I shake the loader on my gun. "I'll bet we can produce a wormhole if we convert these from semi- to fully automatic."

"Let's not do that."

"No, of course, we wouldn't. I'm saying if we did."

"Let's not do that."

"We're not going to do that!" I say. "But hypothetically speaking, how would we—"

"Dear brother."

"Fine, whatever, I'll play along." I search the kitchen for supplies. "It will take me a few minutes to make my cup. I need you to act as a sentinel to cover me. Give me a heads up if they attack."

NicBot thinks or, rather, processes information in a thoughtful manner. "They will have to descend the stairs to start an offensive, so I believe it will be best for me to sneak around to the other side through the library."

The library? I've never heard anyone call that room a library, but it does have floor-to-ceiling bookshelves along the walls. Fair enough. "Sure. Take a position in the library. Hold them off if necessary."

"I will do my best."

"Don't let anything by you," I say, inadvertently quoting my lacrosse coach.

NicBot stands at attention and performs an about-face. Dropping when she reaches the carpet, she combat crawls away.

As entertaining as it is to watch her go, I figure I'd better get started. I pick out the tiniest colander from the cabinet. The metal object is more circular than I had hoped but approximates the size of my cup. After swiping twine from the junk drawer, I measure two arm lengths and cut the twine with a knife. I crouch behind the kitchen island while I loop the twine around the colander handles. I stop a few times when I hear noises. No, I'm good.

Wait, is that something? I guess not.

My heart pounds. I find this sort of thing relaxing in video games. Once again, real-life disappoints. Chill, Jay. NicBot hasn't called out. No shots fired. You're fine.

I kneel to better position the colander over my groin, tightening and shifting the twine around my legs and waist. With my cup secured, I tie the twine into place. This should hold up. When I stand, I realize I left my gun on the floor behind the kitchen island.

That turns out to be the least of my problems.

My dad holds his coffee to his lips and freezes mid-sip. He gawks at the colander strapped to my groin until his surprise fades back to nonchalance. Concluding his sip, he smacks his lips.

"You know I support you in all your life choices," Dad says.

"Uh, right. Good to know. This isn't a thing,

though."

"Isn't it?"

"No."

"All right. What is it?"

"It's, uh." How to explain. "The freaky guy —" Nope. "You see, Nic—" Double nope. "There's a whole squad of—" Not going there either.

I guess I'm not going anywhere. Instead, I rest my hands on my hips and press my pelvis forward to showcase my ridiculous cup in a stance of pride. "Yeah. It's a thing."

Dad rests his mug on the island and steps closer. His eyes glimmer with affirmation. "You know I'll always love you no matter what."

I match his sincerity. "Thanks, Dad."

"Right then. I'm going back to work." Dad retrieves his coffee. "And I will definitely not be distracted by social media or any websites that would upset your mother."

"Cool. And I'm definitely not going to join forces with a robot to combat a time-traveling Prussian platoon in an epic supermassive paintball battle."

Dad had moved to sip his coffee but tents his eyebrows instead. "Wait, is that another, um, thing? Or, no, a video game. You know what? Doesn't matter. Good chat. See you at lunch." He spins away and walks down the hall to his office only to stop and take one more look.

I strike my cup with my knuckle. Dad salutes. "Right," he says. "Good chat."

Once Dad closes the door behind him, I walk over to the counter. Grabbing the knife, I slice the twine and yank off the colander. Screw that thing; the contraption is already pinching me. Time for a new plan.

CHAPTER 17

"The truth is complicated."

I scoop my paintball gun off the floor and slip into the library to join NicBot, who has contorted her body into an absurdly uncomfortable position against the stairwell. She's probably been rooted there the entire time without complaint. Robot soldiers are clearly the future of warfare. I know I'm not the first person to figure this out, but it's still troubling. The German murmuring upstairs heightens my distress.

I settle next to NicBot. She keeps her sights on the Prussians while she speaks. "Was Operation Fashion-a-Cup successful, dear brother?"

"Yes and no, but don't worry about it," I say. "I have a plan to finish them off. I'll go around the other way through the hallway, take a few shots, and retreat. When they counterattack, hold your fire until they're all downstairs. Then you pick them off from behind while I keep them from entering the kitchen."

"Understood."

"Ready to end this, dear sister?"

"Yes, dear brother."

Rolling back into the kitchen, I stifle my amusement. I hadn't meant to say *dear sister* out loud, but whatever. It's so effing hilarious when NicBot does it; how could I not join in?

I tiptoe to the end of the hallway and press against the wall. Here goes. Leading with the barrel, I hug the corner and aim at the last Prussian in the row. I squeeze the trigger, sending him back to where he came from. Blue paint slaps against the walls as I withdraw. I prepare to retreat to the kitchen but hear no footsteps in pursuit. I hold my breath and listen. Still nothing. Guess they didn't take the bait.

I try a few more times, and each time they respond with a bombardment but no advance. We're all entrenched. Bad guys are much less cautious in video games. I have no idea how to break the stalemate. I'm lost in thought when Dad's voice startles me.

"Jay?"

Crap. The office door is closed but opens right into the foyer. I hope he doesn't come out here. "Yeah, Dad?"

"Can you turn your game down? It's pretty

loud."

"Uh." I decide to go with my usual excuse. "I can't reach the remote."

"All right. I'll crank up my music. Give me fifteen, maybe twenty minutes? I'm finishing something up. We'll break for lunch after."

"Cool. No rush. I want to finish the final battle."

If my dad responds, I miss it because a Prussian blasts the gun out of my hands. The gun lands on the floor within reach, but it might as well be in Berlin. Each time I reach for my gun, blue paint explodes around it. I finally give up and crouch down, shielded but unarmed. A rhythmic scuffle announces the advance I've been wanting. Except without my paintball gun, I am doomed.

And another worrisome thought comes to mind. If one supermassive paintball creates a gravitational effect so intense I can't breathe, what would several do? Terror makes me brave. I slap the grip frame to spin the gun toward me, yanking my hand back as blue paint smacks the surfaces before disappearing. The barrel is within reach. I snag it and race into the kitchen, juggling the gun while I spin around the corner. Shots whiz past me.

I flip the gun around and fire blindly into the hallway, aiming up, aiming down, trying different angles, shooting wildly, my fingers cramping and I squeeze and squeeze and squeeze and squeeze.

Then: silence. My gun has vanished. Soft footsteps approach.

"NicBot?" I ask, hopeful.

"Yes, dear brother."

I step into the open where NicBot stands, hands at her side, a placid smile draped across her face. "What happened?" I ask her.

"Your plan was a success," she says. "Dropping your gun was a bold move."

"Bold move, sure. Do you know if I hit any of them?"

NicBot stares at the ceiling for a moment as though she is reviewing the footage. She blinks. "I don't believe you did, but you kept them confused long enough for me to finish them off."

That sounds about right. "Works for me. I'm getting my cup," I say and quickly add, "to drink from. The one in the refrigerator." I open the refrigerator and down the liquid in a few gulps. Followed by few deep breaths. And a brief meditation exercise to keep me from keeling over.

Peering at me is NicBot, the robotic personification of serenity. She doesn't have a pulse, but I'm sure it would be smooth and steady if she did. I, however, am beyond frazzled. "I'm going to crash upstairs until lunch. See you in a bit."

"I look forward to it, dear brother."

I walk through the library toward the

stairwell and spy a hole in the wall, right in the area where NicBot had contorted herself earlier. A lacrosse stick shoots out of the hole and pokes my foot. It's identical to my stick. In fact, I'd say it *was* mine except I know my stick is in my room.

The crosse retreats into the hole and reappears slower this time as if it knew it struck me and is being more careful. Strange, yes, but no stranger than anything else today. I move to the side to let it slide past me. Peering into the hole, I kneel down for a closer view.

The blackness in the hole is absolute, but I think I hear something, a muted pattering that becomes louder. Scruffy charges out of the hole and into my arms. I press my face against hers, and she licks me. It's not gross; it's our thing.

"No! Scruffy, come back!"

Is that NicBot? "Don't worry, I've got her," I say. How did that impish robot get herself stuck in the wall? I left her in the kitchen like ten seconds ago. This day gets weirder and weirder. Scruffy settles into my lap while I stroke her lumpy fur.

"Jay, is that you?"

I freeze mid pet. That is not NicBot. Much to my surprise, I am actually relieved to hear my sister's voice. "Nic? Actual Nic? Ha! I was wondering where you were. How did you get in there?"

"In where?"

Seriously? She doesn't know where she is?

"The hole Scruffy ran out of."

"How? What the—" She cuts herself off. When she speaks again, her tone is thick with suspicion. "Where are you right now?"

"I'm in the library. Where are you?"

"I'm also in the library. A room neither of us has ever called the library before today."

"Seriously, right?" I laugh. "NicBot came up with it."

"NicBot?" she says, and I flush. Oh, crap. Crap, crap, crap. "Jay?" she continues, injecting my name with a fiery venom. "Did you replace me with a robot?"

I grip Scruffy. She trembles in my arms, sensing my distress. "Wow. This is awkward." I often find addressing an uncomfortable situation's awkwardness will make things less awkward. Not this time. Best to come clean. "You see, this commercial appeared. I, uh, assumed it was a joke but then this robot—who looks like you but crushes it with video games— I mean she started out trash so I told her to get good and—doesn't matter. Oh! She helped me win a paintball match against this Prussian team that looked straight out of one of those cosplay reenactments and—you know what? That doesn't matter either. Let me start over. What I'm trying to say is NicBot's pretty cool. We've been having a blast together all morning."

"Yeah, well, JayBot is nice to me. We're having fun too," she says.

"JayBot? Wait a minute. Did you meet Phin?"

"Ugh, Phin. Don't get me started."

Dealing with surly Nic had thrown me off my stride. I'm getting the picture now. "Hold up. So you *also* replaced me with a robot. You did exactly the same thing I did. Yet somehow *you're* upset with *me*?"

"Because you—don't try to sneak out of this."

"Classic Nic. If I do it, it's terrible. But if you do it? No big deal."

"It's not my fault."

I groan. "Your favorite quote. Come on, Nic. Take responsibility for something."

She doesn't answer right away, but I can sense her anger radiating from deep within the hole. I don't miss it. "JayBot is nice to me," she says, more tearfully than I expected. "He doesn't make fun of me or insult me or make me feel stupid. It's been so great to have a brother who cares."

"Cares? Nic, he's a robot. A program. I get that he's cool—NicBot is also cool—but don't pretend there are actual emotions involved. And unlike the robot, I actually do care about you." She doesn't respond, so I continue. "So does Scruffy. Her ears perk up whenever you speak. I was wondering where she had gotten off to. I guess she's been in your world all morning." Scruffy rests her head on my lap. "Don't worry, you can have her back. I'll send your dog through the hole when I'm done petting her."

"Our dog, you mean."

I gasp. Scruffy's ears perk up. "*Our* dog?"

"Scruffy. The family dog." She says this casually as though she had ever before acknowledged joint ownership. "I know you love Scruffy as much as I do."

I pet the tufts on Scruffy's head around her perky ears. She bucks her head to lick my hand. "I don't know what to say, Nic. If JayBot explained that to you, then I am also a JayBot fan."

"No, he didn't—wait, how would JayBot know?"

"JayBot knows everything I know. I mean, I assume he does. NicBot knows everything you know."

"She does? What did you ask her?" Panic quivers her voice. Clearly, there is something she doesn't want me to find out. "I mean, you don't know if what she says is true," Nic adds. "She could be lying. Phin is always saying crazy things."

"Yeah, Phin is pretty extra," I say. "He's all, *I'll give you two choices* and he makes the floor lava. Like, actual lava. Nearly kills me. Next, he sends these freakish birds after me."

"That jerk!" Nic says. I have to admit, her reaction surprises me. I don't think Nic has ever defended me so emphatically.

"Exactly! But it all worked out. He gave me

a much more reasonable third choice."

"I'll bet he did."

"Yeah, it's all good. Anyway, I agree with you about Phin, but I think the robots are programmed to tell the truth. NicBot is a bit too honest, if anything. Oh, I know what you're worried about. No, I didn't ask NicBot about Gavin. I already know more than I want to know already."

Nic grunts. "What's your problem with me dating Gavin?"

"So, so, *so* many things. For starters, never trust a senior who wants to date a freshman." Her silence speaks volumes. "You do understand why seniors shouldn't date freshmen, right?"

"I don't know why *you* think it's a problem."

She has confirmed the obvious. I did the right thing, even if it had backfired on me spectacularly. "There you have it. That you don't know the answer to the question is the answer to the question."

Her huff comes through the wall loud and clear. "I think you don't want me to be happy. Or you don't want me dating your friend."

"Gavin is not my friend," I say, "and you would never be happy with him. The thing about Gavin, none of his ex-girlfriends has anything nice to say about him."

"Maybe he hasn't met the right girl yet?"

"I don't think the girls are the problem."

"Maybe *I'm* the right girl for him."

This is a side of Nic I hadn't encountered until the last week. It is unsettling. "No, Nic."

"Why not? Because you don't think I'm pretty enough?"

"What? How are you not getting this? It has nothing to do with looks."

"I bet you'd fix Brandi up with him."

I stop petting Scruffy. What had JayBot told her? Our dog cocks her head, features taut. Scruffy may have the mental savvy of a toddler who's fallen out of her crib one too many times, but she is remarkably perceptive. She's a canine empath. My sister, on the other hand, is the opposite: intelligent yet emotionally clueless. I choose my words carefully. "Is this about Brandi?"

"No. Maybe a little. Brandi is always the star; she always dates the most popular guys. But if I dated a senior—"

"Stop, no. That's not a good reason."

"I'm not saying it's the only reason, but why should Brandi get all the attention? When is it my turn?"

"Nic, what the hell happened to you?"

"Shut up. What do you know? It's harder for girls. Ugh. Why do I even bother arguing? Admit it. You think Gavin is too good for me."

"That's really not—"

"Admit it."

"Hang on, Dad's coming."

"Yeah, I see him."

Holding Scruffy, I stand. Dad sees me and nods. "I'm going to start lunch. Soup good?"

"Sure," I say. I wait until Dad is out of sight and crouch back down. "Are you still there?" I ask into the hole.

"Yeah. Explain this to me. Why are there two Dads but one Scruffy?"

"You think I understand how this works? Although if I had to guess, I'd say we're in parallel dimensions and this hole is acting as an interdimensional portal. But to get back to the other thing, I never said Gavin was too good for you."

"I have to go help Dad."

"Hang on. Ask JayBot about Amaya and Jenna."

"Gavin's last two girlfriends? Please, everyone knows about them. Amaya was a tease and Jenna cheated on him. What else is there to know?"

"So much more. The truth is complicated. There are two sides to everything."

"Sounds obvious to me."

I take a moment to calm myself down. It doesn't work. "What's obvious is Gavin is controlling the narrative and you're buying in. That is not the whole story."

"Did Jenna cheat on Gavin?" When I don't respond, she grunts. "That's what I thought. Bye, Jay."

"There's more to it."

"Yeah, I know there's more to it. You're putting the moves on Jenna. You're hitting on Gavin's ex because she sleeps around." Nic scoffs. "And you act like you're so superior."

"What the hell? You're quoting Gavin. Nic, think for yourself. How are you so smart and so dumb at the same time? You cannot trust Gavin. Never trust a guy who thinks all girls are prudes or sluts. It drives me nuts that you keep buying into his effing crap."

"Watch your language," she says, her annoyance rising to meet mine. "I'm out."

"Nic, wait."

"Send Scruffy back whenever you want. I'm going to eat lunch with Dad and a brother who isn't a jerk to me."

"Come on, Nic." She doesn't answer. "Nic?" Still nothing. "Nic!"

"Nic's in the kitchen with me," Dad says.

I pet Scruffy while she pitches her head from side to side. Her eyes shimmer with concern. "Thanks, Dad," I call out. "Be right there." I shift forward to let Scruffy jump off my lap before I stand. "Come on, girl. Time for lunch."

PART THREE

NICOLE: EARLY AFTERNOON

CHAPTER 18

*"He'll never know
what hit him."*

One conversation with Jay, Nicole thought, still fuming as she stormed into the kitchen. *That's all it took.* Her father worked the can opener while he gave her a worried look she knew all too well. Nicole softened her lips into the fullest smile she could muster under the circumstances until he eased up.

"Last three soup cans," Dad said, presenting the cans he had lined up on the kitchen island by sweeping his hand as if hosting a game show. He reached over for a pot. The handle drooped as he lifted it. After resting the pan on the counter, Dad rummaged into a drawer and pulled out a screwdriver.

Typical these days. "I think it's time for a new pot, Dad." Nicole yanked the pot by its floppy handle to demonstrate her point.

Dad snagged the pot midair and lowered it to the counter. "Please be careful!" Nicole released it. "We don't need a new pot," he continued, inserting the screwdriver beneath the handle and twisting until it caught. "Good as new." Dad lifted the pan. The handle held, but the rust remained.

Nicole rolled her eyes. *So typical.* As far as she could tell, her father thought everything would last forever if only people were careful. She couldn't recall him buying anything new in the last couple of years, now that she thought about it. Nicole noticed him glance behind her. She tensed, worried about what wacky thing her robot brother might be doing.

"Hey," Dad whispered. Nicole inched closer. "Jay is setting the table." They watched the bot align spoons atop the napkins. "Do you have any idea what's gotten into him today?"

Nicole feigned surprise. It resembled more of a neck seizure. "No, of course not. Why do you ask?"

"Well, Jay did his homework this morning without being reminded. Now he's setting the table without being asked." Dad emptied the first soup can into the pot. He tapped the sides to help the congealed goop along. "Something's up."

"Maybe he's angling for a car?" Nicole meant it as a joke but immediately regretted it. "I'm kidding," she added, hoping to relieve the pained expression that had gripped her father. "He doesn't even like to drive." Pitching in to help, Nicole unloaded the second can into the pot to create a satisfying *sploosh*. "What do you think is going on?"

"I don't know. Maybe the pod people got him." Dad often deadpanned silly things, so Nicole could never be certain if he was kidding. "You know," he continued, "replaced him with a replica that's a trifle too perfect. Like in the movie."

"What movie?"

"It's an old movie." Dad sighed. "Yes, I'm old. But seriously, it's strange. Even you two are getting along unusually well."

Nicole snorted. "Not even five minutes ago, Jay really upset me."

"Oh, all right." Quickly correcting his relief, Dad overcompensated with concern. "I mean, that's terrible. Anything I can do?"

"Nope, I'm fine. Typical Jay stuff. You know, stuff he does all the time like on any other typical day. He has definitely not changed into a pod person or a robot."

"That is a relief." Dad picked up the third can before hesitating. "Wait, who said anything about a robot?"

Nicole backed away. "Jay, let me help you set." She rushed over to the table.

"No need, dear sister."

"Lol! You're such a goof." Nicole gripped his

arm and whispered, "Stop being so considerate. Dad's onto you."

The robot rose to attention. "Say the word, and I shall initiate Subversive Protocol Alpha. I require a codfish and ten cubits of rope. He'll never know what hit him."

"Riiiight." She clutched his arm tighter. "Or stop acting weird. And don't call me *dear sister* in front of Dad."

"Understood. May I call you that when he isn't around?"

Nicole released him and shrugged. "I mean, sure, if you want to." She suppressed a smile. Despite all reason, she kind of liked it when he called her that.

While the robot finished setting, Nicole brushed her hand across at the spot on the table where she had perched not long ago, fearful of stray holes. Her pride swelled, remembering how she had tamed them all. With her awesome new brother's assistance, of course. She didn't mind sharing credit with him, her robot brother. *JayBot*, she thought, satisfied with the new name, even liking it despite knowing the idea came from her brother. Jay was always so arrogant that Nicole hated to give him credit for anything, even in her head.

And what did he mean by saying NicBot knows everything I know? What did she tell him? Probably lies, Nicole presumed. Or worse, the truth. Whatever that was.

Her truth had taken a beating this morning. Nicole had been certain that Jay had been responsible for ending her relationship with Gavin. Now she questioned her assumptions. Of course, she knew one obvious way to reveal the truth.

No, I'm not doing that.

Merely thinking about jumping into another hole made Nicole squirm. No desire to understand her past could be so strong that she would volunteer to self-torture. Absolutely not. Nicole was done with the holes.

Anyway, what could Jay have said to Gavin to get him to lose interest in her so abruptly? *It must have been pretty bad.* A new thought made her gasp. *Was it about Brandi?* A rage burned from within. Nicole drew a deep breath to calm herself. No, she wouldn't assume that. Anything but that. Here lay yet another reason to avoid jumping into stray holes. She was furious enough with her brother already.

"Soup's up," Dad said.

Nicole noticed JayBot staring at her, the ridges around his eyes simulating a deep and abiding empathy. He tilted his head and reached for her shoulder. Nicole pulled away. *Nope, too weird.* She looped around the table to help Dad carry the bowls.

Lunchtime was different, as Nicole expected it would be. Over the last year or so, eating with the family had become strained—

Dad fished for topics to fill awkward silences while Mom and Nicole rarely engaged, and Jay tossed in a few comments with, as far as Nicole could tell, the sole purpose of annoying her. But this meal was surprisingly relaxed and enjoyable.

Dad recounted the plot of *Invasion of the Body Snatchers* with a passion she hadn't witnessed since her most recent trip through the hole. JayBot listened with an intensity Nicole considered excessive. She wondered if the robot had Jay's love of science fiction or his programming obliged him to adapt to any eventuality, including cinematic alien infestation.

While she listened to the story and sipped her soup, Nicole noticed that JayBot had yet to eat anything. He blew the steam off each spoonful before dipping it back into the bowl. Dad hadn't picked up on it as far as she could tell, wholly invested in his movie recap.

"The next morning, we see Matthew walking past rows of gnarled trees when Nancy calls out to him. He stops and stares at her. Then he does this." Dad pointed at JayBot and shrieked like a pig caught in a grinder.

Startled, Nicole dropped her spoon in her bowl, splattering mushy carrot chunks. "What the heck!"

"Sorry, Nic. That's how the movie ends."

Nicole dabbed the area with her napkin.

"So Matthew has also become a pod person? And that's the end of the movie? There's no hope?"

"Not for her. Or for the rest of the city. Maybe not even for humanity!"

"What a horrible ending. Who would watch this?"

Dad shrugged. "It was a popular movie, a social commentary on groupthink and collective paranoia. The seventies were a heady time. Of course, I saw it on VHS in the eighties. The movie made an impact on my young mind. Not sure why exactly." He scrunched his face. "I guess there's a certain magic to being transported into an alternate reality with high stakes."

"I couldn't possibly relate," Nicole said. "Can I get more milk?"

Dad pushed his chair out from under the table, expending more energy than necessary, even with his girth. "Sure."

When Dad left the table, JayBot took to the opportunity to pour the entire bowl of soup down his throat. Nicole stifled her surprise and shoveled in as much of her remaining soup as she could before Dad returned to the table.

"Woah. What the—"

Nicole, still chewing, lifted a finger until she could swallow the bolus. "We were racing to see who can finish faster."

"Why?"

She motioned to JayBot. He blinked at her, as unhelpful as would be expected from a robot not designed for deceptive improvisation. "It's a thing kids do," she said.

"Another meme challenge? How bored is your generation? All right. Looks like Jay won."

"Yes, my brother is very talented. Ready to throw snowballs?"

Dad's face lit up. "Absolutely! Jay, will you be joining us?"

"No, you have fun with Nic. I'll wash the dishes."

Nicole tugged her father's arm before he could point and squeal again. "Show me where Mom put my boots," she said, yanking harder. Dad glanced behind him as Nicole escorted him to the foyer.

"I suppose we could buy a used car."

"He doesn't want a car."

"Or he can borrow mine. I don't drive much since I've been working from home. I don't know, Nic. Something is up with Jay."

"Snowballs."

"Huh?"

"We're throwing snowballs."

"Right." Dad brightened. "Right, of course. Your boots are in the closet. I hope they still fit."

They did, although not by much. While her father bundled up, Nicole wiggled her toes against the sides, took a few steps, and wiggled again. She considered asking for new boots but held back. Something was up with her father. First, she had recognized his sadness and the worrisome shift in his relationship with Mom. Now, the same nagging sensation told her an equally troublesome explanation lurked beneath his uncompromising stinginess.

Dad watched her, immobile, holding his breath. "They fit," Nicole said. The relief on her father's face confirmed her unease. Her father was keeping something from her. Yesterday, Nicole would have let it go, preferring to focus on her problems and push other concerns from her mind. That would no longer work for her. She needed to know everything.

CHAPTER 19

*"The metaphor is not
the problem."*

Nicole joined her father outside a few minutes after he had left to shovel. She found him excavating a path across the porch and over the walkway. The snow flurries had cleared along with many clouds, allowing patches of sun to shine through. Covered in fresh snow, the front yard glistened. Nicole enjoyed the way the frosty air swirled deep within her lungs when she inhaled. She blew out plumes of smoke. Their yard may not have the old farm's grandeur, but Nicole still loved it.

Wind vortexes created by the porch had settled the snow in a looping pattern. One particular chair got the brunt of it. Nicole left the path and crunched through the snow to reach it. Grasping the chair behind her, she launched onto the snow mound and reigned as a winter princess atop her frosty throne.

Once he had shoveled clear to the driveway, Dad spun around to search for Nicole. Locating her, he bowed and extended his hand. "Your majesty."

Nicole grinned. "How did you know I was thinking that?"

"You look regal up there. Are you ready to join me for the royal contest of Hit the Tree with Snowballs?"

Nicole slid down and crunched back to the path. "We need to come up with a better name."

"We haven't played this in ages," Dad said, his words encrusted with somber nostalgia. "Do you remember the rules?"

"Ten snowballs each. Five points for the trunk, three points for the thick branches, and one point for a twig. Whatever you hit first counts. No whining or cheating." Nicole crinkled her nose. "Did I whine and cheat so much that it needed to be a rule?"

"The last rule was for me. I get grumpy when my little girl beats me."

"I don't think that's true."

"Yes, it needed to be a rule."

"Fine."

Dad smiled. "But you're a big girl now. I don't expect any whining, and I solemnly swear I won't cheat unless I'm losing." He placed a gloved hand over his heart.

Nicole did the same. "Agreed." She looked across the lawn to the maple tree by the street. While not as majestic as the old knotted oak on the farm, the snow-covered tree sparkled. "I guess it's a good thing the schools closed."

"Yeah. I'm worried about Mom driving home in this." He reached for snow and pressed it between his gloves. "Maryland drivers and snow, like mixing toddlers with explosives. It never ends well."

"Speaking of Mom, how are things with you two?" Nicole dug her gloves into the snow. She fashioned a snowball while Dad stared at her.

"How do you mean?" he asked, tentative like she was the toddler with an explosive.

Nicole assumed her throwing stance and tossed her snowball, hitting a branch. "Three points." She scooped more snow. "I watched something earlier. Kind of a video but not a video? It's hard to describe. It was from many years ago, the last summer we visited the farm. I saw you and Mom holding hands. But more than that, you were laughing, joking around, and the way Mom looked at you? So sweet and romantic. I've never seen you two like that. Well, not recently. Not that I remember."

Dad rooted in place. When he didn't respond, Nicole took her second shot and winged the trunk. "Five points," she said. "You two aren't like that now."

"No."

"Are you and Mom getting a divorce?"

He sucked in a deep breath. A bird fluttered in and out of the tree. "No," Dad said. He cringed. "I took too long, didn't I?"

"Yes."

Dad took his shot and clipped a branch. After gathering more snow, he compressed it with heightened force. "I'm still going with *no*."

"Then I'm going with *I don't think that's true*."

"Fair enough. How about *I hope not*."

His honesty cut through her as an icy gust. "I guess that's fair too." Nicole suffered the same sensation as when the holes dilated beneath her: freefall, her steadfast support disintegrating into the ether. She shivered. Dad stepped closer and put his arm around her puffy jacket, pulling her close. Nicole slid into him and squeezed. Her Dad, the gigantic stress ball.

Where will I live if they get divorced? Nicole scolded herself for her thinking that. This wasn't about her. She understood that but couldn't ignore the cataclysmic effect on her it would have. If her family broke apart, she'd be alone. She felt an overwhelming urge to text Hannah. Hannah would understand better than anyone. But no, Nicole couldn't text her. They weren't friends anymore. Also, she no longer had a phone.

Nicole stepped away from the side hug. "Hypothetically speaking, if I had to get a new phone, how soon could I get it?"

"Um, we're saving for college. We could also save for your birthday."

"My birthday? That was last month."

"True, but I have exciting news. You get another birthday every year!"

"But my next one isn't for eleven months."

"That does follow. Good thing you already have a phone, so we don't need to worry about it."

Nicole tried a new tact. "What if, hypothetically speaking, something happened to my phone? Like, for example, today."

"Has something happened to your phone?"

"I'm asking a casual hypothetical question," she said, affecting the breeziest nonchalance she could.

"Yes, you are. And I'm countering with a panicky non-hypothetical question."

"I mean, something might have happened to my phone. Hypothetically speaking."

Dad blinked. Several times. "Please be careful!"

"It'll be fine." Nicole brushed it off. "Don't worry about it."

"I wasn't worried about it until you brought it up." He recoiled theatrically. "Tell me you didn't do that dumb thing people do in movies where they get angry and throw their phone across the room."

"No, nothing like that."

"I hate when people do that. Do people do

that in real life? Seriously, I don't get it. Throw a pillow instead. Even better, throw a throw pillow. That is a thing you can throw! It has the word *throw* in the name. Or maybe throw anything else that isn't fragile, costs hundreds of dollars, and is absolutely not meant to be thrown."

"People are not careful." Nicole smiled.

"Exactly!" Dad heaved his snowball clear over the tree and laughed.

"Impressive," she said, "but no points."

They resumed their game. Nicole remembered her strategy had always been to aim for the high branches, but that was back when she had trouble reaching the tree from the walkway. Back when she was little. Her strength surprised her. By aiming lower and more center, she accumulated a few trunk scores. Dad cheered and passed her snowballs.

Before long, she jumped to a fourteen-point lead. Nicole tried to remember the last time they had played this game. Or the last time she had an honest conversation with her dad. She placed her last snowball by her feet. They still needed to talk, to finish what she had started. Dad tended to deflect major topics with humor, and she vowed not to let him distract her. She turned to reengage with her father, but he spoke first.

"What were we talking about?"

"Divorce."

"No, that's not it. I think we were talking about snow. Hey, Nic, check out all the snow! Good thing they closed the schools, yeah? They do get it right once or twice a year."

Nicole pursed her lips. He wasn't even trying to be subtle. "Sometimes I feel like you sugarcoat things to—you know."

"Protect you from the harsh reality of life?"

"Exactly."

"Oh, honey. You feel that way only because it's true."

"Lol. But seriously, how can you expect me to navigate the harsh reality of life if you're always protecting me?"

Dad brushed his snowball with a glove. "That's fair. You're getting older, and I should treat you like an adult." He handed Nicole his snowball, and she hurled it. The throw went wide and snipped a twig. "Tell me what harsh reality you want to know about," he continued, "and I'll lay it on you."

"I want to know what's going on between you and Mom."

Dad picked up more snow. White powder fell from his hands while he worked the rest into a ball. "And you want the harsh reality version?"

Nicole spied the snowball at her feet and picked it up. She brushed off a blade of grass that had become attached. "Yes," she said.

Dad placed his snowball beside him on the walkway. "Let me put it this way. Marriage begins as a fresh bouquet: glorious and lovely, a fragrant representation of your collective hopes and dreams." He peered into the distance while he slapped his gloves together, ridding them of snow. "You return from the honeymoon, arrange the bouquet on the mantle, and stand before colors so vibrant, you can't even conceive the possibility that it might not last forever."

His gaze fixed on Nicole. "But there lies the hazard. If you don't give your bouquet constant attention, tend to its needs, shower it with boundless affection, honesty, and love, it wilts. Subtlety, at first, but later you, well, you notice things. When did the petals start to droop? Is it my imagination or have the colors faded? You try to reverse it, and maybe you can for a time, but not by much or for very long.

"After a while, you learn to accept that whatever you do, your stunning, life-affirming bouquet will shrivel and decay. Before long, you recognize the effort overwhelms the reward. You concede it's a whole lot easier to pretend you don't see, to act as though everything's fine. That works for a bit, but when things get bad enough, when you and your spouse gather to have *the talk* and dare to stand before the bouquet together, you both recognize the painfully obvious. Only one question remains: who will be the first to dump the festering turd in the trash?"

Nicole stared at her father, her mouth agape. The snowball slipped from her hand.

"Too much?" Dad asked. "I'm not great at modulating." He reached for more snow and repeated the compression process. "You didn't like the metaphor?"

"The metaphor is not the problem."

"Are you sure? Because I have another metaphor involving a dying star. You know how a star burns bright, seemingly inexhaustible, but ultimately runs out of fuel and collapses in upon itself to create a black hole that consumes everything in the vicinity? That works too." He crushed the snow between his gloves as though he intended to squeeze out a diamond rather than a snowball. "It's more fatalistic because, you know, you can't stop an imploding star. I shift between the two metaphors depending on how inane the argument Mom and I are having at any given moment." Having reduced the snow to powder, Dad slapped his gloves together. "Sometimes both work."

"Thank you for sharing. Let's talk about literally anything else."

"Sure, honey. What's a more pleasant topic? Oh! Have any of your classmates recognized how awesome and beautiful you are and begged you for a date?"

Nicole frowned. "Tell me more about the festering bouquet."

"You know, that's fine. Better to wait until college to date." Dad bent down for more snow. "High school boys are terrible."

"And you should know because you were a high school boy, right?"

"Exactly correct. Why do you think big brothers are so protective?" Dad asked. He angled closer. "They know."

"Don't you think that's a little hypocritical?"

"A little hypocritical? Nah." Dad shifted back. "More like totally and unabashedly hypocritical, but also honest." He formed a new snowball while Nicole had no response. "How many points do I get for honesty?"

"Zip. You get points for hitting the tree. That's it. And I'm winning."

"By fifteen points. I hit the trunk three times, and we tie."

"You have only three more throws."

Dad flashed a grin. "Guess I'd better not miss." He stretched back and let the snowball fly, nailing the trunk. He picked up his other snowball and smacked the trunk in the same spot.

Nicole was about to compliment him until a memory flashed through her brain. She turned as though watching it whiz by. Dad always got good right at the end. And, from what she recalled, exactly as good as he needed to. "Hey, didn't we tie the last time we played? Actually, haven't we tied every time we played?"

"I pitched for the baseball team in college, remember? Mom came to all my games. Even before we started dating." The memory produced a wan smile, which soon faded. He reached for more snow. "Anyway, we didn't always tie." He continued in a stage whisper, "When you were really little, I let you win."

Nicole groaned. "But now you make sure we tie?"

"You make it sound easy. Tying is a challenge. I have to get the numbers to work. I'm not as good at math as you are."

"Seriously? Was nothing about my childhood what it seemed?"

Dad pressed the snow between his hands. "That happens to everybody. You get older and look back with a better understanding and a new perspective. That happens when you're an adult too."

Another memory rushed forward: second grade when she had no friends and struggled with anxiety. She could relate to her distress because she felt the same way now. Back then, she wasn't popular and had no friends, while now she was popular and had many friends, but deep down, her emotions were identical. Lonely. Frightened. Sure, she had friends now, but she didn't like them very much, and they didn't like her much back. And as in elementary school, she didn't like herself very much either. The joyful time in between was all thanks to Hannah, but even their friendship had arisen from deceit.

"It's been happening more recently," Nicole

admitted. "I used to think Hannah and I became friends on our own, but really you guys set us up."

Dad stopped shaping his new snowball. "Wow, Mom told you?" Noticing Nicole's disappointment, he added, "You and Hannah *did* become friends on your own. Mom and I provided you two the opportunity to get to know each other. That's all."

"I guess."

"I am surprised Mom told you. Actually, I'm impressed. That's not like her. Mom prefers to keep her fiction unmolested."

That's what Phin said about me. The realization hit her hard. "I'm like Mom," she mumbled.

"What's that?"

"Nothing. Let's finish the game."

Dad wound up and let the snowball fly. It struck the trunk in the same spot as his last two throws.

"Strike three!" Nic cheered. They high-fived. "Hey, you're not going to believe it. We tied!"

"Amazing!"

"Yeah, go figure. I'm going inside."

Dad pulled her in for a hug. "Good talk today. I like adult Nic." He stepped back. "I look forward to getting to know her better."

This was too intense for Nicole, and she veered away. "Thanks, Dad," she said, stumbling back into the house. The tight boots bothered her now that her toes were cold. She pulled off her boots as soon as she entered the foyer, followed by the rest of her wet winter gear. *I'm like Mom*, she thought again, sliding to the floor next to her pile. She wished she could be like Mom in the good ways, her strength or her courage. But Nicole understood, now that she chose to see. Mom hadn't just checked out on Dad, she had checked out on the whole family. And Nicole had too in her own way.

Not anymore. Nicole stood, energized by her decision. She would challenge her assumptions, be strong and courageous. She would find out for herself what Jay had done. A cold sweat followed by a frightful drowning sensation washed over her. No, she wasn't ready to go there. She'd try something else first.

Marching into the library, Nicole pulled out the lacrosse stick and peeled off a hole. JayBot hummed in the kitchen. She recognized the tune as the opening theme from one of Jay's video games. *Hold up, is he cleaning? No time to deal with that*, she decided, sliding the stick back into place. The hole rested in her hand.

"Am I supposed to talk, or can you read my mind?"

The hole did not answer.

"Take me to Hannah's Bat Mitzvah party when she betrayed me. Early in eighth grade when she had her public meltdown, and we stopped being friends." Nicole cast the hole near her. The instant it hit the carpet, it vibrated and turned. "Don't hold back. I want to see it all. I need to know everything."

JayBot appeared in the library. "A new excursion? Excellent. One quick suggestion, if I may? It is not advisable to jump into a tall stack of holes."

"It's one hole," Nicole said before remembering that the holes had no tangible depth. "Wait, how many do you see?"

Squinting for effect, JayBot counted silently. And continued counting. Recognizing the danger, Nicole tried to snap up the hole, but not before it dilated. The floor vanished beneath her feet. She swung her hand, snagging carpet. While that halted her fall, it also sent her body careening into the smooth wall, dislodging her fingertips. Hands flailing, a silent scream twisting her lips, Nicole plummeted into the stack of holes.

CHAPTER 20

*"Please don't be
mad at me."*

A larger-than-life image of Hannah as a toddler projected on a screen in the center of a stage. Toddler Hannah perched on her high chair with cake remnants strewn asunder and green icing splattered across her face, her spiky hair as wild as her exalted smile. Next to the screen stood Hannah's mother, who Nicole knew as Ms. Donna. To her right, the DJ crouched over turntables, holding headphones up to her ear as though she was spinning tracks at a club until the early morning rather than working a Bat Mitzvah reception in the early afternoon. Hannah stood off to the other side, swaying with nervous energy in her midnight blue dress.

"This is my favorite photo from Hannah's second birthday," Ms. Donna said. She beamed before the mass of people, who sat at numerous tables around Nicole. "Precious little cake ever made it into her mouth."

"Can you speak up, dear?" A grizzled gentleman with wideset eyes lifted a bony finger. "I don't have my hearing aids."

"Sorry, Uncle Morty. I was saying how little cake made it into her mouth."

Uncle Morty guffawed in a phlegmy but joyous manner. "It made it into her hair!"

"Sure did. Looking at this photo, who could have predicted what a fine young lady Hannah would become." Ms. Donna opened her arms, and a chagrined Hannah sauntered over for a hug.

Cutting through the crowd's collective *Aww*, Nicole heard a harrumph. Brandi, seated between Maya and eighth-grade Nic, bristled. "That dress is not so shiny."

"Shimmery," Nic corrected. "I said it was shimmery."

"It's still not all that." When Brandi leaned back, her rhinestone-encrusted bustier top caught the light and dazzled. Nicole remembered how impressed she had been with Brandi for pulling off such a mature top. Nic's green dress, like Hannah's shimmery blue one, rose to the neck, a more realistic cut for their tween girl bodies.

Observing this a year and a half later, Nicole saw things differently. *Hold up, was that why you chose that dress? Were you trying to out-*

shiny Hannah?

The photo on the screen advanced to a shot of pre-school-aged Hannah in full Little League soccer gear spackled with mud. Nicole remembered this video slideshow ran for a full half-hour on a continuous loop throughout the reception on both the big screen and a smaller screen inside the reception hall. From what Nicole recalled, she and Scruffy made a few appearances.

"I think her dress is cute," Nic said.

Brandi expelled a testy hum, the way a queen might forewarn a rising annoyance with her underling's dissension. Her swank hair covered one eye in a style, much like her outfit, incongruous with budding young adulthood. Nicole recalled how she had oozed with jealousy when Brandi first appeared at school with her new haircut. Hannah called it Brandi's pirate 'do.

Brandi turned to Maya for support. "What do you think?"

Maya stopped chewing and reflected for a moment. "I like the dress," she said and popped another pretzel in her mouth.

"What you like are snacks," Brandi said. Maya withdrew, her face contorting with shame. Brandi put an arm around her. "OMG, I'm trying so hard to be nice, but those carbs are going right to your thighs. You don't need that, do you?"

Maya shoved the snack bowl away from her. Nicole had no memory of this exchange and turned to gauge Nic's reaction, but Nic was otherwise distracted. Nicole followed her sightline and saw Aiden, his tie askew, his road to handsome nearly complete.

Oh, Nic. Don't go there—

The floor gave way followed by a brief, dark interlude before Nicole appeared at the next scene. Dropping through the stacked holes provoked a sensation not unlike collapsing through the floor of an apartment to arrive at the one below. Nicole found the transition jarring but milder than the more familiar sensation of plunging off a cliff.

Darker, quieter, and more sparsely populated, the reception hall took on an otherworldly undertone as after a squall. The remaining crowd shuffled about as dazed survivors. Nicole scanned the room until she found her younger self slouching at a sullen angle by the exit. She peered into Nic's bleary eyes and watched her lower lip quiver, her face illuminated by a yellow glow stick necklace nestled over her green dress.

I remember what you're looking at. Nicole whirled around to face her memory: Aiden and Hannah embracing. *The moment of betrayal.* Hannah faced away, but Nicole could see how tightly she held him. This was no innocent friend hug. Aiden's kind face pressed against Hannah's hair while his hand rubbed her back. Nicole's jealousy rushed back as raw and visceral as it had been the first time around. Aiden should be hugging me. That should be his face in my hair, his hand on my back.

Nicole turned around to watch Nic regain her composure. Nic's movements reminded Nicole of Scruffy after coming in from a rainstorm the way she stretched each body part, primed to shake and spray. Her younger self closed her eyes and pressed her fingers through her hair, sucking in repeated deep breaths until her eyes flashed open. With clear determination, Nic squared her shoulders.

Are you going over there? I don't remember that.

Nic surged forward. In a panic, Nicole leaped away, slamming into the cramped portal. But something stopped Nic cold. Something stiffened her features and shredded her determination. After Nic stormed through the exit, Nicole spun around to discover what had so affected her. Aiden and Hannah, with a hand on each other's shoulder, enjoyed a shared joke. Their glow stick necklaces lit up their smiles, thick as thieves.

Why did you do this, Hannah? How could—

Nicole lurched into darkness. She appeared within the bright reception hall, dynamic once more with overlapping conversations. The crowd sat at tables while Ms. Donna spoke on the stage by the screen, now at a sharper angle. Nicole stood by the boys' table, populated by

Hannah's cousins and a few male school friends. Aiden sat nearby, twiddling his tie between his fingers. Nicole located Nic one table over, checking him out. Staring, really.

Not too subtle, Nic.

"Hey," Hannah said. Startled, Nicole turned to answer her. Aiden beat her to it. "Hey, Hannah. Congratulations."

"Thanks." Hannah flashed a goofy grin. "It's my big day."

"Sure is. Love those baby pics."

"Yeah, aren't they great? My mom has, like, no boundaries. So, Aiden, you're going to dance with me later."

Aiden froze. "Um."

"You know you have to, right?" She pressed her hands together. "And on her big day, thou shalt do as she asks, in whatever she pleases."

"No kidding," Aiden said. "I don't remember reading that passage."

"It's a Jewish thing."

"You know Christians also read the Old Testament."

"Not the Torah, the haftarah." Aiden squinted at her, so Hannah continued, "The haftarah is like a shadow Torah we keep for ourselves. Words of the Prophets, Aiden. Do you dare to quarrel with the Prophets?"

"No, heaven forbid, but I don't know. The half Torah? Like a mini Torah? I feel like you're making stuff up."

"Doesn't matter. It's my day and I say you're dancing." Hannah pressed her hands together once more. "So it has been written."

"I mean, when you put it like that, I guess I have to."

"There really is no choice." Hannah bent down and added cryptically, "My friends also like to dance. Maybe a certain someone will join us?" She winked before walking back to the stage. Aiden twiddled his tie.

Are you blushing? Wait, did Hannah mean me? But Aiden and I never danced. Nicole glanced up and saw her younger self, lips pressed together, tracking Hannah as she walked back to the stage. *Oh, I don't think I liked that wink—*

More darkness, falling, silence. Then last summer's hit pop song blasted in her ears. Hannah and Nic danced atop Hannah's bed, swaying with wild abandon. Nicole didn't have much room to move within the portal so she shimmied in place because really, how could she not? That song was like ants in your pants. Straight away, Nicole recognized her location and time: Hannah's bedroom the day before her Bat Mitzvah.

"Brandi dance!" Hannah yelled over the music, and she and Nic covered an eye with the back of a hand and struck a pose, hip to the side, their other hand outstretched, fingers curled in a kiss-my-hand-you-peasant style, before collapsing on the bed in a heap of giggles.

Hannah tapped her phone, and the music stopped.

"I must wear my hair this way," Hannah said, her hand still covering one eye. "It's for your own protection. I have two sultry eyes, but one is all you petty peons can handle."

"You are so bad," Nic said.

"Dare not gaze upon both my eyes at once! You will be drawn to my rocky shores. Wrecked, I say. Observe!" Hannah pulled her hand away, causing Nic to shriek and crumple before her. They laughed together.

Oh, Hannah. You're such a goof.

Nic sat up. "Seriously, though. You and Brandi need to get along tomorrow."

"I try, Nic, but she pushes my buttons."

"Remember that you're friends."

Hannah looked away. "I don't think we are anymore. It took some convincing to get my mom to let me invite Brandi. You can't fool my mom. She knows all about broken relationships." Hannah turned back to Nic. "I had to time the event with my Dad's weekend to make sure he showed up. At least he bought me—oh, yeah! Let me show you my dress." Hannah led Nic to her closet. She rummaged around until she removed a blue dress. Displaying it over her body, Hannah rocked so the bottom splayed with each sway.

"It's so shimmery."

"My mom insisted I wear a dress. We had a terrible argument until I found this one. The lower part looks cool when I dance."

"You don't like dresses?"

Hannah ceased rocking. "It's not really me. You know that."

Nic didn't argue, and Nicole didn't remember knowing that at all. She still didn't understand why Hannah said that. *Who doesn't like dresses?*

"We're going to have so much fun dancing tomorrow," Hannah said. "I told the DJ all the songs I wanted. And I invited a few boys from school. One boy in particular you might find interesting."

"Yeah?"

Hannah suppressed a devilish grin. "You'll find out tomorrow. So tell me about your new dress."

"Uh—"

"Did you get the violet dress you wanted?"

"I'm wearing my green dress. You've seen it before."

"Oh. I thought—"

"Drop it." Nic walked away.

Hannah hung her dress back in her closet and ran after her. "I don't care what you wear. Nic, look at me. I really don't care at all. Don't be mad at me."

I wasn't mad at you; I was embarrassed. My parents reneged on their promise to buy me a new dress. And I was worried everybody would notice I wore an old dress and make fun of me. Turned out, the only person who might have noticed was Brandi, and she was too focused on herself to care.

Hannah guided Nic to the edge of her bed. They sat together quietly until Nic said, "It's fine."

"You know I only asked because you kept talking about it. I don't care what you wear as long as you come." Hannah hugged Nic's side, resting her head on Nic's shoulder. "Please don't be mad at me."

Nic touched Hannah's hand. "Sorry. I know you didn't—forget it. It's fine. Really. I'm not mad at you."

"Is everything all right at home?"

Nic pulled away. "I said it's *fine*. I don't want to talk about it."

Oh, Nic. Hannah is exactly who you should have talked to.

CHAPTER 21

"Pick a side."

Hannah sat on her bed next to Nic and broke the awkward silence. "How's Scruffy?"

"Scruffy's good. She misses you."

"Tell her I miss her too."

"Sure." Nic fought a smile. "She's a little offended you didn't invite her."

Hannah lit up. "OMG! I wish I could invite her. I like her better than most of my relatives. Some of my friends too."

"Really, Hannah?"

"I didn't say who."

You can't resist a dig at Brandi—

When the bottom fell out, Nicole moaned until muted by the hole's inky silence. She didn't want to leave. Nicole wanted more, more of when she and Hannah were still friends, more of the time before things went sour.

When Nicole reappeared at the reception, she faced Nic and Hannah, their body language markedly different from the day before. A slow song played in the distance.

"Why are you taking Brandi's side?" Despite Hannah's anger, Nicole couldn't help but notice how pretty Hannah's dress looked all lit up by her blue glow stick necklace. "She can't stand any day that isn't all about her. She won't let me have one day!"

"I know it's your day," Nic said, "but that doesn't mean you can do whatever you want."

Stunned by the comment, Hannah reeled. Off to the side, the photo slideshow played on the small screen. Ten-year-old Hannah and Nic held Scruffy in their arms, Hannah in mid-shift to keep the squirmy dog aloft, Nic unaware, still beaming at the camera. "What do you mean? What have I done?"

"Don't pretend you don't know." Tears formed in Nic's eyes, horrifying Hannah.

"Nic, I really don't know." Hannah touched Nic's arm. "What do you think I've done?"

"What do I *think* you've done?" Nic yanked her arm away. "I saw you put your moves on him, dancing, make him laugh—he's supposed to be *my* guy."

"Your guy? Wait, do you mean Aiden?" Hannah drew back. Nicole did not remember Hannah being that good an actor. "You still haven't talked to him?"

"Don't play dumb. You know I like him. Why are you trying to steal him from me?"

Wow. Hannah seems genuinely surprised.

"How—" Hannah shook it off. Tears formed in her eyes too. "How can you think that?"

"I've seen you with him. Ugh! You're such a hypocrite. You go off on Brandi all the time, but she'd never do that to me."

I sure got that wrong.

Hannah shook her head faster, tears streaming down her cheeks, but her denial only served to infuriate Nic more. "And the worst part is you don't think you've done anything wrong."

"No," Hannah said. Her voice erupted with blazing intensity. "The worst part is we've been friends for years, and you don't know me at all."

Yeah, I didn't know you'd do that to me.

"Brandi's got you so spun around," Hannah continued. "I don't even know who you are sometimes."

Brandi? What does she have to do with—

Another drop, more nausea. Nicole

wondered what would happen if she vomited while in the hole and decided to try her best not to find out. She appeared back where she had started, at the girls' table during the reception. Ms. Donna spoke on the stage by the screen, which displayed a new photo: Ms. Donna and Hannah's father holding infant Hannah, the family with all their potential happiness still intact. Although Hannah had said that her father's affair began before she was born, so maybe not.

Looking over to the boys' table, Nicole and Nic watched Hannah wink at Aiden. Distressed, Nic scrutinized Hannah as she made her way back to the stage. "Hannah, what are you doing?" she asked aloud.

That got Brandi's attention. She wasted no time. "Good for Hannah, making her move early. She's smart."

"What? No, that's not—"

"It's Hannah's big day, right? She can do what she wants. OMG, is that Aiden? Wait, isn't Aiden the boy who liked you?" Brandi covered her pouty lips with exaggerated alarm. "I guess not anymore."

Oh, I do not like where this is going.

"I mean, maybe he liked me," Nic said. Her sad attempt at nonchalance made Nicole cringe.

"Oh, my gosh! Do *you* like him?" Brandi asked, astounded.

"No. I mean, maybe."

Brandi lifted her one exposed eyebrow and moaned as if she had seen a baby bird leap from the nest and splat beak-first on the pavement. "Listen, Nic. This is super important. Does Hannah know you feel about Aiden?"

"Um."

"Because if she doesn't, I mean, you can't blame her. Aiden's gotten so much cuter this year, don't you think?"

"Um."

"I mean, good for Hannah. Boys love it when girls make it super obvious. I bet she'll be dancing a lot with him later. I'm so happy for her, aren't you?"

"Um."

"Unless you *did* tell Hannah. Wow! I mean, if you think about it, that's so mean." Brandi chuckled to herself. "Boys, am I right? Always causing trouble. At least now you know who your true friends are. I mean, I would never steal your guy."

"Um. Thanks?"

"Of course, Nic. It's super important for true friends to stick together." Brandi flipped her hair back. Her one exposed eye shifted. "I can't even imagine how Hannah can say she's your friend and do something like that." When Nic looked away, Brandi's lips curled into a cunning smile.

That was devious, but if all she did—

Another drop, another rush of nausea. Nicole couldn't tell if reliving the ordeal or the actual falling had provoked her queasiness. She appeared again at the reception. The DJ spun tunes on stage while adults and teens bounced on the dance floor, most lit up by glow stick necklaces. Huddling together by their table stood Brandi, Maya, and Nic. Ms. Donna walked toward them, clutching assorted glowing necklaces.

"Hello, girls. Are you enjoying the party?"

"Yes, Ms. Donna," the girls answered, although not in unison or with equivalent enthusiasm.

"Let's get you all lit up so you can join Hannah on the dance floor. I'd say red for Brandi. Red should match your rather mature dress."

Brandi popped the necklace over her head. "Well, you know what they say. If you've got it, flaunt it. Oh, I'm sorry, Ms. Donna." She draped a hand over her breasts, now lit in a demonic red glow. "I didn't mean it as a dig at your dress."

Ms. Donna smiled the way assassins do

before they slit your throat. "Quite all right, Brandi. If that's what you need to feel good about yourself."

Yikes! Go, Ms. Donna.

"I think orange for Maya. Orange should match your lovely earrings." Maya's smile glimmered orange. "And Nic. Yellow should light up your pretty green dress." As she handed Nic the necklace, Ms. Donna gripped Nic's arm. "Thanks for coming. I know how much this means to Hannah."

"I wouldn't miss it," Nic said.

"Terrific! Have fun, girls." Ms. Donna moved on to illuminate other guests.

Nic fiddled with her necklace and swayed from one leg to the other. "We should get out there," she said to Brandi and Maya.

"Definitely," Brandi agreed, syrupy sweet. "Look, aren't Hannah and Aiden super cute together when they dance?" Nicole watched Nic's excitement drain until she sagged. "Oh, Nic, you know how much I hate conflict but I really felt that needed to be brought to your attention."

"I—I can't believe Hannah's doing this."

"Come on, don't stare. Don't give her the satisfaction." After pivoting Nic away from the dance floor, Brandi noticed Hannah motioning for them to join her. Brandi shook her head.

Hannah pointed at Nic, beckoning her with her hand while nudging her head toward Aiden. Brandi gestured that she'd let Nic know. Brandi whispered in Nic's ear, "That's right. Ignore her. She doesn't deserve your attention." Brandi turned back and shrugged at Hannah. What else could she do? She'd tried her best.

Seriously? This blows. How many holes are in this stack? Am I going to be trapped here forever? Ugh, can this get any—

As she descended, Nicole hoped not finishing the sentence might save her, but she didn't have high hopes. The holes followed her thoughts, this much was clear. And of course it could get worse. And of course it did.

Nicole appeared outside the reception hall. The bright glare in this room contrasted with the hall's dim mood lighting. A bar extended along the far wall, where a few adults congregated in clusters. Near the doorway, Nic watched Hannah and Aiden laugh together, each resting a hand on the other's shoulder.

Nic stormed through the exit and into the brightly lit room, marching past Nicole. Nicole spun around as she passed. Brandi and Maya sprang from their chairs to meet Nic.

"We were waiting for you," Brandi said. "Finally had enough?"

Nic sniffed. "Yeah." Her voice sounded

weak, drained.

"Good. Now take off the damn glow stick."

Nic lifted the necklace over her head and placed it in Brandi's outstretched hand. After glaring at the glow stick in disgust, Brandi hurled it across the room. Nicole remembered how startled she had been to see Brandi furious. Brandi was always in control, coolly commanding every situation. Except now.

"I've had it with Hannah. How dare she yell at us? In front of everybody!" Brandi paced as though a lioness confined in a cage. She swung her head, daring anyone to mess with her, but no one did. Besides the three girls, the other people in the room were adults at the bar, all several drinks past any condition to judge. Brandi's voice strained with fiery rage. "I've never been more humiliated!"

Maya watched Brandi in terror. She kept her mouth clamped shut.

"We should ghost Hannah for a week," Nic suggested. "It's like, I don't even want to deal with her right now."

"No."

"No?"

"No. Not just a week," Brandi said, indignant. "And not just ghosting. We need to cut her out forever—social and IRL. She's out.

She's finished."

"I mean—"

"Forget it, Nic. You always defend her, but I'm done. Pick a side."

Nic stared at her. Nicole didn't remember taking so long to respond. Brandi pulled Maya closer. "We're doing this for you, Nic. Hannah said mean things to me, to us, but what she did to you was unforgivable. That friendship is over."

"Yeah," Nic said, "I guess you're right."

Brandi relaxed, her confidence restored. "I mean, you can't let her walk all over you."

Right. That's your job. Hannah, I'm sorry. Why couldn't I trust—

Nicole plunged through the muted blackness and emerged back in Hannah's bedroom near where she had left Hannah and Nic the last time.

"I like her better than most of my relatives," Hannah said. "Some of my friends too."

"Really, Hannah?"

"I didn't say who."

Hannah and Nic sat together on the edge of Hannah's bed. Nic peered at her askance. "Come on. Brandi's cool"

"Sure, Brandi's cool," Hannah said and

added in her silliest Brandi voice, "She's *super* cool." Nic laughed. Hannah continued, "But she isn't very nice."

"What do you mean?"

"I mean, don't you think Brandi's stuck-up?"

Nic considered this. "Maybe she's a little stuck-up."

"A little? Lol. She's stuck-up like a Post-it note on the roof."

Nic stifled a laugh. "Not that much."

"No, more! Way more. She's a Post-it note on the Washington Monument."

"Which part?" Nic asked and pressed her lips together while Hannah smiled. "The tip," Hannah whispered. Nic covered her mouth. "The tip of the phallus!" Hannah yelled.

Nic shrieked, and the girls flopped on the bed.

"OMG, stop! You're so bad," Nic said. Hannah stopped. She and Nic smiled at each other, ready to burst. Nic finally spoke in a low whisper. "Where is she now?"

"On the Eiffel Tower." Hannah rolled over and stood on her bed. Drooping a hand over one eye, she continued in a thick French accent, "Ooh, la, la! You trivial nothings bore me. I shall now recite a poem whilst I dance." Hannah cleared her throat, and Nic sat up. "Why can't you be / so chic as me? / The hu-manity!"

Nic jumped on the bed with her as they recited the poem together, each time louder than the next—WHY CAN'T YOU BE / SO CHIC AS ME? / THE HU-MANITY!—before collapsing on the bed with peals of laughter. Nic could hardly catch her breath. "Oh, Hannah. You are so funny."

"We need to hang out more." Hannah took her hand. "Just the two of us."

"It's been too long," Nic agreed.

Hannah hugged her close. "I am so happy to have my friend back."

Nicole pressed her head against the smooth wall. *I miss you too, Hannah. Who cares about a stupid boy? I wish you never had your meltdown. Then we could have stayed—*

As she cascaded down the hole, Nicole knew precisely where and when she would end up. Everything led to this moment.

CHAPTER 22

*"I want to rip this
thing off so bad."*

"The worst part is we've been friends for years, and you don't know me at all." Hannah fixed on Nic, her disappointment cast in a blue glow. "Brandi's got you so spun around I don't even know who you are sometimes."

The DJ played a familiar slow song. A few adults in the background swayed in pairs on the dance floor. Nic and Hannah stood together by the screen, still projecting photos from Hannah's life on an endless loop. Prepubescent Hannah and Nic held Scruffy in their arms. The image dissolved into the next: Hannah, Nic, Brandi, and Maya at twelve years old, smiling together at a table with fashion magazines splayed open before them.

"Talk to me," Hannah said. "Whatever it is, we'll work it out." Hannah spotted Brandi and Maya closing in, and her expression dropped. "No. I cannot deal with *her* right now."

Brandi greeted them with sticky sweetness. "Hello, girls." She turned to Nic and continued with overwrought concern, "Is everything all right?"

"Uh, huh," Nic said, but her tone suggested otherwise.

"Your makeup is blotchy," Brandi said and rubbed Nic's cheek. "Wait, were you crying?"

"Leave her alone." Hannah stepped between Nic and Brandi. "I don't know what you're telling Nic, but you better stop."

"Let me get this straight. *You're* criticizing *me*?" Brandi draped a hand across her chest. "After everything you've done."

"What have I done?"

Brandi flicked her wrist. "Whatever."

"No, tell me, Brandi. What have I done that's so terrible?"

"Really, Hannah? You know you've been, like, super stuck-up today."

Hannah glared at her. "How rich coming from you."

"What's that supposed to mean?" Brandi

asked, her umbrage as thick as her feigned innocence. "You know, Hannah, I am so tired of your attitude. I get this is your big day or whatever, but that doesn't give you the right to be full of yourself."

Hannah sidled up to her, her pique fused with a chilling calm. She smiled at Brandi the same way her mother had earlier. "Oh, Brandi. You pretend you're so mature, so much better than everybody else, but I know you do that to hide how frightened you really are." Hannah's calm slipped. She gripped her dress. "You don't care about anybody but yourself. You boss us around like we're your petty little peons. Yeah, Brandi, everyone's afraid of you, but no one likes you!"

Once Hannah yelled in Brandi's face, all other conversations in the room ceased.

"Look what happens when people get close to you," Hannah continued, seething, her voice strained. "Poor Maya's on the verge of collapse. Nic's so contaminated with your lies, she's all spun around. You poison everybody and everything near you. How sad to be you. No wonder you lash out. No wonder you're insecure. Maybe you have everyone else fooled, but I see through you, Brandi. I know what you are. You're toxic!"

The song had finished midway through

Hannah's outburst, and the DJ remained immobile, hunched over her turntable, as stunned as everyone.

"Get out of my life!" Hannah screamed.

Gaping maws surrounded the girls. The lull stretched.

"Is Hannah still talking to the mean girl?" Uncle Morty shouted. "I can't hear anything."

Brandi stepped back, visibly shaken. "Come on girls," she said, her usual confidence tainted by uncharacteristic fragility. "We're not wanted here." She bolted for the exit. Maya followed right after her, but Nic lingered. Hannah fixed on her, eyes pleading.

Nicole also wanted Nic to stay, but she knew it wouldn't happen. The holes were view-only. No editing. She would be forced to bear witness.

Nic shook her head, her anger and confusion too great to bear. When Nic walked away, Hannah deflated like a balloon, drifting to the floor. Ms. Donna sprinted over and caught her, guided her to a chair, and hugged her daughter while she sobbed.

That was so horrible. I shouldn't have walked away, Hannah. I realize that now. But I still don't understand what you and Aiden were so chummy ab
—

Nicole shot through the floor and appeared back at the dim reception hall. On stage, Ms. Donna and the DJ huddled together. No music played over the few hushed conversations. Glancing around, Nicole located Hannah standing alone by an empty table. Aiden walked over to Hannah. He poked her arm, and Hannah faced him.

"I guess you and Nic had a fight," Aiden said.

"Yeah, you could say that. Nic thinks I'm hitting on you."

"Really?" Aiden turned away, suddenly distracted by the floor, the wall, the table. Eventually, he looked back at Hannah. "I mean, do you like boys?"

Hannah pursed her lips. She shifted her weight from foot to foot. "Um." She crinkled her nose. "I'm still working out my sexuality."

"Yeah, I get that. I was surprised to see you in a dress."

"I want to rip this thing off so bad."

"That's cool." Aiden edged closer and continued in a hushed voice, "Since we're being honest and all, I used to have a thing for Nic."

"You don't still?"

Aiden winced. "Wow. Was I that obvious?"

"Nic and I used to be besties, remember?" Her voice caught and her tears flowed. "Used to." Hannah sucked in air. Aiden lifted his arms to offer a hug, and Hannah lunged forward, bawling into his shoulder.

Nicole searched for a yellow glow by the exit and found herself glaring at Hannah and Aiden, enraged at what she misconstrued as a betrayal. *I did it again. I jumped to the worst possible conclusion. My best friend is crying, and I let my insecurities get the better of me.* Nicole realized this had become a theme. A disheartening, destructive theme.

"Yeah, I did like her," Aiden said once Hannah had pulled back. "She's pretty. And she used to be nice."

"She was," Hannah agreed. "Spending time together was awesome. We danced and sang. Every second was so much fun."

Aiden's eyes widened. "I think you and I liked the same girl."

"No, not like that." Hannah brushed off the suggestion. "I loved spending time with her. Nic and I were like sisters. Sisters argue, but they always—" She allowed her sentence to trail away.

Oh, Hannah. You're right. We were like sisters.

Hannah smacked her thighs. "Doesn't matter what I thought. Anyway, Nic likes boys. In fact, Nic had a thing for this annoying boy who would say hi but was always too shy to, like, actually talk to her."

Aiden hung his head, taking the dig in stride. "Seriously, right? I totally suck."

"You do."

"Guess I'd better find a new crush." Aiden looked at her expectantly. "Hey, is Maya seeing anyone?"

"Seriously, Aiden? WTF! Pick a new group."

"Can you blame me? I have a thing for hair bows." A smile peeked through his otherwise earnest expression.

"No, you don't."

"No, I don't."

They burst out laughing at the same time. "You had me going there," Hannah said. Aiden rested his hand on her shoulder and Hannah returned the gesture, allowing joy to break through her heartache. "Just, wow," she said, and they laughed again. "Thanks, Aiden. I needed a good laugh."

Nicole turned to the exit and watched her younger self recoil from what she had mistaken as more betrayal. *I messed up again. Why didn't I know you were still working out your sexuality? If we were like sisters—ugh! I was so focused on myself, I didn't think about you at all.* Nicole gasped. *I'm like Brandi.*

Recovering her poise, Hannah stepped back. Aiden's hand slipped off her shoulder. "It's too bad for Nic. She loves to laugh. She blew it, you know? You two might have worked. Before, I mean. You know, before all this."

"Yeah?" Aiden sounded hopeful. Nicole perked up. "I mean, maybe later when we're older?" he asked. "You know, when we get to high school and grow up?" Hannah frowned and Aiden drooped. "Nah, probably not," he agreed. "What was I thinking?"

Seriously?

"You and I are still friends, right?"

"Sure," she said, "of course we are."

"Cool. Happy Bat Mitzvah. You're a woman now!"

"I'm a mess."

I'm a mess too. And I messed up everything. Again. Nicole looked toward the exit, but her younger self had already slinked off. *I'm gone. I walked away from my best friend, my only friend who truly loved me. How could I have let it get so bad?* Nicole let her question hang in the air unanswered while she waited. When she dropped, it lasted longer, which made sense. The holes had revealed the full story, as requested. Even her nausea faded, replaced by a vast sorrow.

Nicole shot out of the hole and flopped onto the brown couch. JayBot swooped down to peel the hole off the carpet and somersaulted over to snag the next. Before long, he had stacked the holes against the wall with extraordinary efficiency.

Nicole sat up while she watched. "My new brother, the robot ninja."

Having secured the holes, JayBot sat on the floor to face Nicole. "You should rest. I performed additional research while you were away.

Jumping into a stack of multiple holes is not recommended. The psychosis risk accelerates in a nonlinear curve with each additional hole beyond three."

"How many holes did I—?"

"Eleven."

Nicole curled her arms around her legs. "So now I'm crazy?"

"Potentially, but I think not. I have assessed your condition and detect moderate despondency with lingering nausea and disorientation. Your mental state appears to be otherwise intact. However, I recommend a rest period before your next foray through time and space."

"Rest sounds good," Nicole said and flopped onto her side. JayBot continued to stare in a way that struck her as considerate yet way too intense, so she closed her eyes. Nicole reflected on the negative things Hannah had said about her this morning or, more accurately, a week ago. Nicole conceded Hannah was right to accuse her of betraying her trust, of focusing too much on herself, and of not being a reliable friend. But she was wrong to say Nicole would never change. She would and she had.

More than anything, Nicole wanted to text Hannah and make everything right. Except Nicole had no phone. Also, what would she say? *It's all so impossible*, she thought. On the other hand, maybe not. She'd been mired in the impossible all day, and that had yet to slow her down.

What about Jay? Had she misjudged him as she did with Hannah? Nicole had good reason to think Jay was responsible for Gavin's sudden indifference. Gavin had said as much two days ago after lunch, after Gavin humiliated her, after she chased after him into the hallway to demand answers. Their devastating conversation seared into her brain, leaving a festering wound. Nicole remembered the scene vividly.

Over the bustle in the hallway, Nic called out to Gavin. "We need to talk."

Gavin stopped in place but took his time before turning around. Until he did, she still held out hope that he would come to his senses and tell Nic she was the one he wanted all along. She read enough romance to know how this was supposed to go. Gavin would gush that it was her, it had always been her, it could never be anyone but her, and beg Nic's forgiveness.

But when Gavin faced her, his expression withered all illusions. "There's nothing to talk about, Nic. I've moved on."

"Why? What's wrong with me? I thought you liked me."

"You're fine," Gavin said, his concession both nominal and condescending, "but I can do better." His mouth contorted into a malignant smirk. "Even your brother thinks so." Gavin left her with his enigmatic jab.

"What's that supposed to mean? What about Jay? Hey, come back." Nic chased after him.

Spinning around the moment Nic reached him, Gavin laid into her. "I considered asking you out, but Jay convinced me I should aim higher." He grunted in her stunned face. "What a family. Jay acts all superior but he's not above cutting you down. Like he's the team's moral compass. As if. He's got the same filthy porn on his computer, same as the rest of the guys. What a snob. Oh, what, you don't believe me? Check for yourself. He leaves his laptop unattended during lunch when he's playing video games."

So many emotions rushed through her head, Nic didn't know what to think. Gavin took a step back, and Nic took a step forward. He did it again with the same result and scoffed. "Quit following me like a lost dog. Pathetic. You and Jay, a couple little bitches." Gavin took another step back. Nic remained in place, devoting all her energy to holding still, to holding it together.

Gavin took off while Nic sagged against the wall, battling an emotional tsunami, desperately trying not to bawl in the middle of the hallway. Until an idea entered her mind, a fitting scheme to get even with Jay. A satisfying rush soothed her. Nic knew exactly what she needed to do. And the next day, she did it.

And why not? Jay blocked her from dating Gavin. This was bad enough, but pushing him towards Brandi? Unforgivable. Jay knew what it would do to her. What did he expect? Jay wouldn't allow her to be happy, yet he thought it totally fine to make his move on that loose girl, Jenna? Oh, heck no. Now, thanks to Gavin, she had the perfect way to get Jay back.

Nicole reasoned that what she did was perfectly fair. Jay came between her and Gavin, so she came between Jay and Jenna. All well-deserved, assuming Nicole had the first part right. But did she? Had Gavin lied or tricked her somehow? Nicole no longer trusted herself. She needed to know for sure.

Nicole opened her eyes and sat up. "I need to ask you something," she said to JayBot.

"I recommend a longer rest period."

"Duly noted. Did Jay try to stop Gavin from dating me?" Nicole waited for an answer. The robot's lack of expression unnerved her more than his hesitation. Eventually, JayBot responded, "I am unable to answer your question."

"But I'm asking you to tell me," Nicole said, incredulous. "Don't you have to?"

"I am programmed to respond truthfully, but my primary directives take precedence. I cannot answer your question without upsetting you. The best I can say is the answer is complicated."

"Complicated? That's what Jay said." Nicole groaned. "What's so complicated about a yes/no question? You know what? Don't bother. It's fine.

I need to see for myself anyway. Peel me a hole."

JayBot removed the lacrosse stick from the wall. "I shall endeavor to assist you to the best of my ability." He held the stack of holes in one hand. "May I suggest we limit the stack to no more than three?"

"Definitely. I want one hole."

"One will be challenging. The holes are sticky." JayBot peeled and flipped them back as he counted. "Five ... thirteen ... seven ... four ... eleven ... three." He paused. "Are three holes acceptable?"

"No, I want one."

"Understood. Twelve ... six ... thirteen ... five—" The numbers washed over her hypnotically. Nicole wondered if it would ever end. "Sixteen ... ten ... eighteen ... two—"

"Stop! Two is fine. I'll take two."

After removing two holes from the stack, JayBot replaced the lacrosse stick. He guided the holes to the carpet. Nicole edged closer. "Take me to when Jay and Gavin talked about me," Nicole said. The holes vibrated. "When Jay changed Gavin's mind about dating me, or whatever actually happened."

JayBot stepped back. "I hope you find what you're seeking, dear sister."

CHAPTER 23

"Do it, coward!"

Florescent tubes buzzed overhead, bathing Nicole in an unflattering light. She stood in the school gymnasium next to the mat by the near wall. A dank musk suggested morning classes had already sweated through. Nicole heard a faint but familiar titter mixed with a provocative male voice coming from the hallway. She jammed her body against the hole to find the best angle to observe the couple through the open double doors.

And Nic and Gavin were undeniably a couple, Nicole noted with pleasure. She hadn't remembered wrong after all. Gavin rubbed Nic's pretty peach blouse between his fingers, commenting on the soft material.

Nic squirmed beneath his touch. "It tickles," she said, but Nicole knew that wasn't truthful. His touch didn't tickle her so much as thrill her in a way she had been unprepared to acknowledge. Even from inside the gym, physically separated and two days removed, Nicole flushed. This scene dated back to when Gavin was still sweet, before he had humiliated her. An hour before, at most.

"Swing by the cafeteria during lunch," Nic said. She captured Gavin's hands to still them. He rubbed her fingers, and she melted against the wall.

"Maybe I will," Gavin said, cheeky as though he might consider granting her the favor of his company.

"You better." Nic parted her lips, her arousal evident in her plea. Gavin laughed. He sounded careless and cocky, but she remembered thinking him racy and provocative at the time. He smoldered the way a strapping protag from a steamy romance novel would.

Exhilarated, Nic slapped his chest. "You better," she repeated emphatically. Gavin chuckled again. She reached out as if to give him another slap but let her hand linger instead. They both stared at her hand on his chest. Nic pushed him away, continuing her motion as though this had been her intent all along and he had merely distracted her. She slid away, her thrill aglow. "I *will* see you later."

Gavin watched her leave, his brazen gaze directed to her rear. From her new perspective,

Nicole observed two things she hadn't at the time: Gavin's hungry stare and the fullness in his pants. *I guess he was into me.* Nicole remembered how he had swung by the cafeteria as she requested. But not in the way she desired.

Nic had been the first at her table to see Gavin coming. She preened, boasted about her new guy as he approached, and beamed while her friends congratulated her. All her friends, including Brandi, her delectable envy evident. Gavin made his usual flashy entrance.

And then? Gavin ignored her, focusing all his attention on Brandi. Like he was any other boy. Nic had been so stunned by Gavin's reversal, so utterly devastated, she kept silent. She didn't even cry, although she did chase after Gavin to demand an explanation once he had strutted away, completing her mortification. After Nic spoke to Gavin, she understood.

Somehow, Jay had ruined everything. Nicole would find out how soon enough.

Right on cue, Jay passed the double doors and stood before Gavin. Jay got right into it. "What's this I hear about you and my sister?"

Scrolling on his phone, Gavin didn't even glance up. "She's into me."

"She's a freshman."

Gavin shrugged. He shoved his phone into his pocket. "That's all right. I don't mind a challenge." He began to walk away until Jay snagged his arm. Gavin spun back and shoved him. His jovial expression persisted, but irritation strained his tone. "Something you want to say to me?"

"I mind. She's a freshman."

Why do you keep saying that?

"Relax, bro. Lots of people dated in middle school. She's not too young to date."

"They dated other middle schoolers," Jay said, exasperated as though having to explain to a three-year-old why he shouldn't bite. "Dating a high school senior means something different."

"Yeah, I guess it does," Gavin agreed, a twinkle in his eye. "Don't worry, I'll be real gentle. You know how I am." When Gavin walked away, Jay seized him again. This time Gavin collected Jay's collar in his fist. "I'm getting real tired of this. Don't touch me again unless you want to start something."

"I do know how you are," Jay said. The calm in Jay's voice startled Nicole. She had never witnessed this side of him: driven, even fearless. The way Jay brushed off the taller, broader Gavin, whose fury radiated danger, astonished her. "I know exactly how you are. My sister's too young for you. And I don't mean her age."

Gavin chuckled and released him. "Yeah, I figured that about Nic. Don't worry. Girls like an experienced guy for their first time. I'll bet that's what she needs: a guy who knows what she wants." Gavin's smirk emerged, as radiant and disdainful as ever. "Same thing they all want."

He stepped away. The instant Jay grabbed him, Gavin whipped around and slammed Jay into the wall. Gavin curled his lips into a menacing sneer. "Hit me. Do it, coward!"

Jay clenched his fist near Gavin's face. Jay's rage flashed until extinguished by the same preternatural calm that had awed Nicole before. He uncurled his fist. "No. Coach said anyone who fights is automatically benched. If we're both out, we'll never beat Dulaney. I'm not risking my scholarship."

Gavin released him. Gavin's shirt had shifted in the scuffle, and he tugged it back into place. He brushed a finger against his shoulder as though flicking a gnat. "Yeah, all right. We'll friend fight."

"What's that?"

"Same as a regular fight but no throwing punches."

Jay considered this. "So, wrestling?"

"First one to tap out loses."

"Fine. If I win, you do not date my sister."

There it is. That's how you made Gavin drop me.

Gavin flashed a cocky grin. "You're not going to win."

"Say it. If I win, you do not date my sister."

"The famous Hallett confidence! Sure. If you win, I will not date your sister." Gavin shifted closer, bringing his contemptuous sneer beside Jay's ear. "No matter how much she begs me." Gavin brushed by him and entered the gym. After Jay followed, Gavin reached back to pull the doors shut behind them. They advanced to the matted area in the corner by where Nicole stood. "And when I win, you're my bitch."

"What does that mean?"

"It means when I call you *my bitch*, you take it like a bitch."

"Fine, whatever," Jay said. "If you win, I'm your bitch for a week."

"A week?" Gavin scoffed. "Where did that Hallett confidence go? Did Gunner and Fat Boy scare you?" Gavin flexed and kissed each of his biceps. "One month."

"Two weeks. And I won't make fun of you for naming your biceps Gunner and Fat Boy."

"This one is Fat Boy," Gavin said, pinching his right biceps while flexing rhythmically. "Look how fat he is. What's that, Fat Boy?" He mashed his ear against his swollen arm. "Fat Boy says two weeks is good."

The boys circled, Jay focused, primed to pounce, and Gavin cavalier. "I can't wait to introduce Nic to Gunner and Fat Boy," Gavin said. He bucked his pelvis. "And another friend."

"Are you ready, asshole?"

"Sure, bitch."

"I'm not your bitch."

"You will be soon enough."

No, he won't. You didn't know Dad taught Jay how to wrestle.

In one fluid motion, Jay kneeled and yanked the back of Gavin's legs. He drove his head against Gavin's hip to slam him on his back.

Gavin took the hit and rolled Jay over him. He leaped to his feet. "That all you got?"

Jay bounced back up and locked Gavin's arm against his chest. Pushing forward, Jay hooked his foot around to trip Gavin, knocking him on his back again. The impact created a thud so massive the vibration shook Nicole. But Gavin never lost his taunting smirk, unruffled by either blow. This time, Jay pinned his full weight against Gavin's torso to hold him down.

Come on, Gavin. Get up!

Gavin wedged his hands under Jay's shoulder and heaved, his arms swelling under the strain until Gavin created enough separation to slip out. They both scrambled back to their feet and circled. Gavin laughed, his haughty pride intact. "You got some moves, Hallett."

Jay stepped in and out while Gavin reacted. Each time Jay ducked Gavin's counter until he found an opening to wrap his hand behind Gavin's neck and shove his head down. Gavin reacted by bucking up. Jay used the opportunity to loop his arm under Gavin's armpit and flip Gavin over his back, slamming him to the mat.

Two buff boys wrestling. Nicole smiled, enjoying the show. *This would be much more fun if one boy wasn't my brother, and I didn't already know Jay wins.*

Jay held Gavin in position. "That's three takedowns. Give up."

Gavin's smirk twitched. "I'm bored. Enough foreplay." Using brute force, Gavin thrust Jay sideways. Jay struggled, expending energy to slow the sudden pressure but unable to sustain his advantage. Once Gavin arched over him, Jay lost his leverage and flattened. Gavin seized Jay's wrists. Shifting Jay's arms above his head, Gavin clutched both wrists with one hand to free up an arm. He balled his fist over Jay's face and punched the air above his nose. "Pop, pop, pop," Gavin said, providing the sound effects for what would have been multiple facial fractures. "You give?"

"No."

Gavin let out a cocky chuckle. Nicole found herself enjoying this less and less, no longer sure who to root for. As much as Jay deserved it, she didn't enjoy watching him get beat. Gavin struggled to roll Jay, lacking the moves. Instead, he kicked his legs into the mat, ramming his chest into Jay's side multiple times until dislodging him. Once Gavin had Jay prone, Gavin twisted Jay's arm behind his back, causing him to cry out in pain.

"Tap out."

"No."

Gavin twisted harder. "Tap out."

Jay screamed.

Tap out, Jay!

"You lost, Hallett. Tap out!" Gavin jammed his weight into the arm, creating an unnatural bend.

Jay hit the mat with his free hand, and Gavin leaped to his feet. His swagger energized, Gavin bounced as if he had been warming up and was anxious to start. After flipping over, Jay rubbed his shoulder. Gavin bounded back, planting his hands on his thighs to get in Jay's face. "This is going to be a fun two weeks, my bitch. At least for me." He spun away, passing Nicole as he flexed.

I don't get it. Gavin won? So Jay had nothing to do with it? Then why did Gavin lose interest in me?

Nicole turned to her brother. Beaten but not defeated, Jay glared. She could sense Jay's turmoil, his intensity. Her skin went cold.

"Nic's best friend is Brandi."

What! Nicole cupped her hand over her mouth.

Gavin hesitated but did not look back. "Oh, yeah? Brandi Moldenado?"

"Yep."

No. Don't do it, Jay!

"Cool. Brandi's hot. Maybe I'll have her next." Gavin pushed open the gym door.

"Not if you date Nic first," Jay called out. "Brandi doesn't do seconds."

Gavin stopped. He pulled the door shut and turned around. "That tracks. Go on."

Jay rose to his feet, grimacing as he held his arm. "I'm sure Nic's been texting Brandi all about you. Bragging, making Brandi jealous, not that Brandi would ever admit it. If you make your move on Brandi now, she would welcome the chance to best Nic."

Gavin's eyes widened. "I'll bet you're right, you evil fuck. I have underestimated you." He snickered. "You know, when you wanted to fight, I thought, *Damn, Jay must really hate me*. But now I think you must really hate your sister."

I'm wrong again but in a different way. This is all worse than I imagined.

"You have Brandi's info?"

Jay pulled out his phone and noticed Gavin's raised eyebrows. "I've given rides to Nic's friends," Jay explained.

"Brandi shot you down, huh?"

"It's not like that. Anyway, Brandi's not my type."

"No? Not your type? You don't like hot and popular?"

Jay pressed his lips together, bottling whatever response he chose not to share. "There. I sent it."

Gavin glanced at his phone. "Thanks, my bitch. This day gets better and better." He stepped back into the gym door, pressing it open. "Sucks for Nic, though. Cute kid. I almost feel bad for her." He grinned. The door banged shut behind him.

"Yeah," Jay said, his shoulders sagging.

How could you? Nicole slugged the invisible wall. *I'm glad I got you back, you jerk. I can't believe I worried I might have taken it too far. And I was afraid you would find out? Forget that. I want you to know I did it. You deserve so much worse.*

Nicole dropped through the floor. She struck the hole with her fist as she descended, her rage mixing with tears. Her motion ceased, and a new location appeared. Satisfaction calmed her. At last, the hole brought her to a scene she could enjoy.

Jenna stood at her locker, shifting books around, stealing eager glances down the hallway. Casually stylish, Jenna had an undeniable natural beauty. *Just like Brandi.* Nicole swallowed her jealousy. No need, she knew what was coming, and her revenge would be glorious.

Nicole turned towards the sound of footsteps to find Nic from yesterday dressed in a modest sweatshirt, her phone clutched in her fist, a familiar rage etched in her face. *You get her, girl.*

"You're Jenna, right?"

Jenna froze. "Yes. Do I know you?"

"I'm Nic, Jay's sister."

"Oh, hi! Nice to meet you." Jenna smiled warmly.

Nic glared back. "You should know about Jay before you get mixed up with him." She tapped her phone and held it so Jenna could watch the video she had recorded. "That's Jay's computer." In the video, the shot opened with the sticker Jay had affixed to his laptop, the one the lacrosse recruiter from the University of Maryland had given him. Jay had written his name at the bottom. The video shifted to the front, where Nicole pulled up his browser history and scrolled. "And those are all the sleazy, disgusting porn sites he's been to."

Jenna recoiled. "Why would you show that to me? Why would you do that to your brother?"

"Jay isn't the person you think he is. I know he acts caring, and sometimes he can be, but he'll betray you in the worst possible way whenever it suits him." She stuffed her phone into her pocket and pulled out a folded piece of paper. "Go on, take it. I listed all the sites. Read it and learn all about Jay."

"I don't want that. Please go away."

"You like him." Startled by her realization, Nic sneered. "No kidding, I figured he was one more guy to you." Jenna's face dropped. Her hands fell to her sides. "Well, whatever," Nic continued. "At least *you* can walk away. Not me —I'm his sister. I'm stuck with him. What I wouldn't give to replace him with a brother who doesn't upset me, one who helps me instead of working behind my back to hurt me." She unfolded the paper. "Go on, take it. Read about Jay before it's too late." Nic forced the paper into Jenna's hand before marching away.

Justice. You don't get to win, Jay. You mess with me, and I will always get you back. Count on it.

Nicole smirked in righteous indignation. Jenna peeked at the paper, twisted away, and looked again. Her hands trembled, and she shuddered as she read. Observing Jenna's distress, Nicole's contentment faded. She tapped the floor with her foot. *My part's over. Let's go.*

The more Jenna read, the more furious she became. Nicole heard footsteps from the other direction and saw Jay round the corner. He bubbled with anticipation. Nicole couldn't remember the last time she had seen him so energetic and happy. Against her better judgment, regret seeped in.

The floor opened up, and darkness engulfed her. Nicole was relieved that she didn't have to witness any more of that scene. Jay deserved it, of this she was certain, even more so having watched Jay's wickedness for herself. But Nicole didn't feel as righteous viewing it the second time around. Something nagged at her. No, she rejected her unease. She knew the truth. And for once, what she had seen confirmed it.

Nicole flew out of the hole and twisted to her feet. She and JayBot worked in tandem, each peeling a hole off the floor. Nicole passed her hole to JayBot, who slapped it against his hole while she yanked out the lacrosse stick. JayBot attached the holes to the stack, and Nicole slid the stick into place.

JayBot's baseline pleased expression faded into one of concern. "Are you injured? What happened? I detect several telltale signs of a recent cry."

Nicole brushed him off. "Doesn't matter. I'll be fine as long as you're around instead of my horrible brother."

"Understood." JayBot rested both hands on her shoulders. While his hands felt the same as Jay's, JayBot had never touched her before that moment. Nicole found the sensation more disturbing than unpleasant as if her phone had kissed her fingertips.

"That explains the message I received from Phin," JayBot continued. His tone struck Nicole as distinctly ominous.

She wavered as she spoke. "What's the message?"

"Phin wishes to speak with you." JayBot looked deep into her eyes. "The moment has come to determine the course of your life. Good luck, dear sister."

PART FOUR

JAY: AFTERNOON

CHAPTER 24

*"Trust your intuition,
dear brother."*

I don't know if Scruffy has learned the word lunch, but she definitely understands what it means when I walk into the laundry room. Especially when I snag her food bowl on the way. Scruffy pounces in the air, leaping, bounding, beside herself with excitement.

How fortunate to be so thrilled with life's basic functions. Can't say I'm anywhere near that excited about soup. Or about much of anything besides video games. And Jenna, yes, but let's not go there.

As I loop my arm deep into the economy-sized bag of dog chow, I can't help but think about my intense conversation with Nic. She sure did panic when she thought I had asked NicBot questions about her. I figured she worried that I had asked NicBot about Gavin, but that didn't seem to be it. I'll bet she thought I asked NicBot about yesterday. Hells no to that. I already know more than I want, thank you.

When I dump the chow into Scruffy's bowl, the rattling makes her twirl and bark. "You act as though we starve you," I say but really I'm relieved by her reaction. Scruffy wouldn't be this hyper if Nic had already fed her. I spin the food in the bowl while I walk it over to the kitchen by her water. Scruffy asserts her inner wolf and charges the bowl the moment it hits the floor. I yank my hand away as though she might chew it off. This is a thing I like to do because it's fun to pretend my small dog is ferocious. "Attack!" I command redundantly.

Back in the laundry room, I squeeze the bag and seal it up, recoiling as the briny air gusts into my face. The fish-flavored chow must have been on sale last month. I hope the as yet unopened chicken-flavored bag beside it has a less vile odor.

Through the open door, I notice NicBot setting the table. Watching NicBot makes me wonder what Nic will say to JayBot, now that she knows she can ask him questions about what I know. I hope she takes my suggestion and asks him about Amaya and Jenna. Probably she won't, but she should. If Nic had any idea what those two went through, she might understand why I couldn't let her anywhere near Gavin. Of course, if she had known what Gavin was really like a week ago, she might not have gotten mixed up with him in the first place.

That insight gives me pause. Yeah, I might be partially at fault here, but it's not as if I've been intentionally hiding things from Nic. She and I never talk about that sort of thing. Sex, I mean. Nic's my little sister. And yes, I know she's in high school, but I have trouble thinking about her in that way. Guess I'm not doing her any favors treating her like a little girl.

Still, talking to Nic about anything sexual is asking for trouble. She lives in a self-imposed fantasy world. You drag her out of her bubble at your own risk. I can't simply have her download Urban Dictionary and be done with it. Speaking of which, there's one more thing I need to do before lunch.

While Dad stirs the soup over by the stove, I walk over to the kitchen table. NicBot aligns spoons atop the napkins with a precision that would be pathologic if she didn't have the convenient excuse of being a robot.

"Hey," I say quietly but loud enough to get her attention. "Do me a favor and don't use any new words you've learned for male genitalia in front of Dad. He'll know right away something's off."

"So don't say *love piston* or *spunktrumpet* in front of Dad?"

Cringing as if she punched me in the gut, I take a moment to breathe. No galaxy exists where I'm cool with my little sister saying *spunktrumpet*. "No. Or to me. Or to anyone, ever. Delete it all."

"Understood. And shall I extend sexual parity and also refrain from saying *vagoo* and *vijayjay*?"

I squint at her while I take a breath, partially to question if she is serious but mostly to resist the impulse to vomit into my mouth. "I feel like you already know the answer and you're just messing with me."

"Trust your intuition, dear brother."

"Right." I groan. Lunch should be fun.

"Soup's up," Dad says.

Lunch is pretty routine, at least at the start. It's been mostly Dad and me talking at meals these days anyway. In the past, I pulled Mom into the conversation but that led to awkward moments. Or her getting frustrated with one of us, usually Dad and sometimes me or Nic. Eventually, I did the family a favor and learned to go with the flow. Stress and food don't mix well.

Between swallows of soup, Dad talks about how he watched the snow accumulate from his office window. "We had quite a blizzard going for a few hours," he says. Dad doesn't get easily impressed by snowfall, so I believe him. "It will be a while before the county clears the roads. Oh, and Mom texted from work. She'll be coming home late."

Mom works as a therapist at the hospital.

Not a therapist you talk to when you're stressed out, the kind that teaches you how to stand from a chair after you've had a stroke. At least that's how she first explained what an occupational therapist does. I was six or seven at the time, old enough to grasp what she was saying on a superficial level but not old enough to process in a way that made much sense.

As a result, I spent much of first grade standing from a chair using the strength of one leg. I figured I'd better start practicing right away. You know, before my stroke. It's pretty easy to stand using one leg when you're a healthy child. I couldn't understand why her patients spent so many weeks practicing this.

Bursting with pride, I shared my extraordinary talent with Mom. She suggested I try again but imagine I have severe arthritis and couldn't support all my weight on one knee. That bumped the difficulty level to near impossible. I tried over and over again, and the only way to avoid face-planting was to cheat.

I protested as any child would, at least one naïve and privileged enough to believe in a just world. I said, *That's unfair!* and she said, *It sure is!* So I spent the rest of first grade worried my stroke would happen before I had mastered the technique. Whenever I hyperventilated about it, I would settle myself with the understanding that I didn't also have arthritis. Yet. I was also unclear about when I was to get arthritis.

When Mom recognized my distress, she sat me down for a long talk about how strokes and arthritis were adult things. *You have many years before you have to worry about it*, she explained. And for many years, I found this reassuring. Then I turned eighteen and everyone cheered, *Welcome to adulthood!*

Hurray for me. So much to look forward to.

"She texted me from the Room of Toys," Dad continues. He and I have made good progress on our soup while NicBot hasn't taken a sip. She is moving the contents around her bowl. I'd better work something out before Dad picks up on it.

"Do you remember calling it the Room of Toys?" he asks. "Back when you two were little, Mom brought you to work and showed you all the devices they have in that huge rehab area in the hospital. Contraptions for squeezing, pulling, pushing, lifting—you two ran around and played with everything. You called it the Room of Toys." He looks at me. "I remember you were obsessed by the chair that inclines to stand by pushing a button."

I do remember. "Yes, helpful for people with arthritis. Like a regular chair but *new and improved*." I wink at NicBot. I figure she'll enjoy the reference but neglect to account for her cyber precision and recent download.

"*New and improved* is nonsensical," NicBot says. "To improve something implies revising something that already exists. If something is new, it cannot also be improved."

"Nic makes a good point," Dad says.

"Oh, it is not *my* point," NicBot corrects with robotic rigor. "The dictionary regards that expression with contempt."

Dad's forehead crinkles. "What dictionary expresses contempt?"

"Delete! Delete!" I flail my arms for good measure. But unless I can figure out a way to type it into her mainframe, she is not getting the message.

"The dictionary," she repeats, mystified by his confusion. "By your age, I would think you've read the dictionary."

"Excuse me?"

Responding to Dad's tone, NicBot lifts her hands. "Don't @ me."

Dad's forehead crinkles deeper. "Why would I *at you*? That doesn't make sense."

"Delete! Delete!" I say and turn to Dad. "She means *no offense*."

"Oh. Is that a thing?"

"Yes."

"Really?" He mulls it over. "Don't at me? I feel like you're missing a word."

"Hey, Dad. Can you get the milk? I'm out."

Dad pushes his chair back and walks to the refrigerator. He mumbles, "Prepositions can be verbs now?" Snagging NicBot's bowl, I dump her soup into mine and chow down as much as I can before Dad returns.

"And it means *no offense*," he says, still preoccupied as he hands me the milk. I pour a splash in my cup for show. I'm getting the impression that lunch needs to end soon. Better chug my milk. "All right," Dad says. "Say something offensive and I'll try it."

It's as if he wants me to do a spit take. I choke instead. Before I can speak, Dad says it for me: "Delete! Delete!"

I wipe my mouth and laugh.

"I like that one," Dad says. "Makes more sense than the other thing. I like it even more than *on fleek*."

"Stop," I say. "No one says *on fleek*. No one in the history of decency has ever used that expression."

"Someone must have said it," NicBot chimes in. As with actual Nic, she does not know when to quit. "It's in the dictionary."

Dad arches his eyebrows. "What dictionary are you talking about?"

"Delete! Delete!"

"Ha, ha! Right? But seriously," Dad says, his expression slipping from lighthearted to stern in a flash. "What dictionary?"

For once, NicBot doesn't answer. Her minimum clueless setting must have finally kicked in. Before she can make things worse, I propose an answer. "Webster's?"

Dad is not impressed. "I highly doubt Noah

Webster ever said *on fleek*."

"Right, no. But they do update the dictionary."

Dad lets his head bounce. "Fair enough."

NicBot rounds her mouth, evidently not computing. I try to communicate via brain waves. *Stop. He's ready to move on.* But no, she is not programmed with telepathy. I can only imagine what screwy hazard that premium upgrade would cost.

"According to the dictionary, people did say *on fleek*. He might have been one of them. Was Noah Webster an uncultured idiot with large quantities of diarrhea vacating his body?"

Dad lowers his spoon. "Wait, what?"

"All done." I push my bowl away. "Hey, Dad. Let's throw snowballs."

"Hang on, why—oh, you want to throw snowballs?"

NicBot stands. "And I'll do the dishes." She brings her dishes to the sink while Dad gawks in disbelief. He drifts over and whispers, "Are we in an alternate universe?"

"Maybe," I whisper back, "Although I was thinking a parallel universe or at least a parallel dimension. I'm not sure how to tell the two apart."

This does not relieve his concern. More the opposite. "You know I'm joking, right?"

"Sure," I say, dubiously given how I am not at all sure. "So am I?"

We stare at each other. Dad grimaces. "Can you wink or something? You're starting to worry me."

I stand and tap his arm. "Come on. We'll meet outside. I'll get my crosse and gloves."

CHAPTER 25

"Out of sync."

Technically, my crosse pokes out of the wall in the library, but I leave it alone and head upstairs. I'd rather not risk a cross-dimensional paradox by yanking out the stick. Plus my gloves are in my room so I'd have to go upstairs anyway. Sure enough, my stick and gloves are both in my room where I left them. JayBot must have snagged the crosse from my parallel bedroom. I mean, if he knows everything I know, he'd know where I keep it.

This again makes me wonder what JayBot has told Nic. Not that I have anything to hide. Except for recent events with Gavin—I do not see that going over well—but JayBot would know why I did what I had to do. For a second, I wish Nic were here so we could talk. Better for her to hear it straight from me. I glance over to the library where my crosse marks the conduit between our worlds. But my Nic-related irritation soon overwhelms any fleeting interest. I leave it alone.

Dad is already outside shoveling. I listen to his rhythmic scraping while I pull on my boots. I also hear humming coming from the kitchen. NicBot has composed a pop medley of Nic's favorite songs. What a wacky thing to program a robot to do. Then again, it's those unexpected details that give artificial intelligence its character. Much respect to the coders.

The moment I open the closet door, Scruffy is underfoot. I step back while I put on my jacket, trying not to squash her. "Hey, girl. Do you want to go outside?" I crouch down. "Do you want to go outside? Does Scruffy want to go outside?" Scruffy erupts with manic energy. Her joy grows by leaps and bounds, most of them into my ribs. "Do you want to go outside?"

Scruffy must think I'm the dumbest human she's ever met. At this point, her energy level is somewhere between me popping off after I've defeated the final boss and a toddler mainlining sugar. Yeah, I've probably revved her up enough. "Come on, girl."

I open the front door and she's a rocket. However much she wants to relieve herself, Scruffy still bides her time, sniffing and pawing at the snow. Dad has shoveled the length of the walkway, but Scruffy expresses her personal esthetics and digs out an area by the shrub. Once she has cleared a grassy patch to her satisfaction, she rotates and squats.

"Good girl!"

In her haste, Scruffy didn't give herself quite enough space to scoot her entire backside in there. I dodge the flowing yellow river on my way to the lawn. My boots crunch deep into the snow.

Dad sees me and drops his shovel to the side. "I'll make snowballs while you get ready," he says. "Remind me about the goal area."

When I reach the tree by our street, I flatten the snow around me to approximate the goal area. Dad is working on his second snowball by the time I've finished. I call out, "From here to here." I position my stick to give him a visual. "Bring the heat, old man."

He launches his shot, which pegs the trunk well over my head. "The goal is not that tall," I say. "This isn't soccer."

"Just warming up." Dad picks up his other snowball but doesn't throw it. I guess we're in for a talk. "I don't want to jinx it, but I have to say how great it is to see you and Nic hanging out this morning."

I blow it off. The water vapor from my breath makes a physical representation of my dismissal in the air before me. "Cabin fever, you know? Like when we were little. If a child can play with a box for five hours, why not play with the other kid who hangs around the house all day?"

I figure Dad will appreciate that shiny pearl of wisdom I polished up this morning. Instead, his expression reads less agreeable and more appalled. "No, no, no. You and Nic were never two children stuck in the house together playing with a box. You two were best friends and playmates." He shakes his head. "You don't remember."

No, I don't, but who knows? He could be right. "I guess we've changed."

"Of course you have. You go to school and make friends your own age. That's normal. But you and Nic genuinely loved playing together. I'm sorry you stopped. I really am." He rotates the snowball in his hand. "Until today. Whatever happened to make you two enjoy each other's company again, it's not cabin fever. I've seen you and Nic stuck in the house many times before and you two might as well be in different zip codes. I've always found it sad. But today?" Dad flashes a smile. "I think it's fantastic that you and Nic found a dash of the old magic again."

What's fantastic is to see Dad so cheerful. No point in taking that away from him by troubling him with the whole robot business.

"I know it's easier when you're little," he continues, dusting the snowball with his fingertips as he rotates it. A more spherical snowball emerges. "And sure Nic's changed. We all change. You've changed too. Changing isn't the problem, it's being out of sync. You either change with somebody or you change without them."

Having seen my pearl of wisdom and raised it with a pearl of his own, he winds up. I shift into position. The ball curves down and left, and I snatch it with the net. Out of habit, I whip it back. The ball streaks the way a meteor slices the atmosphere, disintegrating into a snowy arc. Flakes sprinkle down on Scruffy, who leaps beneath the powder.

"Cool," Dad says and collects more snow.

I should probably let it go, but the truth is Nic and I aren't the only people out of sync. "Like you and Mom," I say.

He hesitates. "What about me and Mom?"

"Out of sync."

Dad mashes the snow. "Yeah, out of sync."

"Dinner's gotten awkward," I say. "Why is Mom always so angry? You didn't do anything." Dad stops mashing and stares at me. His surprise is understandable; I've never been this blunt before. Spending the morning with a brutally honest robot must have set me off.

"That is one way to look at it," he says agreeably but at the same time clearly not. "Another way is I was unemployed and depressed for nearly two years. We blew through our savings even with Mom picking up more shifts. I guess I wore her down. But I'm doing better now. I mean, the meds help. I can get out of bed in the morning. And my web business is starting to pick up, although it's still feast or famine. Mostly, it's nice to have a purpose, to be contributing. I'm trying to make it up to her," Dad says, dubious. "I may be too late. Which stinks, but there it is."

"You're giving up?"

"I'm not—I'm not giving up." His shoulders slump while he stares down the street. I look too. We're the first ones outside since the blizzard let up. The block is otherwise empty and still. Maybe our neighbors are waiting for the county to plow our stubby side road. Bracketed by trees on either side, the street is a sparkling white cloak, extending to a blinding infinity. I squeeze my eyes shut and feel the burn.

"I'm accepting, not giving up," Dad clarifies. "What's done is done. I put Mom through a lot."

"Yeah, but isn't that how marriage works? For better or for worse? And as you said, you're doing better now. She has to forgive you."

Dad rests the snowball by his feet and scoops more snow. "That's not how forgiveness works, Jay. It isn't something you can demand. You can offer it. You can ask for it." He thinks for a moment and frowns. "That's about it. Forgiveness is a tricky and powerful thing." He scrunches the snow, periodically rotating the ball. "The way I see it, if you want others to forgive you, the first step is to forgive them. Forgiveness always works both ways. And next, if you can swing it, the second and more challenging step is to forgive yourself. That's still a work in progress. I'm getting there."

Dad's always been a bit of a philosopher but I never considered him passive. "I still think you should *do* something," I say.

"I am doing something. I'm giving her time. It might be too late, but I'm not giving up. And always remember both Mom and I love you and Nic. That will never change. Mom and will I always have in common whatever happens." When I don't respond, Dad bends over to pick up his other snowball. "Are you ready? I've got two."

I assume my stance. "Bring it."

He fires in a breaking ball. I shift the crosse in time to knock it away, but I've lurched out of position. He's already winding up with the next one, and I sense it'll be a fastball. Sure enough, he hurls it in. I snag it in the net and flip it over Scruffy where she has curled up by the shrub. She leaps in the air, intending to chomp the ball, but it's already powder. It sprays down on her. She shakes her head the way a cartoon character might show surprise.

"Scruffy." Dad chuckles. "She's such a goof."

She is a goof, but I'm too distracted to laugh. All this talk about their marriage is heightening my anxiety about the future. I wait for Dad to look at me. "I am excited about college but not so much about becoming an adult," I say. "It seems complicated and, no offense, kind of blows."

"No offense taken. I am not the arbiter of adulthood." Dad gathers another handful of snow. "Adulthood can be rough, but it's less complicated than you think. When you break it all down, when you decide what is and isn't important, it all becomes pretty simple. Be a good person. The rest will work itself out."

"Be a good person," I repeat, incredulous. "That's it?"

Dad shrugs. "That's the brunt of it, yeah."

Wow. This guy. "Thanks, Dad. You've solved life."

"You go ahead and make fun," he says. "Thirty years from now, you'll look back and realize I was right the whole time."

"All right, go off," I say, laughing. Then I stop. Dad's logic has an obvious flaw. "I have to ask. Did the rest work itself out for you?"

"In some ways, yes. Others, no, but that's on me. I wasn't always a good person."

"You were always a good person to me."

"Well, yeah. And that part worked out."

I knock my glove into my head and stagger for effect. "You just blew my mind."

"I'm going to blow this snowball right past you."

"I'd like to see it," I say, and he does. I was not expecting two fastballs in a row. The ball clips my shoulder, slamming into the trunk and spraying my neck. "Sweet throw! You still got it."

"It's nice to be good at something."

"Yeah, I get that. You should do this more."

Dad makes a sweeping gesture with his hand. "First legitimate snowfall this winter and it's already March."

"Not with snowballs. I mean, you should join a league."

"A league? Of what, old guys past their prime who want to relive their former glory?"

"Exactly. Don't they have a league at the rec center?"

Dad considers this. "You know, I think they do."

"There you go."

"Sure. Maybe I'll join after you go off to college." His smile drops for a moment before he replaces it with a forced one. I don't know why he thinks I can't tell the difference. I've looked at his face as for as many years as I've looked at my own.

"I won't be far," I say. "Easy drive to College Park. It's like fifty minutes."

"Fifty-four if you avoid the toll roads," he says without hesitation.

I lower my stick. "Not that either of us checked Google Maps."

"I sure didn't." His genuine smile returns. "So my son's going off to college. Whatever. It's not like I'm so proud of him I can burst."

Neither of us says anything for a bit.

I lift my crosse into position. "Throw another one."

"Yep."

Dad rushes to create another snowball and wings it at me. I snag it and fling it high into the air. Lying in wait for the chance to redeem herself, Scruffy pounces into the fragments, her paws swatting the air. Snow has coated her fur, and she crouches for a full-body shake. Convulsions begin at her head and transmit section by section until released through her tail.

"So Scruffy wants to play in the snow, but she doesn't want any snow on her?" Dad asks. "I don't understand her plan here."

"Yeah, I don't think she's thought it through."

Scruffy slips into one of the deep footprints I made when I stomped across the lawn. Her tumbling triggers a memory, one which grips me with such immediacy I gasp as though I'd been struck by another space-time-warping paintball.

Nic and I sled at Pine Woods Middle School, back when we're both in elementary school. Our future middle school looms behind us, casting imposing shadows. We mount the sled and shoot down the hill, same as we had throughout the afternoon, except this time we hit an irregular patch and the earth veers, jolting us apart. I stand, taking a moment to find my center. After snagging the sled's handle, I search for my sister.

Nic's whimpering on her side, flopped over like a sad flounder. I assume the worst and spring into action.

Tossing that droopy fish over my shoulder, I sprint up the hill, the sled bounding behind me. The incline is steep, especially the last bit, but I don't stop until I crest the hill. I collapse at the top, exhausted. Mom checks Nic out and declares all bones intact with no yucky bleeding parts. Nic giggles.

After catching my breath, I ask Dad, *Why didn't you come down and help me?* He arches closer until our hats and noses touch. *You do a great job taking care of your sister,* he says. *She wanted you to do it. Nic loves you so much.*

I shake off the memory, not in stages like a snow-powdered Scruffy but equally violent. The memory is a moment in time from a billion years ago, Precambrian even. I shove it down and replace it with a more relevant notion: a hypothetical world without Nic.

"Did you enjoy being an only child?"

Dad scoops more snow. He works the snow between his gloves. "I did while growing up, yeah. As a child, it's nice to have everything to yourself. Not until I went off to college did I understand how much I was missing out."

"Missing out?" I ask. I don't see it.

"My friends with siblings seemed less alone in the world. I mean, consider Mom. She's got a squadron of brothers. Maybe that's why she's such a together person. All that love makes her strong. You and Nic have it too, with each other. Whether you recognize it or not."

"We used to," I say. Dad inhales as if he's about to interrupt, and I hold up my hand. "Save it. Nic did something awful recently. Something that—well, the sole purpose was to hurt me."

"I'm sorry, Jay. Sometimes good people do bad things. I've already shared my views on forgiveness."

"That's just it. I don't think Nic wants forgiveness. I don't think she believes she did anything wrong."

Dad nods. "I hear you. You should talk to her about it. I'm sure she'd look at it differently if she knew how hurt you are." He notes my expression and adds, "Unresolved conflicts fester, Jay. Don't ignore them. The longer you wait, the more intractable the problems become."

I brush it off. "The last time I talked to Nic, we argued more. I don't think it helped."

"Really? You two seemed fine at lunch."

I freeze. Crap. No way to explain my way out of that. Time to bug out. "My hands are getting cold. These gloves aren't for warmth. Thanks for the goalie practice."

"Of course," Dad says. "I enjoyed it."

"Come on, Scruffy. We're going inside." Scruffy crosses the yard with me until we reach the shoveled path. She veers over to her private cleared area, pressing her rump firmly into the shrub while she squats. "It's poop time."

"Do you have a bag?"

"Uh."

Dad pulls a bag from his pocket and inverts it for me. When I walk over, he places a hand on my shoulder. "You and Nic are great kids. And more importantly, you're family. You'll work it out."

"Sure we will," I say. But I'm not a good liar, and I fool nobody.

CHAPTER 26

"Is that fun?"

After dumping the stinky bag in the garage, I peel off my winter clothes. I keep rehashing what Dad said about forgiveness. I didn't do anything to Jenna that she needs to forgive, but I hope she can find a way to trust me again. I don't know if Jenna could even if she wanted to. Or if I could forgive Nic even if she wanted me to.

I place my boots by the door to dry. Scruffy has curled up on the floor near Dad's office. What did Dad mean by forgiveness works both ways? I did nothing to Nic. Well, maybe not nothing. It pains me to admit it, but I wonder if things would have worked out differently if Nic and I talked as we used to. If I had told her what I know rather than acted on it behind her back.

It's not all on her, I guess. I never explained my relationship with Jenna to Nic. But what if I had? Would it have made a difference? There's no way to know.

NicBot still hums in the kitchen. Must be her screen saver.

Oh yeah, I guess there's one way to find out. I walk into the kitchen where NicBot idles. Her eyes pop open. "How may I be of assistance, dear brother?"

"Would you be interested in hearing the story of me and Jenna?"

"Yes, of course." She takes a step in my direction and stops when I raise my hand.

"Hold up," I say. "How much of your answer is Nic and how much is NicBot?"

"I am unable to separate the two. My programming is based on Nic, but confounding variables make a response to your question inconclusive. Speculating with a moderate to high degree of confidence, I believe Nic would want to hear your story. Her hostility toward you is primarily based on you criticizing her or you not talking to her. Neither applies in this situation."

Criticizing her? Yeah, fair enough. But I only do it because she's so much better than she acts. If I didn't think highly of her, I wouldn't bother. I wouldn't care. Let her be a vapid Brandi clone. Then again, that may not be how Nic sees it.

"Good enough," I say. "Let's sit over there." We walk over to the blue couch and are soon followed by paw pattering. Scruffy rounds the corner but does not join us directly. We sit and wait as she sniffs the carpet, crouches, shoots her tail in the air, and repeats the process, carefully making her way over. I have no idea what she is searching for, but its importance cannot be overstated.

"Do you know what she's doing?" I ask NicBot.

"I do not."

Scruffy leaps onto the couch next to NicBot. She circles next to her and sniffs. Abruptly changing her mind, Scruffy struts over to me and presses her nose into my side until satisfied. She circles before settling against my thigh.

I rest my hand on Scruffy's fur. "I guess the coders haven't mastered scent. Scruffy has sniffed you out."

"Is that a request?"

"No."

"It's no bother, dear brother. Pheromones do not register as a premium setting. I shall initiate presently."

"No! Please do not sweat like my sister."

NicBot flashes an eerie smile. "That was a joke. I have no chemical capabilities."

"Funny," I grumble. "You're a laugh riot. You must kill at the robot conventions."

"We do not have robot conventions. Also, I'm programmed not to kill or engage in other forms of violence."

"Got it. So you can make jokes but you don't get them?"

NicBot widens her eyes. "Ah, I understand now. You were being humorous."

"Wow." I shake my head. "Way to gut the vibe. Do you still want to hear this story?"

"I am most interested in your story, dear brother. Please proceed."

I scratch Scruffy behind her ear. She lifts a paw toward the ceiling. That's dog for *I'd rather you scratch my belly*. I move my hand as directed, and she twists with pleasure.

"Settle in," I say. "We have a lot to cover."

I rarely talked to Jenna until recently because I could never find the perfect moment. She had too many people around her, or I was too nervous, or some other lame reason I bailed. But a few months after Jenna and Gavin broke up, I notice her alone at her locker at the end of the school day. I recognize this as the perfect opportunity. Jenna drives home, and I have time after school before lacrosse practice starts, so I figure, now or never.

Even then, it takes me time to build up the nerve. I make up my mind to go for it a week ago Monday. Jenna usually ignores me when I walk by her, but this time I walk right toward her. She notices and stiffens. I fight the urge to swerve to the other side of the hallway, to cut my losses and bolt. But I stay on track. This is it, I decide, my one and only shot.

As I walk closer, Jenna drops a textbook. When the book slams the floor, the bang is as if she shoots me in the gut. Her attitude gives off the same intent. But I've already committed. If she wants to shoot me down, she can do it with words.

"Hi, Jenna," I say.

Her response is a scowl, measured by begrudging respect that I hadn't fled the scene like a sane person. Jenna is silent, practically daring me to say another word. Even worse, I realize I had been so focused on gathering the courage to talk to her, I hadn't planned anything to say past hello. I rack my brain for a topic. We've had classes together, although none this year. I can't think of any mutual friends beyond the lacrosse team and I know better than to bring that up. I've got nothing.

But right when I'm about to panic, I have a moment of clarity. None of it matters. Whatever I say, Jenna is poised to brush it off, reject it, or have some other hostile reaction. My situation is so predictably disastrous, there's only one solution: be unpredictable. So I do the absolute last thing any sane person would do in this situation. I tell her a story about clovers.

"Human girls enjoy stories about clovers?" NicBot interrupts.

"No, you're missing the—why don't we hold all questions until the end."

"Understood. Do continue, dear brother."

The story isn't about clovers exactly. It's about the time my family visits the Walt Whitman house during a trip to one of my parents' college friends on Long Island. Nic and I are way too young to care about a long-dead poet. I'm nine—old enough to suffer quietly for an hour if I have to—but Nic is three years younger and there is no way. Sure enough, in no time she's two sniffles shy of a raving fit. So they send us outside, where she and I crawl around the lawn for an hour inspecting the clovers.

The docent comes outside after their tour and quotes a line: *the powerful play goes on, and you may contribute a verse.* I am too young to understand. In my child-brain, I think she's giving me homework. What? Now I have to write a verse? She explains that the line is from a Walt Whitman poem, not meant to be taken literally. I remember being relieved, and maybe that's why the quote sticks with me.

I tell Jenna, "Not too long ago, I saw *Dead Poets Society.* My parents like to make us watch old movies. It's the Family Time activity least likely to result in an argument because, you know, no one has to talk. Anyway, the Whitman quote turns out to be pretty famous because it's in the movie. I recognize it right away but had never understood what it meant. The powerful play is life, and we all contribute a verse because we're all part of it. Now that I get it, I think the line is great. I mean, it's cool that in a world where we're so small and insignificant, we all have a chance to contribute something."

The whole time I'm rambling about clovers and poetry, Jenna moves things around her locker. Not once does she acknowledge me. She doesn't leave, but I have no idea if she's even listening. Softly, almost to herself, she says, "I don't like my verse."

I'm so startled when she speaks that my throat closes up. "We're young," I say, forcing the words out. "I've barely started mine."

Her expression softens. "Did you really crawl around the lawn for an hour looking at clovers?"

"We were searching for one with four leaves," I say. I'm defensive but on the other hand, Jenna keeps talking to me, so, you know, score!

Despite Jenna's confusion, her beauty overwhelms, even with her eyebrows all bunched up. "And that's fun?" she asks.

I shrug. "It's not *not*-fun." For a split second, she nearly smiles before overcompensating with a harsher scowl and finally leveling out into a blank stare. This is such an improvement from her initial scowl that I can't help but grin at her.

"I have to go," she says. She's not angry exactly, more like she'd rather not stick around and risk a laugh.

"All right if I come by and talk to you again?" I ask. This is pretty bold, I know, but her almost-smile has intoxicated me.

She looks away. "It's not *not*-all right." Despite the playful reference, her expression remains vacant.

"Good," I say. "Then I'm not *not*-unhappy."

Our shared joke does the trick. Jenna snaps her smile back, a moment too late, clamping her lips. She frowns as though her face is defective and she had better get the thing fixed before it breaks down and smiles squirt out her ears. "If you come by, Jay, I'll talk to you, but it's not like we are going to be friends."

"I'll take what I can get."

"That's all you're going to get," Jenna says. She walks away. I wait a bit to see if she turns around but no such luck. She's done with me today. Still, she left an opening for tomorrow, and the way I see it, my first attempt went better than it could have.

"It also went much worse than it could have," NicBot says.

"Hold up. Aren't you programmed to be my supportive sister?"

"If you would prefer, we can change my comment setting from honest to positive-only.

Ask Phin to send an attendant, and we will revise your request."

"Revise?" Her comment surprises me. I didn't realize I had anything to do with her programming. Scruffy stirs. I rub her belly until she settles back into canine nirvana. "Is your current programming based on my request?"

"Yes," NicBot says. "I am to joke around and not take everything too seriously, be interested in things you enjoy, and not be moody or manipulative. As you specified."

That does sound familiar, although I don't remember specifying any of it. At least not out loud.

"I also have an obsequious setting favored by egocentric siblings with low self-esteem."

Admittedly, I consider the setting for a moment before I laugh. "This is you joking around and not taking everything too seriously, right?"

"Yes, dear brother."

"Good one. I'm going to continue my story."

"Please do."

I arrive at Jenna's locker around the same time the next day. Jenna ignores me, but no reaction is such an improvement from yesterday's hostility, I consider it progress. And even better, I'm prepared this time. I open with a story about my English teacher who's pushing forty but acts as if she's still in college. She's plastered her classroom with college posters like it's her dorm room. Go Towson Tigers!

Jenna says she's never had her for English but has seen her in the hallway dressed as though she's hitting the clubs after work. Jenna peppers me with questions. It's fantastic to have a conversation with her that isn't so one-sided. But at the first pause, she tells me she has to go. She's almost apologetic as if she would have preferred to keep talking to me, but, you know, things to do.

I wait by her locker to see if she turns around. I'm more optimistic this time but nope. Just like the day before, Jenna is done with me. Still, I note more progress when I come by the next day and catch her peeking down the hallway. And when I arrive on Thursday, Jenna starts a conversation with me before I even reach her locker. She tells me about her little brother in middle school and how she worries about him.

Jenna is easy to talk to when she's less guarded. The next time there's a pause in the conversation, I expect her to bail again, but instead, she says, "If you're going to keep talking to me, I suppose we can be friends, but that's all we're going to be. Maybe I'll date again in college." She stares past me down the hallway. "I'm so done with high school, you know?"

"Sure," I say. "I'm pretty done with high school myself."

"Yeah, well, I'm *completely* done," she says.

I suppose this conversation should disappoint me, but I'm too flattered. When she looks back at me, she tilts her head the way Scruffy does when she can't quite figure out what is going on. "What is up with you?" she asks.

"Sorry. Can't help it." My joy is so intense, I have to force my words out. "Jenna Zielinski, the most awesome girl in school, told me we're friends."

She tries to suppress a smile, but for a brief moment, she fails. We share a glorious, fantastic moment. "I said I *suppose* we can be friends," she clarifies. When Jenna realizes she has not tempered my joy, she adds, "Don't be too proud of yourself."

"I'll try, but no promises."

"We're friends," she says. "Nothing else is going to happen."

"Got it. I'll take what I can get."

"Jay Hallett, don't be cute." Jenna piles her things into her locker. Once she notices my expression, she pouts. "*Now*, why are you smiling?"

"You called me cute."

"No. No, I didn't," Jenna says, adorably defensive. "I told you *not* to be cute."

"Sure, but you have to be the thing before you can be told not to be the thing."

She closes her locker and fiddles with the lock. The lockers lock automatically, so I'm not sure why she is doing this. When she looks at me, her cheeks are flushed in a way that takes my breath away. "Are you going to come by again tomorrow?"

"I'm going to come by every day if that's all right with you."

A faint smile curves her lips, and for once, she lets it linger. "It's not *not*-all right," she says, scarcely above a whisper. Jenna's pretty even when she scowls, but when she's happy, her beauty overwhelms. She pulls away. I wait by her locker to see if she turns around. She never has, but I still don't want to miss it.

I'm stunned when Jenna stops. She turns, and I wave. She walks back to me, slowly at first, then faster. I can't tell if she's going to hug me or punch me in the gut. Whichever she chooses, I realize I'm thrilled she is coming back because now I get to spend more time with her. I also realize I was so focused on offense, I forgot to play defense. Here I am trying to get Jenna to fall for me, and, well, I've got it pretty bad for her.

She stops in front of me and grips my arms. "You think you know what you're getting yourself into, but you don't," she says.

"I don't care." I say this with such conviction, she hesitates.

"You should," Jenna says with matching sincerity. "You know what people say about me. I'm some trashy girl who screwed her boyfriend's buddies. And you know what they are going to think about you if you hang around me."

"That's their problem. I know Gavin's a liar. I know what happened." I can tell she's about to call me out, so I add, "Paulo told me what went down."

Her mouth opens beneath her shimmering eyes. She fixes on me as though seeing me for the first time. "I didn't know. I thought—I was worried you were like everyone else."

"I'm many things," I say, "but like everyone else is not one of them." I smile at her. I want to wipe away her tears, but I literally can't because she's still holding my arms. "Jenna, I've liked you since Spanish class freshman year. Didn't you ever wonder why I enjoyed conjugating verbs so much?"

"I did think that was a bit weird," she says.

"That's fair. I can be a bit weird."

"No. You're pretty great." Jenna squeezes my arms and steps away. "But we're just going to be friends. I can't—I can't." She races down the hallway. This time she doesn't look back. And me? I can't wait to see her again. I am in serious trouble.

I pause to allow NicBot to say something before I move on. She does not. Much like Scruffy, NicBot has curled up on the couch. She's engrossed in my story, which makes me wonder again what Nic's reaction would have been. I'm not sure it matters. If I had attempted to tell Nic this story, I doubt I would have gotten far. Nic made her biased view of Jenna clear when we spoke through the portal. I doubt I would have tolerated her insulting Jenna for long. Brushing away the issue, I continue.

The next day, Jenna and I talk as though we've been friends for years and this is just another Friday. She tells me about the physics assignment she has to do over the weekend. She's flirty and unguarded. I've seen her like this with other guys before she dated Gavin. Now she's like this with me. My heart pounds as if I've won the lottery and I'm the only one who knows.

The conversation remains casual, but I sense an underlying depth. I can tell that she also notices the shift between us. Within each sentence, so much is unsaid, each word carries so much extra weight, the conversation collapses in on itself. We smile at each other. For once, the silence isn't awkward at all. It's actually quite delicious.

"I have to get my book," Jenna says. She pulls her textbook out of her locker and spins around, hugging it to her chest. I have never been so jealous of *The Principles of Physics*. "Why are you smiling?" she asks.

Here is one of those moments I wish I was good at lying. I have no choice but to own it. "I'm jealous of your textbook."

"Why would you be—?" Jenna flushes. She

lowers her book a little and steps closer, resting a hand on my shoulder. Her lips are dangerously close to mine. "You're not supposed to say the quiet parts."

I shrug. "It was pretty loud in my head." Her lips quiver while she struggles to contain a smile. As Jenna is about to lose the battle, she slams my chest. I lose my balance, distracted as I was by her lips. She steadies me by grabbing my hand. She doesn't let go, and I don't either. Our fingers brush together.

"It would be easier to be just friends with you if you weren't so funny," Jenna says.

"I'll have to remember that."

Our eyes lock. For a moment, I allow myself the fantasy that we are going to kiss. Instead, Jenna drops my hand and closes her locker. "You can text me later if you want, buddy."

"Sure, pal," I say. When she walks away, I call out, "Hold up, I don't have your number."

She flicks her hand into the air without breaking her stride. "I guess you can't text me then." Jenna doesn't turn around this time. And the worst part is, I have to wait until Monday before I can talk to her again.

Except that I don't. Jenna texts me the next day: "Hey, you. I got your number from Amaya." I immediately panic. She and Amaya are not in the same social circles. I didn't even know they even knew each other. So as casual as one can text anything, I write, "I didn't know you knew her." And she responds, "The two of us have something in common." I'm in my room, screaming in my head: *crap, crap, crap.*

Seconds pass by. I have to say something, so I text, "I am so sorry. Gavin's an asshole." Right away, she responds, "I don't want to talk about him," and we wind up chatting for the next hour about nothing and everything else. She's so easy to talk to that I'm embarrassed it took me so long to try.

We text several times over the weekend. Mostly it starts with her writing something like *hey, I was doing this thing, and I thought of you.* It's never any big thing, whatever it is, but that doesn't matter. Every time she contacts me, I'm staggered. For years, I had built her up in my mind as an unapproachable goddess but she's really a sweet girl who's been hurt too many times.

CHAPTER 27

"People suck."

"You should tell Nic this story," NicBot says, sitting bolt upright to simulate excitement.

"Yeah, I was thinking about that but I don't think she'd want to hear it."

"She would. She reads romance all the time."

I squint at NicBot. "Romance? What are you talking about? This story isn't romance. It's high drama. It's an epic tragedy for the ages."

"Oh, no, it's full-on romance." She says this with the same dreamy air Nic gets. "The story has all the elements. Picture the cover: you perched on a cliff, your shirt torn, your muscles rippling, a brisk wind mussing your hair. On one side, you grip your lacrosse stick, and the other stands Jenna, fiery and impassioned, clutching your shoulder."

"Nice. Now let's picture you having full-on blown a circuit. This is not romance. Not once do I describe a heaving bosom. At no point do I drive my manhood into her flowering petals."

NicBot performs a flawless simulation of a wide-eyed Nic gasping. "You know, for a boy who claims not to read romance, you sure do know how it sounds."

"I know romance memes, not romance novels. Do you want me to finish the story or not?"

"Oh, yes, dear brother." She settles back on the couch. "Please continue."

So anyway, Monday comes around, and I'm not sure what to expect. I worry all those texts were her way of banishing me to the friend zone. I admit I'm disappointed, but I meant it when I told her I'll take what I can get. The last thing I want to do is pressure her, especially after all she's been through.

My last class runs late, and I race down the hallway, worried I'm going to miss her. When I round the corner, I see Jenna standing by her open locker. She slams the locker shut when she sees me coming. Jenna's pissed, and I worry that she's going to storm off before I get the chance to say anything. Instead, she crosses her arms and waits for me to walk closer.

"You're late," she says.

"I got caught up."

"I thought you weren't coming." Her expression is unreadable. She is scary good at keeping her face blank.

"Not coming?" I say. I stare back at her as though she's insane because she would have to be insane to think that. "This is the highlight of my day."

Her lips part, but she doesn't say anything. I realize she was worried, not angry. Jenna wanted me to show up. She was waiting for me. I have this joyous sensation she likes me more than she is letting on. Right away, I brush it aside. I don't want to slide down the wishful-thinking rabbit hole. But the warmth I sense from her deep brown eyes, I can't help it. Allowing even a glimmer of hope lights me up.

We share the moment, ambiguous yet intimate, until she breaks the silence. "Come with me," she says.

Jenna leads me to the nearest classroom and closes the door behind us. She guides me against the wall. I smile at her. She smiles back but quickly suppresses it, twisting into profile instead with an adorable pout. "Don't look at me like that," she says. I still question if she means to discourage me. Her pretend-annoyed act is way too sexy. "Stop it," she says. "We're just friends."

"Right," I say, but it is so wrong and I'm such a lousy liar that we both laugh.

"I mean it," she says. Jenna tips toward me until her breath brushes across my lips. I hold still, drawing in her warmth, willing her to cross the line. Instead, she rocks back and rests her hand on my shoulder. Then she says the strangest thing.

"Can I touch your face?"

No one has ever asked me that, so I go a bit overboard. I say, "You can touch any part of me any time you want." I'm trying to be romantic. Fine, yes, romantic, let it go. Nobody likes a smug robot. Anyway, whatever I am trying to do, it does not have the desired effect.

"Really," she says, and not in a sexy pretend-annoyed way. This is actual-annoyed, fierce and stormy. "Any part of you any time I want? So if I pass you in the hallway, I can kick you in the balls?"

Her body tenses. Her hand grips my shoulder as if she's primed to rip it off. I've triggered her in some way, this much is clear. Here is the moment when I blow it, I think. We are too good to be true. With any other girl, I'd want to escape—nuts intact—but this is Jenna. There isn't any other girl. Throughout high school, I haven't been interested in anyone else. I mean, there are many other girls, a few almost as pretty, but I'm not interested in them. Not enough to bother with a relationship. I have lacrosse and video games and friends. I'm fine. Relationships are not worth the effort. Except for Jenna, I mean, she was always worth it. And now that I've gotten to know her better, I cannot screw this up. So I don't bail. Instead, I risk her ripping off my shoulder, or kicking me in the balls, or whatever crazy shit she's going to do. I don't care. For her, I don't care.

"Why would you kick me in the balls?" I ask, nice and slow, the calm to her fury. She relaxes her death grip. "*I* wouldn't," she says, stressing the *I* as though she knows a faction of girls restless for the opportunity to pop my scrotum, "but if you say things like that, people will take advantage. They'll see it as a weakness to exploit. They'll use it as an opportunity to destroy you."

"Who?" I say without thinking and instantly regret the question because I know. I know exactly who she's talking about. Everything she did—her explosive reaction, her rage—it all makes perfect sense. "This is because of Gavin," I say. I'm not asking her; I state it as fact. I want her to know I get it.

She stiffens, furious again, but not at me. "I'm going to tell you what happened," she says. "You know part of it, but I'm going to tell you everything." Her eyes shimmer. "Then we'll see what you think of me."

Jenna takes a deep breath and begins. "I convinced myself I loved Gavin, and I told him I'd do anything for him. He says, *anything?* I should have heard it in his voice. I should have known. In a way, I think I did know, but I ignored my intuition. Instead, I say, *anything you want.*

"*Prove it,* he says, that jerk. I convince myself he's playing with me. My inner voice is screaming, *get away*, but I'm too invested. I want to be a good girlfriend, so I ask him what he wants me to do to prove it. I hope it's something like stand on a table in the cafeteria and belt out a cheesy love song. But no, Gavin isn't angling for a silly romantic gesture. He wants to humiliate me.

"When he first tells me what he wants, I figure he's joking. *Really, you want me to screw your friends?* He must be messing with me, or at least that's what I want to believe. It's all a sick test. *Don't be silly*, I say. *I'd never cheat on you.* I kiss him all over. *I'd never be with anyone but you.* I offer him my body, wishing that it would be enough, that I would be enough, but he tosses me off him as if I've betrayed him because I didn't want to betray him. *It's not cheating if I tell you to do it*, he says. Angry, yelling. *If you really love me, you'll do anything for me, even that.* Like he wants me to be his whore. And then I get it. That's exactly what he wants. And I—I feel like I have to. To prove my love. To prove I'm worthy of him."

I remain silent while she flicks away her tears with such force, I worry her fingernail might take out an eye.

"He made me hate myself. I let his desire become more important than mine. More important than me. I let him take everything from me, and after, after I degrade myself, he is so disgusted with me that he dumps me. Right there. Right after I give him everything. He tosses me away like garbage. But even then—it's still not enough. It's not enough for *him* to treat me like garbage. He needs everyone else to do it too.

"The next day at school, he spreads it around that I'm a skanky slut he dumped because I screwed his friends. Everybody feels sorry for him. And they all look at me as if I'm trash instead of him. That's who he is. That's your friend Gavin."

"Gavin is not my friend," I say. I know this is a minor point in her story, but I can't stand the possibility she might think it. I touch her arm and say, "I'm so sorry you went through that."

Jenna breaks down, sobbing into my chest. I hold her gently, but at the same time, I want to rip Gavin to pieces. I want to tear out his cold, dead heart. I don't know how long we stay huddled together, but my violent fantasy is interrupted when she pulls back. Her eyes are red and intense. "Do you still want to be my friend?" she asks.

Her question stuns me. "What? Of course, I do." I think of how I can convince her, so I remind her I already knew all this. Well, not all this. I hadn't fully understood what she was going through, but the part about Gavin lying, that I knew.

"You're one of the few people who do," she

says. "Another person is Amaya. She came up to me the day Gavin spread it around. When everyone else was being horrible, she told me what Gavin did to her. How he tried to rape her when they were dating and she barely escaped. How he spread it around that he dumped her because she was a frigid prude. How horrible he made her feel. She told me I could tell her what happened and she would believe me because she knows Gavin's a liar. It took me a few days to open up. She may have saved my life. I wanted to die. I mean, really die."

I am beyond horrified. I don't even want to imagine a world without Jenna.

"To answer your question from this weekend, yeah, I'm friends with Amaya. We've talked about many things. Including what you did, how you and Yasmine helped her escape." Jenna stares right at me. Her eyes are piercing. "That's the only reason I let you talk to me. When you first came up to me, it took all my strength not to yell at you to leave me alone. Because ever since Gavin, that's what I do when guys come up to me.

"You're not the first guy, Jay. Not by a long shot. Guys come up to me all the time. They either want to insult me because they think I'm a slut, or they want to date me because they think I'm a slut. So I scream at them and chase them the hell away. Now people think I'm crazy." She shrugs wildly, hands flailing. "And that's fine by me. That's better. I don't care if they think I'm crazy; it's better than what they thought before. And at least it's true. I mean, at least it's based on something *I* decided. So now you know who I am. That's the verse I contributed. I'm a crazy bitch."

The air is electric as after a storm. I experience a piercing clarity. "That is not your verse," I say. "And I think you're the sweetest girl I've ever met."

Jenna squeezes her eyes shut and shakes her head. When she speaks, she spits out each word with the contempt it deserves. "I. Hate. People."

"Yeah. People suck."

She opens her eyes and leans into me, resting her hands on my shoulders. As I'm about to hold her, she pulls away and slaps my chest. "Where were you a year ago?"

I respond meekly, "I was...here?"

"No, you weren't! You were skulking in the background. Yeah, I noticed you, Jay. Why wouldn't I? You're sexy and strong and smart. But so what! You say you liked me for years? How the hell was I supposed to know? You rarely spoke to me!" Tears streak down her cheeks. I reach out and bring her back for a hug. "How was I supposed to know?" she asks again into my shirt. "I could have dated you instead of him? I don't even know how to process that."

"You would have dated me over Gavin?" I ask. "I mean, back then?"

In my arms, her chest rises and falls. It feels so good to hold her, but at the same time, I draw in her misery, and it becomes my misery. I realize my view of Gavin has shifted from an obnoxious jerk I tolerate because he's the best attackman on the team, to someone I deeply loathe. Her rage is my rage.

"Of course I would have picked you over Gavin," she says. "In one week, I'm closer to you than I ever was the whole time I dated that asshole." She laughs, but it's an angry laugh, directed in the most vicious way, against herself. "I went out with Gavin because I thought that's what I deserve. I stayed with Gavin because I thought that's what I deserve. I let that jerk control me because I thought that's what I deserve. I thought I loved him. I don't know if I believed it or wanted to believe it, that I deserve love." She pulls away from me. "See, this is why I can't trust myself. Do you understand? This is why we can't be more than friends."

I nod. "I got it. Like I've said, I'll take what I can get."

Jenna presses against me, her mouth so close to mine, I can smell her lip gloss. "Jay Hallett, don't be cute." She pulls back again. "I mean it. You have no idea what you're getting into. It takes everything out of me to get through the day." Tears well in her eyes. "Everything. And sometimes, I have nothing left, and I want to die." She rolls next to me. We stand flat against the wall, side by side as though lined up for a firing squad.

I want to console her, but I have no idea how, or even if I could. I am deeply unsettled. My agitation eases when she slides her hand into mine. We stand next to each other, holding hands and not talking for several minutes. Her staccato breathing slows and steadies. She drops my hand. When she opens the door, she spins around and leans against the doorjamb to say one last thing. "Thank you for being my friend, Jay. It means so much to me."

"This was three days ago," I tell NicBot. "The next day, Paulo gives me the heads up that Gavin is honing in on my sister for his next conquest. There is no way I will let that happen. Nic can hate me for as long as she wants—I did what I had to do. And I have the bruises to prove it."

"Bruises? Am I going to hear that story?" NicBot asks.

"No. But I will finish the story I'm telling. We still have one more day before everything unravels. You're going to enjoy the last bit. It is, well, romantic."

NicBot leans in. I know she replicates emotions but watching the animated way she has listened to the story, I regret not sharing this with Nic. Not sharing anything with Nic. It occurs to me that this is the critical failure in my relationship with my sister. It's not the fighting or the competing or even the backstabbing—that's all sibling stuff. You can come back from sibling stuff. It's that we stopped talking to each other. We stopped sharing our lives. We stopped being family and became two people stuck in the same house, marking time until we're old enough to escape. And then what? Then she'll be out of my life. No more Nic.

The worst part is, I'm not even sure how I feel about that.

CHAPTER 28

"It's not not-fun."

When Jenna sees me walking towards her on Tuesday, she brightens. Her happiness is my happiness. She shuts her locker. Before I can say anything, she takes my hand. "Come with me," she says and brings me into the same classroom as yesterday.

Jenna closes the door and approaches me, guiding me against the wall. She holds her body against mine. For the entire day, I've been thinking about how incredible it would be if she touches me again, and now the pleasure overwhelms.

"Can I kiss you?" she asks. "As a friend."

Yes, yes, yes! I think. But then I think, *Hold up. As a friend?* It's such a lie. It was a bit of a lie yesterday, to be fair, but now it's a total lie. So I say no. She draws back, clearly hurt, and I speak rapidly to preempt whatever damaging thing she might say next.

"Yes, I want you to kiss me—that would be incredible—but not as a friend. I'm sorry. I can handle the flirting and holding hands and, you know, pretend like I'm cool with the just-a-friend thing, but to do that *and* kiss you?" I shake my head. "Impossible. I can't do it, Jenna. Every time we touch, you light me up. I'm barely hanging in there, as it is. I—"

Mercifully, she shuts me up with a kiss. There is no tongue, but she lingers a moment before pulling her lips away. Our fingers intertwine. I've missed this as much as anything.

"That's for being honest," she explains. "I promise I won't kiss you again."

"Why the heck not?" I say.

She squints as though gazing through a fog. "Give me one good reason to kiss you again," she says, but not as a challenge. It's a request. She wants to kiss me. She wants a good reason! The realization makes me brave. Crazy brave.

"I'm in love with you," I say.

Her body trembles against mine. "That's a really good reason," she says. We kiss again, this time deep and passionate. She tastes like spring, a vast sunlight warming me to my bones, everything blooming. I've never experienced this before, yet at the same time, it's familiar, natural. For a fleeting moment, the world makes sense. When she pulls away, I make it clear I was not kissing her as a friend.

"You better not be," she says. She rests her head against me, and we hold each other. I'm so content that I don't realize she's crying until I hear a whimper. Now I'm surprised and confused. I try to make eye contact, but she keeps shifting. "What's wrong?" I ask her. "What happened?"

She presses her hands into her tears. "I haven't let myself feel anything for so long. I've been numb. Numb is safe. But I can't be numb with you no matter how hard I try. It terrifies me, Jay. I've cried every day since you started talking to me."

"Oh, no," I say, horrified. "Smiling a little too, I hope."

"Yes. Yes! Smiling, crying, laughing—all the emotions I've held inside, it's all pouring out. And I'm scared, Jay." She touches me as though I'm a bomb that might explode. "I still don't trust myself. Can we take it slow?"

"Of course."

"It's not that I don't want to have sex with you, I just need to take it slow."

It takes me a moment to start breathing again. This may sound improbable coming from a hormonal teenage boy, but sex was not on my radar. I was hoping she would kiss me again. But sex? Holy shit.

"Um," I say, as suave as I can, meaning not at all, "I've never dated anyone before."

Her eyes widen as if she's discovered the lost city of Atlantis. "Are you telling me you're an 18-year-old virgin?"

"There are a lot of 18-year-old virgins," I tell her.

"No, I know, I'm—" She buries her face into my shirt, but I can still hear her laugh. "I'm not laughing at you," she says, muffled but still laughing.

"Yeah, I can tell," I say.

"No, no, really, I'm not. I'm—" She cuts herself off and looks at me. Her smile lights up the room. "I'm so relieved. I feel like I hit the jackpot."

"I know the feeling," I say.

Jenna presses against me. Her lips brush against mine, so close to kissing me. Again and again. Just shy of kissing me. I had never imagined playful teasing could be so erotic. "You don't mind taking it slow?" she asks.

"No."

She kisses me gently and taps my lips with her fingertip. "That would be so much more believable if you said it without a huge erection."

Ordinarily, this sort of thing embarrasses me. This is not an ordinary moment.

"That's on you," I say. "Be less sexy." We kiss again, deeper this time, until I gasp for air. "And maybe don't rub against it." She flashes a devilish grin and bites her lower lip. At that moment, I recognize how completely and utterly in-over-my-head I am.

"You mean like this?" she asks. "I shouldn't do this?" I kiss her neck while she grinds against me. I have transformed into one throbbing mass. Her fingertips brush my lips. She holds me closer until her warm breath tickles my ear. As she gyrates, she whispers, "I look forward to seeing you every day," and, "I'm so happy we're together," and finally, "Yes. Go ahead. Let me feel how much you want me." The warmth of her hand cupped against my pants causes my body to spasm. She muffles my moan. I slump against the wall.

Jenna is pleased with herself, as she should be. "Did you enjoy that?" she asks. This has to be the most rhetorical question ever. I stare at her while I catch my breath. She grins. "Is that fun?"

This time, I know my line. "It's not *not-fun*," I say, and we share a laugh.

She pushes off me and opens the door. Like yesterday, she spins around at the doorway and settles against the doorjamb. "I think you're going to want to clean yourself up."

"I think I'm going to want a fresh pair of underwear."

Jenna flashes another glorious smile at me. It makes me so happy to see her like this. "Are you going to text me tonight?" Her eyebrows crinkle.

"Are you kidding? I'll text you as soon as I'm out of the bathroom."

Jenna drops her gaze to the floor. "I meant

what I said. I look forward to seeing you every day. That's my favorite part too." She gets serious, shy. "Do you understand what I'm saying?" She peers up at me expectantly.

"Yes. You don't have to say anything else."

"No, I want to. I need to." She straightens up and takes a deep breath. Jenna acts so nervously that all I want to do is hug her. And grab a few tissues considering how sticky things are getting down there.

She looks me straight in the eye, more determined than I have ever seen her before. "Jay Hallett, I'm in love with you," she says. I smile at her, but it doesn't last long. "Don't make me regret it. I couldn't stand it if you let me down." I start to tell her I won't, I wouldn't, but she silences me with a stare so cutting I can feel it slit my windpipe. "It will break me," she says and dashes away.

"The next day was yesterday," I tell NicBot. "The day Nic—" I shake my head. My attempt to finish the sentence fires me up to a full boil. "What Nic did was unforgivable. She didn't hurt only me. I mean, if that's all she had done, you know, whatever. I can take her crap. I'm used to it, you know? I'll get over it. But she also hurt Jenna. In the worst possible way."

"I'm so sorry," NicBot says. "Speaking for both of us."

"You don't speak for Nic," I snap. I don't

want to rip NicBot, but the sheer audacity of this robot. I rest my hand on Scruffy's back. She has burrowed her face between me and the couch cushions. Even her warmth can't still my rage. "Retribution will come. And Nic will have to answer for herself."

For reasons I don't understand, this terrifies NicBot. The TV clicks itself on before I can ask her why. Phin appears, as dapper and disheveled as ever.

"My dear Jay. We have come to the conclusion of your trial period. I trust you've enjoyed your new and improved sister thus far?"

"Yes. Wait, trial period?" Figures. "What's the new offer? Wait, let me guess. Continue for the low, low price of $29.99 a month, and—if you act now—we'll throw in this handy set of kitchen knives!"

Phin bows slightly. "As always, your unparalleled wit overwhelms. No, Jay, no kitchen knives, no ham sandwiches, and no money involved." Phin tugs his suit, which serves only to slant it in the other direction. "What's with you two and money? Don't be so eager for free. Free means the true cost is hidden. Like latent trauma. Or a landmine."

"Phin, wait," NicBot chimes in. Her terror has not diminished. "He's not ready."

With a flick of Phin's wrist, NicBot crumples on the couch. "We'll power her down. This isn't a proper conversation for robots."

I lift NicBot's hand and let it drop to her lap. She's so lifelike. "NicBot is impressive," I say. "I'm blown away by the technology. It's effing beautiful."

"Indeed. The effing beauty of ineffable marvels. My dear Jay, at last, we agree." Phin bows again, this time deeper. "Our time has reached its apex. All that remains is a parting decision." A grin slithers across his face like an eel marooned on a beach. Sinking into the couch, I have my first inkling of NicBot's terror. "A simple decision to be sure," Phin says, his eyes glimmering, "but perhaps the most important one of your tender, young life."

PART FIVE

NICOLE: LATE AFTERNOON

CHAPTER 29

*"Who could have foreseen
such a catastrophe?"*

"How lovely to see you again, my dear Nicole. To whom shall I direct your compliments?"

Nicole stood before her mirror, her hands pressed to her hips. She was not in the mood. After witnessing her brother's treachery, an ordeal intensified by her robot brother's unsettling urgency, she'd scarcely had time to catch her breath. "Skip it. I'm here because JayBot said you wanted to talk to me."

"JayBot," Phin repeated, eyes widening. "How curious. A new moniker for your new brother. How did you come up with it?"

Nicole stiffened. "I was, um, you see, he's a robot and, you know, I—ugh! What do you care? I can call him whatever I want!"

Phin thrust a finger under his hat and

scratched. He brightened and shifted his hat back into place. "That is a reasonable and appropriate response to an innocuous question, raising no suspicions whatsoever. Consider me unequivocally satisfied and ready to press on with no lingering concerns. Now then—"

"Fine! I talked to Jay."

Phin cocked an eyebrow. "Fascinating. How did you manage it?"

"I used the interdimensional portals you gave me."

"The holes are most assuredly *not* interdimensional portals. Although," Phin said, gazing upward in thoughtful contemplation, "if one were to stack multiple holes, rotate along the horizontal axis, and allow, shall we say, a small dog to pass through, then I suppose the holes could act as a portal between two dimensions." He looked back at her. "Hypothetically speaking."

"So the holes *are* interdimensional portals."

"Most assuredly not."

"They are! You said the holes could act as a portal between two dimensions. That makes them—" Nicole thrust her hands towards Phin and shook them as if to wring his neck. "—interdimensional portals!"

Phin's eyebrows shot up. "On the contrary, acting like something is not the same as being something. You could say a book is a plate because you ate dinner on it. But after your meal, it's still a book. You just *misused* it." Phin slanted towards the glass, his ill-fitted suit billowing.

"And while we're on the subject of misusing things, we must also address your disregard for the read-only directive. No editing, remember? To compensate, I have dialed up the wall integrity, reducing the possibility you might inadvertently initiate a cosmic cataclysm." Phin tugged the brim of his hat. "The least I could do. But back to the matter at hand. You spoke with Jay! Remarkable, my dear. Quite remarkable. I am astonished beyond measure." Shifting to a softer, conspiratorial tone, Phin continued, "Less surprising was when you said how you wanted to date Gavin so you could be the star and get all the attention like Brandi."

"That's not the only reason. Gavin is dreamy."

"Dreamy, you say?"

"Wait, how did you—so you already knew I talked to Jay!"

"Did I?" Phin asked, crinkling the corners of his eyes.

Nicole squinted back. "You don't seem too surprised."

"Why should I be surprised?"

"You said you were astonished beyond measure!"

Phin's slippery grin squirmed into place. "Ah, yes. I suspect I may have overstated the degree of my astonishment."

"Uh, huh," Nicole said, shooting him a side-glance. "And I suspect there is something you're not telling me."

"Your suspicion is wholly unfounded."

"But you've been tricking me all day!"

Phin scratched his chin until he nodded. "Fair enough. Allow me to rephrase. Your suspicion is partly unfounded with a chance of deception."

"OMG, you are so frustrating! Why can't you admit the truth?"

"The truth?" Phin's eyes sparkled. "Perish the thought. We both know better than to fiddle with something so hazardous. Troublesome truths are pesky shards of broken glass. Why risk getting cut to the quick when you can smooth it over with a bit of mischief?"

Nicole brushed away his question. "Mischief is more your thing."

"Indeed, I am the Maestro of Mischief. But my dear Nicole, a bit of mischief lies within you as well. You simply choose not to recognize it." Under Phin's withering stare, Nicole dropped her gaze to the floor.

"But I digress!" Phin exclaimed, startling Nicole with his explosive vigor. "New business demands attention. I regret to inform you that your trial period has come to a close. I trust you've enjoyed your new and improved brother thus far?"

"Yes. JayBot is awesome."

"Excellent. Then you'll relish this next part. You must choose between Jay and JayBot. Permanently."

Nicole regarded him suspiciously. "Permanently? So if I choose JayBot, Jay will continue in his world, and I'll continue in mine with JayBot?"

"Well, not exactly." Phin's wrist flopped from side to side as if a fish out of water. "How to explain? Splitting the timeline into parallel dimensions is entertaining but unsustainable. The splintered dimensions will converge soon enough and cannot withstand two Jays. There's an exclusion principle in play. Like in quantum mechanics, except involving robots rather than fermions. Yes, I know physics is wonky, but let's not get into it. I find it best not to split hairs—or atoms, if you can avoid doing so. Which, let's admit, is not so easy. Especially when you *really* enjoy doing it. My point is, one Jay will have to go."

The prospect of Phin splitting atoms for kicks disturbed her, but Nicole concentrated on her primary concern. "So, wait. What will happen to Jay if I choose JayBot?"

"He'll be lost forever," Phin said.

Nicole stared at him. "What do you mean by lost forever?"

Phin raised his arms as though preparing to conduct an orchestra for its closing requiem. "Lost forever has only one meaning of which I am aware. I await your decision."

"Do you mean dead?" Nicole shuttered.

"Dead. Listen to you! *So* dramatic. And in this case, *so* accurate."

"Hold up! You're going to kill my brother?"

Phin lowered his arms. "Of course not. You are, my dear Nicole. Or at least you'll finish the process you've already started. What did you think would happen to your old brother when you replaced him with a new one?"

"I—I didn't think about it."

"You didn't think about it," Phin said, eyes wide. He allowed his forehead to touch the mirror and pressed his face through it, stretching the glass around him. Popping snaps reverberated in the air until Phin's nose jutted against Nicole's. She watched in horror as he spoke. "You didn't think about it. Truer words have never been spoken, certainly not by either of us. But actions are tricky, especially with all their irksome consequences wiggling about. So easy to miss until it's too late, so lamentable, such a shame." Phin jerked back into the mirror. The glass reverberated much like the surface of a lake after swallowing a rock.

Phin brushed himself off, hat askew. "Now then, which will it be? Old brother, new brother, new brother, old brother." He sang it as a song. "Oh, what others would give for the choice you have."

"I refuse to choose," Nicole said. She

smirked, thinking Phin stumped, but her hopes withered under the mockery of his sparkling eyes.

"So your action is inaction. Inactions have consequences too, and equally wiggly. No matter, we'll pretend not to see them, shall we? I'll simply decide for you."

"Wait, no, I'll choose. I'll choose! But not until you've told me everything."

A sickly grin twisted sideways across his lopsided face. "Indeed," Phin said, leveling his hat. "There is more. There is always more, but why the sudden interest in everything? You have always been satisfied with less. Do you wish to rattle your sensibility with the full force of everything?"

Nicole squared her shoulders, resolute. "Yes."

"How exciting! My dear Nicole, you never cease to entertain. If you must know everything, here's the remaining bit: I gave your brother the same choice."

"The same—" Her throat caught. She forced her words through clenched vocal cords. "You mean Jay could get rid of me?"

Phin stumbled back, aghast. "In theory, I suppose, but that would never happen. You two may not always get along, but it *is* always his fault, am I right? Never yours. You merely react. How could he blame you? You had no choice!"

"Right, but—"

"But nothing, my dear Nicole. Problem solved. He will choose you, you will choose the bot, and all will work out as desired. For you, anyway, but that's what matters."

A dizzying sensation gripped Nicole. Try as she may, Nicole did not share Phin's nonchalance. "Jay might not see it like that. What if he chooses NicBot?"

Phin rested his hand on his chin and tapped his lips with a finger. "Oh, my. How unfortunate."

"Why? What would happen?"

"I think you already know, my dear." Phin glowed with the euphoria of a prince perched atop a gold mountain. "You would be lost forever."

"What?" Nicole glared seditiously. "That's not fair."

"Not fair! My goodness, am I not being fair? This simply will not do. A moment, please, to appraise the logic." Phin wrote with his finger in the air when he spoke. The words appeared backward and reversed on the glass. "If you choose the bot, then your brother will be lost forever. If your brother chooses the bot, then you will be lost forever." He tapped his lips while he read over what he had written. "I fail to detect injustice. My proposition appears equitable, even-handed, and—dare I say—*fair*."

Nicole rested her hands on either side of the mirror to keep herself upright while Phin used the side of his fist to wipe the words from the glass. Her knees wobbled. When Nicole spoke, her quivering voice exposed her emerging panic. "What if we both pick the bot?"

"Why, you'll both be lost forever."

"Wait, what?"

"I don't understand your concern. That would never happen," Phin reassured her.

"That is exactly what's going to happen!"

"Will it? My, my. How unfortunate for you both. Who could have foreseen such a catastrophe?" Phin's crooked smile widened.

"You're scaring me," Nicole said. Her eyes welled with tears.

"Life is full of frights, my dear. It will all work out in the end, one way or another. Soon your worries will be over."

Nicole slumped to the floor and cried. Someone unfamiliar with Phin might have mistaken his curious expression for concern. "Worry won't help you. The beasts that bump and bray in the night know nothing of your worries—they wish only to *eat you!*"

"What!"

"Pay it no heed, my dear. I'm merely reciting a nursery rhyme parents intone to their babes to assist them in their slumbers."

Nicole's anxiety transformed into frustration. She shrieked, "It's a lie! Everything you say is a lie! You tell one lie after another with enough truth mixed in to string me along."

"But of course," Phin said, pleased by her insight. "The best lies are the most plausible."

She pulled strength from her anger, straightening her knees until her head was level with his. "How considerate of you to save your best lies for me." Nicole glowered at him.

"Absolutely, my dear. Putting in the effort shows how much you care." Phin tipped his hat. "Only the finest lies for you."

Nicole stiffened. "I would never do that to you."

"No. Alas, you wouldn't," Phin agreed. "You hoard your finest lies for yourself."

"Hey! No, I don't."

"And there's another one!" Phin exclaimed. As he did, the room darkened. A reddish glow cast deep shadows across the carpet. "Your lies pop up as misty mushrooms festooned with nibs on scarlet parasols. Their white gills inspire the beguiling miasma. So dainty, yet so poisonous." A mist rose from the carpet, hissing. Nicole gasped.

"Ah, to be young!" Phin continued, his glee spilling into his quivering fingertips. "How glorious to skip through life without the guidance of experience or the dread of consequences. Those who don't pay attention amass a collection of heedless blunders, but you exceed expectations. Your brain deflects! You don't just shirk responsibility, you trundle onwards unfazed. I am favorably impressed, my dear Nicole. I bow to your ability to swallow your deceptions with nary a choke." When Phin bowed, he twirled his hand before him, creating hypnotic finger waves.

Nicole lurched back to break the spell. "You insult me."

"Not at all. As Head Honcho of Hustle and Hokum, I recognize a fellow traveler when she graces me with her presence. You rival me in splendor." Phin bore down on her. "We're quite a pair, you and I. Such a shame our time is coming to a close." His grin twitched with exultation. "Or, at least, yours is. I know who I am."

Nicole collapsed to the floor, inhaling the savory, earthy mist. "What have I done?"

"You have touched bottom at last. Welcome."

Dread overwhelmed her weary body. Dejected and beaten, Nicole raised her chin to engage with Phin once more. "I tried," she said through her tears. "I jumped into the holes and learned things. Things I didn't want to know."

"Too little, too late. Too late for so little. Oh, yes, you tried a little. I will credit you for your brief jaunt outside your comfort zone. If only you were willing to challenge yourself more."

A thought flashed through Nicole's mind. While more desperate stall than an explicit idea, her thought inspired hope. Nicole rose to face Phin. "I would challenge myself if I had more time. I still have questions about Jay I'd like to ask. And I'm willing to go wherever it takes me."

"Wherever? Perhaps you mean whenever. Either way, you are considering an exploration deep into dangerous territory. A journey far removed from your comfort zone will invite observations and facts certain to shatter your worldview."

"I know. And I'm willing to take the plunge."

"Quite literally in your case," Phin said. His grin softened. "I must admit, this presents a remarkable curiosity, most remarkable indeed." The mist cleared. "A curiosity worth an hour of my time." The room brightened, its ruby glow extinguished. "Then it's settled! I shall extend your trial period by one hour." Phin tapped the glass with a fingernail as one might do to get the attention of a goldfish or, more likely, irritate one. "Do be sure to make the most of it."

Phin's image zapped from the mirror, leaving Nicole alone with her reflection. She sunk back to her knees, her energy spent, overwhelmed by the futility.

The image of her wild hair distracted her from her funk. While she pressed her fingers through her tangled curls, she noticed a hole slip out from under her bed and drift towards her, a hole that sized her up in a way she found eerily familiar.

"Tess? Is that you?"

CHAPTER 30

"You don't want to do this."

At the incantation of its name, the hole came to a halt and spun. Tess fled to the extent a slowly gliding hole could flee.

Nicole twirled around. "Wait, please don't go. I need you." The hole rotated to face her. "I need you to take me someplace terrible. Will you help me, Tess?"

The hole's edges vibrated.

"All my life, I've known that people betray *me*, not the other way around. I've always been sure, except I wasn't right about Hannah. Am I wrong about Jay? I watched him destroy my chance with Gavin—I *know* that was true—but Jay never denied it. He said it was complicated." Nicole stood. "Did he think he was protecting me? Jay told me to ask JayBot about Gavin's ex-girlfriends, but I know a better way." Nicole stepped to the hole's edge. "Show me what happened between Gavin and Amaya. Why did they really break up?"

The hole dilated, and Nicole dropped into the inky blackness. For once, she suffered no dread, only nervous anticipation.

Nicole arrived in an unfamiliar hallway. The tang of flat beer and the clamor of a party accosted her senses. She turned toward the clomping of footsteps ascending the stairs and was soon face to face with her brother.

Jay? What are you doing here?

Nicole knew Jay couldn't hear her but, recognizing his befuddled expression, wondered if he knew what he was doing here either. They stood silently, waiting for something. A break in the music revealed muffled sounds coming from the room across from where Nicole stood. Jay lunged at the door and flung it open.

From her angle within the hole, Nicole observed a cluttered room, the end of the bed, and two lacrosse posters on the far wall, one declaring I BEAT PEOPLE WITH A STICK and the other a marginally more considerate BLOOD HELPS THE GRASS GROW. Jay also had a lacrosse poster in his room, a University of Maryland poster that implored you to FEAR THE TURTLE. Nicole had always questioned why anyone would choose a terrapin as their school mascot if they wanted to inspire fear. She figured the University of Maryland must have neglected to consult the lacrosse team.

Nicole smiled at her joke, but her amusement gave way to unease when a shaky, female voice said, "Please don't."

"We good in here?" Jay asked.

A new song opened with a bass beat, but Gavin's voice overpowered it. "Hey! Get the hell out, perv!" Jay raised his arms to protect himself against a barrage of clothing. He retreated from the room, pulling the door shut. An agitated Jay yanked out his phone and put his thumbs to work. After dropping his phone into his pocket, Jay rested against the wall.

What did you see? Nicole slapped the invisible wall, annoyed by how it limited her mobility.

Jay and Nicole waited together, both uneasy, until a girl Nicole recognized as Amaya's friend raced up the stairs. Jay put his finger to his lips and beckoned her closer. When she made it to the hall, Jay spoke in hurried tones barely audible over the music.

"Amaya's in there and looks scared. Wait, Yasmine, don't leave the room without Amaya. I'll jump in if things get physical but, you know."

"I know. I'll leave you out of it if I can." Yasmine twisted the knob and cracked open the door. She peered inside while Jay flattened himself against the wall. Nicole lurched to her side for a less obstructed view and saw jerky, aggressive movements on the bed. Above the clamor, the same shaky voice pleaded, "You don't want to do this. Please, stop."

Yasmine dashed into the room. Gavin shouted, and Nicole held her hands over her ears to muffle his vulgar cussing. A tearful Amaya soon stumbled into the hallway, pulling up her pants. When she spotted Jay pressed against the wall, she spun away from him, facing Nicole instead. Nicole recoiled at the totality of Amaya's shame.

Yasmine and Gavin shifted to the doorway, both still shouting. Gavin wore nothing but his underwear, a spectacle Nicole would have relished as recently as a few minutes ago. Now he terrified her. Gavin flailed his arms, bellowing, his face flushed a raging scarlet.

Yasmine backed out of the room. She wrapped an arm around Amaya and guided her down the stairs. Gavin glared at the girls while Jay and Nicole, both unseen, each held their respective breaths. Still seething, Gavin stormed back into his bedroom. Jay peered into Gavin's room, waiting until the coast was clear before bolting for the stairs.

Hurry, Jay. Oh, no! He's coming out!

After making it down a few steps, Jay spun and acted as though he was on his way up. The timing was perfect. Nicole cheered.

"What's going on?" Jay asked Gavin. "I saw Yasmine and Amaya on their way down."

Now wearing pants, Gavin pulled his shirt

over his head. "Why? Did they say something?"

"No, but Yasmine looked pissed. Amaya was crying."

Gavin brushed it off. "Usual girlfriend drama. All my bitches take some shots." Jay cringed. Lucky for him, Gavin was too busy peering over the railing to notice. "Amaya's a prude. I had to dump her, you know? That's why she's crying. And Yasmine, she's crazy. Everybody knows that. Who knows what bullshit she'll say next, amirite? I mean, you saw us. I was fooling around with my girlfriend. Come on, let's go down."

"Nah, I gotta pee."

"There's a bathroom downstairs."

"Occupied," Jay said and shot past Gavin. "That's why I came upstairs."

"Uh, huh."

Nicole watched Gavin regard Jay suspiciously, menacingly. She had never heard Jay lie more convincingly, but he still sucked at it. And he blew it by adding the last bit. Seasoned liars know better than to explain anything they don't have to. *Seriously, Jay. You came upstairs to use the bathroom twice?*

Gavin flexed. Nicole recoiled, forgetting for the moment that he couldn't see her. She remembered watching Gavin wrestle Jay, and how Gavin toyed with him even after getting thrown to the mat repeatedly. And how Jay, as strong as he was, lost. Amaya never stood a chance. Realizing she would have been next, Nicole shuddered. She wouldn't have stood a chance either.

I get it now, Jay. I wish you had told me. The moment before the floor opened up, Nicole wondered if she would have listened to her brother even if he had.

Nicole took deep calming breaths as she descended. Once she shot out of the hole, she swung her arms like a seasoned acrobat, landing squarely on her feet. Nicole dove for Tess and the new hole, peeling both off the floor and merging them. She flung the stacked holes against the wall and tossed the end of a power cord inside. Nicole waited. The holes remained in place.

Once satisfied that she had secured the holes, Nicole raced downstairs to the library and kneeled next to the lacrosse stick. She placed her hands in a bullhorn shape around her mouth to direct her voice. "Jay! Are you there? Jay!" She waited in vain for a reply, calling again and again.

Nicole gripped and released the lacrosse stick. Thinking about Gavin made her furious. She loved romance. She cherished the fire inside her, the one that had surged whenever Gavin came near. But no longer, he had snuffed it out. This was not how her story was supposed to go. In the books she read, the boy wanted the same thing as the girl, the same thing as Nicole. Passion. One true love. But Gavin, he had it all twisted. He exploited the yearning and devotion he inspired, corrupting it into violence and control.

Her desire extinguished, Nicole stewed in a smoky rage. It took her a moment to spot JayBot observing her from the brown couch.

"You've returned, dear sister." JayBot stood when Nicole approached him.

"I don't have much time," she said. "I need to ask you something important before Phin comes back."

"Anything you wish."

Nicole took a deep breath. Phin hadn't been wrong about her not wanting her worldview disturbed. Although after what she had witnessed, maybe a disruption was exactly what she needed. "If I asked you to help me date Gavin, would you do it?"

"Certainly," JayBot replied. "As I've said, I shall endeavor to do whatever you request to the best of my capability."

"But, you also said you know everything Jay knows."

"That is correct."

Nicole forced a hand into her tangle of hair and squeezed. "Then you already know what I learned. Gavin almost raped Amaya."

"Would you be so kind as to permit a suggestion?" JayBot waited for her consent and continued, "I find it more precise to state the actions a person does take than what they do not. Consequently, a more factual statement is that

Gavin is guilty of sexual assault and attempted rape."

Nicole stared open-mouthed. "And you would help me *date* him?"

"If you asked me to. Certainly."

Nicole placed her hand before her face, palm out, as though physically trying to restrain her anger. She reminded herself that JayBot was a robot devoid of malice, one who had always sought to help her and, therefore, must have a logical explanation for this glaring inconsistency. Her outrage simmering at a low boil, Nicole lowered her hand and spoke deliberately. "Your programming is faulty if you think *that* is being a good brother."

"My programming may be faulty but please understand. What it means to be a good brother is based upon your specifications. I have two directives," JayBot explained, "say nothing to upset you and do whatever you request to the extent of my capabilities. I agree that a sexual predator is not the boyfriend I would have chosen for you had you solicited my opinion. However, telling you the truth about Gavin would have upset you. It follows that if you had asked me to help you date him, I would have complied with your request to the extent of my capabilities."

Nicole scoffed. "That's not what Jay did."

"No," JayBot agreed. "I think it's fair to say that he and I are wired differently."

"That is fair to say." Nicole had never quite thought about it in that way, but as she did, she realized it explained a lot. Jay and JayBot were wired differently. As were she and Jay.

Nicole stepped closer and hugged him. "Goodbye, JayBot." She looked him in the eye and smiled. "You've been an awesome robot brother."

"Thank you, dear sister. I shall forever cherish our time together, right up to the moment my memory is deleted, and I am reprogrammed."

Nicole gaped at him, her brow justly furrowed. JayBot tilted his head. "Do you wish for me to complement your hair?" he asked. Nicole squeezed JayBot's arm before heading toward the stairs. "Nope, I'm good."

CHAPTER 31

*"People believe what
they want to believe."*

Back upstairs, Nicole yanked out the power cord and peeled the stacked holes from her wall. She pressed a fingernail into the edge, attempting to find a groove or some other way to separate them. Nicole glanced from the holes to the mirror, fearful Phin would appear before she was ready. "How much time do I have left?" Instinctively, she reached for her pocket. No phone. And, of course, no clocks in her room. She had never needed one before. Nicole resumed pinching and poking while her anxiety surged.

"Forget it. No time." Nicole dropped the stacked holes on the carpet. "Tess and friend, I need you to take me to when Jenna cheated on Gavin. I want to know why Jay thinks this was complicated." Tess and friend vibrated. Nicole stepped to the edge, and the floor gave way. She descended into the void.

Nicole arrived in a bedroom and inhaled an unfamiliar, sharp scent. The bedspring creaked rhythmically. The holes had brought her to the requested moment in time, but *where* was she? Nicole strained to get a good view from her position near the foot of the bed. All she could see was the back of Devin poking above the covers.

Why does this room look familiar?

Nicole had assumed this was Devin's bedroom, but now she wasn't so sure. Something about the clutter reminded her of a place she'd seen recently. Nicole turned and gasped. Taped to the far wall, she observed the same two lacrosse posters from her last trip through time: I BEAT PEOPLE WITH A STICK and its companion, BLOOD HELPS THE GRASS GROW.

Hold up. You cheated on Gavin in Gavin's *bedroom? No wonder you got caught.*

Devin yelped, and his hips jerked. Nicole stared, intrigued yet uneasy. She had never been this close to sex. Devin slunk out of bed and snapped off the condom. Nicole gawked at his hairy butt until he lifted his underwear. Jenna tugged the covers to her neck below her flushed face and red, glistening eyes.

Were you crying?

"Thanks," Devin said, not even glancing at Jenna, and tossed the condom into the trash. Jenna curled into a ball. The air crackled with tension, rage. Devin put his pants on, jarringly oblivious. Even with her limited carnal experience, Nicole knew something about this was way off.

Devin picked up his shirt and smirked at Jenna. He bent over for a kiss. She recoiled, furious, causing Devin to snicker. "Don't pretend you didn't enjoy it."

"Get the hell out!"

Devin brushed her off and split, leaving the door open. Jenna sat up at the edge of the bed and rocked, back and forth. Claustrophobia lurched over Nicole while she watched Jenna sway. Nicole extended her arms and pressed against the smooth walls.

Gavin entered the room, startling Nicole. She braced for yelling. Instead, Gavin sat next to Jenna on the bed. Jenna put her arms around him.

"I didn't like that," Jenna said.

Gavin smiled. "I'm so impressed you'd do that for me."

What the heck?

Jenna kissed his cheek. "Can we stop? Please."

"One more."

"No, please. Gavin. Please."

Gavin shushed her. He stroked her hair and kissed her forehead. "It will all be over soon. Don't worry." He kissed her nose. "This is getting me so hot."

"Yeah?" Jenna said.

"Oh, yeah." He kissed her lips. She kissed him back, and he pulled away.

"Please, Gavin. Stay with me a little longer."

Gavin tugged her hair, making Jenna wince. "Don't get clingy. You know you're a party girl." Gavin wrenched Jenna's hands off him and stood. Jenna and Nicole watched Gavin walk to the doorway. "I'll be back after." He leered at her. "Super hot."

Jenna wiped away her tears and forced a smile. After Gavin left the room, she rocked on the edge of the bed. Back and forth.

Nicole pounded the walls and stomped on the floor. *Tess? Phin? Anybody? Let me out of here. I don't want to see any more.* She had never more wished to be anywhere else in her entire life.

Footsteps approached, and Jenna and Nicole froze. Paulo entered the room. Closing the door behind him, he sat next to Jenna on the bed. When he spoke, his voice quivered. "I guess I should take my clothes off?"

"Get it over with," Jenna said, clinging to the sheets wrapped around her.

Creases extended across Paulo's forehead. "Wait, I thought—" He shook his head. "Gavin said you wanted this." Jenna shot him a dirty look. Paulo threw his hands up. "He said this was your sex fantasy."

"You watch too much porn," she said.

Paulo mouthed the f-word. "Yeah, I probably do. I totally believed him. Sorry, I'll go." He shifted forward to stand, and Jenna yanked him back.

"Sit down! I didn't let Devin rape me to have you blow it."

They sat silently. Paulo hugged his chest and stared at the floor. He whispered, "I don't know what you want me to do."

"Make sex noises."

He drew back. "I can't. I'm too embarrassed."

"How do you think I feel?"

Paulo looked away. He moaned. "Louder and more believable," Jenna encouraged. Paulo moaned more, each time with increasing urgency. "Oh, baby!" he said.

Jenna smacked his shoulder. "What?" he whispered. "Don't say anything," she scolded, "moan."

Paulo moaned again while Jenna bounced, creating a familiar rhythmic creaking of the bedsprings. "How long should I go?" Paulo whispered.

Jenna sized him up. "I'd say a minute, tops."

Paulo sighed but didn't argue. He moaned a few more times until Jenna motioned with her hands for him to wrap it up. Following her lead, Paulo mimicked finishing grunts. Jenna stopped bouncing. They sat together quietly.

"Thank you," she said.

Paulo shook his head. "Jenna, this is so screwed up. You should get out of here."

Jenna hugged the sheet. Her eyes glistened. "I'm almost through this, and once it's over, everything will go back to the way it was."

Nicole could tell Paulo didn't believe it. She couldn't understand why Jenna did. Then again, Nicole knew all about wanting to believe something because you wished it, whatever the reality. As Phin had said, troublesome truths are pesky shards of broken glass. Phin, that devious trickster, sure knew how to cut through other people's deceptions.

Paulo stood. Nobody moved. He whispered, "I'm getting dressed," and Jenna nodded. After a bit, Paulo moved his hand toward her shoulder. Jenna recoiled. He mouthed the word *sorry* and left the room.

While waiting for Gavin, Jenna wiped her eyes and adjusted her hair. She was a hot mess, radiating natural beauty through the wreckage. *Like Brandi.* That thought usually provoked Nicole into explosive jealously, but not this time. For once, Nicole had no desire to be like Brandi or Jenna. She no longer wanted any part of that world.

Gavin entered and sat next to Jenna on the bed. Jenna put her arms around him. When he ignored her, she kissed his neck. "I need you to hold me," she said.

"Check you out. Fucked twice and ready to

go a third time."

"Not like that." Jenna stroked his hair. "Please hold me. I feel horrible."

"Yeah, right. I know how much this turned you on." Gavin chuckled. Derision oozed down his muscular arms. "You're so trashy. We should make this a regular thing."

Jenna recoiled. "No! I'm never doing this again. I hated it."

"You loved it."

Shaking her head, again and again, Jenna struggled to hold back her tears.

"Cut the crap," Gavin said, his thrill collapsing. "You know you loved it. It was your idea." Jenna burst out crying. Gavin grabbed her arm and yelled in her face, "It was your idea!"

"You're hurting me."

"It was your idea!"

Jenna swatted his hand until Gavin released her. While Jenna rubbed her arm where he had restrained her, Gavin glared, daring her to contradict him. Jenna shrunk back at first, then gathered per poise. Thrusting her chin, she focused directly on him. "You know that's a lie."

"Bitch." Gavin leaped off the bed, scooped her clothes from the floor, and whipped them at her. "Get out of here."

Jenna clutched her clothes to the sheets around her. Her body trembled, but Nicole could see courage surge in Jenna's features. When Jenna spoke, her ferocity sliced through the air.

"Everyone is going to know what you did to me."

"What I did to you?" Gavin scoffed. "I didn't do anything. You're the slut who banged my friends." He veered toward her, causing Jenna to cower. "People believe what they want to believe. You think anyone is going to believe you over me?" Gavin sneered at her. "I had to dump you. I can do better."

I can do better. That's what you said to me. And I believed you. I thought I wasn't good enough, but you're an insecure jerk.

"Asshole," Jenna said.

And that.

"Get dressed and get the hell out of here." Gavin blustered to the doorway and swung around. He stared her down. "You disgust me, you pathetic whore."

Jenna stared back, defiant. The moment Gavin left, she collapsed, dropping her hands to her sides, allowing her clothes to tumble down. Curvy-fit high-rise jeans. A pretty floral blouse. Lavender panties and bra. An ensemble thoughtfully crafted lay crumpled at her feet. Jenna sobbed.

Nicole cried with her. *Jenna, I'm so sorry. Gavin tipped me off about Jay's computer. That's where I got the idea to—Oh, no! The terrible things I said to you. I was trying to get back at Jay, and I hurt you. I didn't think about your feelings at all.* Nicole gasped. *I'm like Gavin.*

The floor gave way, and Nicole fell.

Passing through the inky blackness, she took deep breaths to calm herself. When the motion ceased, Nicole flailed her arms to flip onto her feet. Instead, she banged her hands against the invisible walls. *Oh, yeah. Two holes.* A familiar scene appeared before her, causing Nicole to gasp. *No! I don't want to see this! Tess, get me out of here!*

With a satisfied sneer twisting her face, Nic from yesterday offered Jenna a folded piece of paper.

"I don't want that," Jenna said. "Please go away."

No! Not again! Nicole closed her eyes and screamed. She held her hands over her ears and shrieked some more.

Nicole tentatively opened her eyes. Her former self was gone. Jenna stood by her locker, her mouth contorted with disgust as she read the paper Nic had given to her.

Don't read that. I take it back.

Footsteps approached. Nicole remembered how joyful Jay appeared when he rounded the corner. She couldn't bear to watch again. The footsteps slowed.

"What's wrong?" Jay said. "What happened? Talk to me."

Jenna folded the page. She gripped it in her fist. "This is a list of the porn sites on your laptop."

"There aren't—oh, right. That wasn't me."

She twisted her lips. "Don't lie to me. Do you expect me to believe you've never watched porn?"

"On my *school* computer? No one is dumb enough to—well, some guys are, but I'm not. Listen, Gavin pranked the team. He went on our laptops during practice and pulled up all that trashy stuff. I'm going to wipe the thing clean before we have to turn it in. I haven't had the chance to—" Jay trailed off. Recognizing he had not appeased her, Jay tried a new tact. "You know how Gavin is. Why would you believe him?"

Jenna brandished the paper. "*He* didn't give this to me."

"Oh. Someone else on the team?" Jay looked confused. "I don't know who else knew about it."

"Someone who knows you better than I do." Jenna bent over. Her anguish contorted her features. "What was I thinking? I'm so stupid." She smacked herself with the paper again and again until Jay reached out to still her hand. "Jenna, please," he said. "You have to believe me."

Jenna pulled back. "Don't you think I *want* to believe you? I mean, the way you look at me." She met Jay's gaze with a similar yearning. Nicole watched, mesmerized. "Don't you think I want to believe this is real? Of course I do. But I can't trust myself." Jenna unfolded the paper and trembled as she read. "Abuse porn? Rape fantasy? No. No, no, no. I can't, Jay. Not again. I can't—I can't risk it again."

"Jenna, please." Jay brushed her arm. "It's me."

Jenna let him touch her for a moment, her breath stilled before she tore her arm away. "It's you? It's you? Who are you, Jay? I don't know you. I want to believe you're different so much. I can trust Jay; he's for real. But you're not, are you? You're the same as everyone else, and I'm the same idiot who fell for it." Jenna yelped. Her anguish reverberated down the empty hallway. "Why am I so stupid? I promised myself I'd never let this happen again. Never! But I let you in; I let you make me feel something. And now, here I am, fooled again. What is wrong with me?"

Jenna didn't wait for an answer. Bolting towards Jay, she slammed the paper against his chest and held it there. Jay touched her hand, his eyes pleading. Jenna shook her head. "Jay Hallett, you broke my heart." She spun around and ran. The paper fluttered to the floor.

Jay watched her flee, unable to breathe. He bent over, hands to his knees, gasping for air.

*Gavin put it on your computer? I thought—ugh! Gavin tricked me. It wasn't my—*Nicole cut herself off and pressed her lips together. *No, I'm not doing that anymore. This is my fault.* She braced for the floor to open, but nothing happened. She waited while Jay caught his breath. Nicole tapped the floor with her shoe. *Is there more?*

Jay spied the paper on the ground and

reached for it. When Jay flipped it over, he blanched. A cold sweat spread across Nicole's skin. Her memory flashed to what JayBot had said: "I know whatever Jay knows," and earlier this morning, more ominously, "I know your handwriting well, dear sister."

You knew. You knew it was me.

Jay stumbled back as though punched in the face. He slammed into the lockers, righted himself, and lurched closer to where Nicole stood in horror. Nicole pounded on the confining invisible walls and screamed.

Jay gripped the paper in both hands. He read what Nicole had written as quickly as she could, to jot down as much as she could, to hurt her brother as ruthlessly as she could. The sheet crinkled between Jay's fingers. He spoke with a quiet sorrow. "Nic? You wrote this?" His expression went blank, all emotion drained. "I didn't know you hated me."

No! No! Nicole slammed herself against the portal, again and again, her nerves blazing with every jolt, the physical pain folding into her torment. She lost all sense of place and time. Tears blurred her vision. The sharp tang of blood intensified her movements, thrashing with more power, more ferocity. Separate pains merged into one indistinguishable, all-encompassing agony, suffocating her screams, blistering deep within her.

Nicole lunged headfirst toward Jay,

accepting in advance the blow that would end it all. But instead of splattering her brains, the wall stretched. She found herself a breath away from Jay and reached for him, yanking him bodily into the air. Jay grabbed her back, and they floated, suspended between Jay's body in the hallway and Nicole's body in the portal.

"Can you hear me?" Nicole asked.

"Yes."

"I'm so sorry, Jay. I'm a terrible sister."

"Yeah. Even for you, that was shocking."

A force yanked them further apart. Jay's hand slid down to her wrist. Nicole clutched the nape of his neck. Her legs flailed as if a banner in a storm.

"We're out of time," Nicole said. "It's too late."

"It's never too late for us. That's the great thing about family. Whatever happens, we'll always be brother and sister."

The pull intensified again, causing Nicole to lose her grip and Jay's hand to slide off her wrist. Their fingers entangled, blanching under strain.

"I'm so sorry for everything," she said. "But listen, Phin is going to give you a choice."

"Oh. Yeah. That already happened."

"No! What did you—?"

Their fingertips snapped apart. Nicole launched back into the portal, trapped once more. Jay slammed into his body and shuddered as though snapping back from a daze. He crumpled the paper in his fist and stuffed it in his pocket. Jay noticed Jenna's open locker. Stepping over, he tossed a book inside and closed the door. His hand lingered on the locker door before he walked away. Nicole waited for the floor to give way. Nothing happened.

She remembered how Phin had warned her that stepping out of her comfort zone would shatter her worldview. What a talent he had to be a consummate liar and yet so accurately reveal the truth. His prediction described her perfectly: shattered.

Seconds passed. Nicole listened to Jay's footsteps fade. When the floor mercifully opened, she barely registered her fall.

CHAPTER 32

*"The finest lies come
home to roost."*

After realizing a tic too late that she had shot out
of the hole, Nicole struck the floor, simulating
the thwack insects make when they collide with
the goggles of a motorcyclist. Woozy from her
collision yet aware of the danger, Nicole reached
for the nearest hole. But the hole levitated,
avoiding capture. Nicole stared aghast at the
holes hovering above the carpet.

In a flash, the holes flew towards the
mirror. Her door sprang open, and a queue of
holes rounded the corner behind them. One by
one, they sliced into the mirror where Phin
stood, hands outstretched to collect them. Each
layered over the others until the final hole
entered. The door slammed shut. Clutching the
edge, Phin compacted the stack to the size of a

silver dollar. With a flourish, he produced a case from his pocket. Phin pressed a button, popping open the palm-sized box, and placed the tiny hole in its center.

Phin snapped the case shut with a finger. "You might think platinum or titanium would work best, but no. Only plastic can contain them." Tapping the box, Phin chuckled to himself. "Ah, plastic. Is there any limit to its usefulness?"

Nicole stood. She stepped forward, apprehensive and silent.

"Yes, of course, I'm well aware," Phin continued, waving a hand in the air as though he had stepped into a gnat swarm. "Plastic will disrupt every ecosystem on earth and hasten the collapse of humanity—blah, blah, blah—but you have to admit, it is *quite* handy." He slid the case into his pocket. "Worth it. Now then, where were we? Ah, yes! What an adventure you have had. I must say, Gavin is quite the charmer."

Nicole shook her head. "Gavin is a nightmare."

"A nightmare? Didn't you say he was dreamy?"

"I was wrong," she said.

"Wrong?" Phin chuckled. "No. Wrong is when you think Kansas City is the capital of Kansas. You, my dear, were catastrophically mistaken. Let's not mince words." Nicole stewed, and Phin bowed. "Enough pleasantries, I agree.

You've had an hour to mull it over. The time has come for you to make your decision, and we shall conclude our business. Do you chose Jay or the bot?"

Nicole realized she had been so focused on what Jay would do, she hadn't come to a decision. "JayBot is everything I wanted in a brother," Nicole reasoned. "At least everything I thought I wanted." Nicole stepped forward, head held high. "JayBot makes an excellent robot, but he isn't much of a brother. I choose Jay."

Phin remained impassive. "Is that so?"

"Yes, it is. I know this all started because I got angry at Jay. I know you came here because of me."

"You know?" Phin scoffed. "You know?" His eyes narrowed, focusing the gleam. Phin's abrupt anger terrified Nicole. She inched back.

"The sheer breadth of your knowledge could fit on a pin's head and leave enough elbow room for a coterie of dancing angels. No, my dear. As usual, you have it backward. I didn't come because of *anger* and I didn't come because of *you*. Jay caught my attention. More specifically, Jay's reaction to your treachery. When Jay realized what you had done to hurt him, he had every right to be angry. But—" Phin let the sentence dangle in the air as the condemned from a noose. A grin twitched between his lips. "—he wasn't. No, he blew past anger. His reaction was so much worse." Phin could no longer contain his excitement. The twitching spread down his torso and radiated to his limbs. His fingertips quivered when he pointed. "Jay gave up on you. He cut you from his heart. He severed the bond."

Nicole tensed. She understood what Phin was saying but refused to believe it. Had she lost? Had Phin tricked her again? When she spoke, her thin voice wobbled. "What did you do?"

"Me? Why nothing at all. I am but a passive force in life's grand spectacle. At most, I mop up the mayhem. As Jay said, it's already happened." His grin expanded, no longer restrained. "Oh, yes, I know all about your chat between parallel dimensions, my dear Nicole. You knew you weren't supposed to do that. The holes are view-only, remember? No editing!" Phin tsk-tsked with delight. "You created a colossal gash in space-time. *Terribly* irresponsible. *So* naughty. But fear not! After much exertion, I have mended the breach. Antimatter makes a marvelous epoxy. Truth be told, I use it all the time."

Phin brought his hand to his mouth to affect a dramatic aside. "In case you were wondering why so much antimatter has gone missing." He winked in slow motion, reminding Nicole of earlier this morning, the way Phin winked when he had first appeared on her screen. Back when he made her an offer she found enticing. When she had tossed Jay aside, never contemplating her action's consequences, the effect of her disregard for others. Nicole wished she could take it back. And not just today, gobs of it. Years.

"Another tragedy," Phin bemoaned. He swayed as he spoke as though bewitched by his melodic voice. "Another relationship stifled by the accumulation of petty annoyances, each minor grievance displacing another sliver of love until resentment expanded to suffocate you both. A moment to breathe may have helped, a moment to reflect on what is important and what is fleeting. Alas, we'll never know what might have been. All is lost. Jay has already chosen." Phin shifted his ill-fitting suit, pausing for dramatic effect. "He chose the bot. You have been discarded."

When Nicole gasped, Phin pressed a hand against his chest with stylized concern. "Do not be overspread with gloom. Certainly you saw this coming? You had predicted it." Nicole shook her head but in dismay, not disagreement. Tears streamed down both cheeks. "There, there. I understand," Phin said, drawing his words through a discordant blend of sympathy and farce. "When one is forsaken, the world looks dark indeed."

"I—" her voice cracked. She tried again. "I regret so many things."

"Inadvisable, my dear. Regret is but a half-potion of physic, making the patient sick and affecting nothing. You would do better to dose with humility. While equal in bitterness to regret, humility can at least affect a cure."

"What would you know about humility?" she barked. "You've been toying with me all day. You knew I was doomed, trapped in your sick game. Why even bother to put me through all this? Obviously, you have the power to do whatever you want."

The sparkle in Phin's eyes magnified tenfold. "I do have the power, as do you. Free will, my dear. I've told you time and again. You have it, yet you cannot relinquish it fast enough. *I had no choice*, as you like to say. This deflection is but a convenient fiction, a salve for passive minds. True, your choices may be poor, the inevitable consequence of previous poor choices heaped upon earlier reckless decisions cast atop a teetering tower of imprudent indiscretions. Be that as it may, you always have a choice. Several, if you'd hazard to extend the effort. But no, you'd rather blame me? So be it. Time and again, you squander the greatest gift life has given you. Had you dabbled with introspection, you might have noticed you have not asked for your brother back. Not once. The request hasn't crossed your mind." Phin's eyes gleamed. "What does that tell you?"

"I didn't know I could."

"You never asked."

"You never told me!"

Phin tented his eyebrows, heavy with

ersatz sorrow. "Lamentations of the lazy. You must do better."

"Fine. I'm a terrible sister." When Phin did not respond, she pressed on. "What? No snide comment?"

"If recognizing your failing as a sister is your attempt at epiphany, I'll hold out for your next revelation. You may well have concluded stars are hot and space is cold."

"Sure. You mock while I'm trapped in the most dangerous situation of my life."

"Yes, my dear. Your astute sense of calamity is most endearing but regretfully true." Phin swelled as a stage actor eager to deliver his favorite line in a play. "You are in imminent personal peril, precariously perched on the precipice of perdition. On the other hand, consider the positive. At least you had a snow day."

Despite her despair, Nicole felt a surge of joy when she remembered the snow day. Where all else had failed, it soothed her. "I do love snow days."

"Don't we all?" Phin agreed with a manic exuberance. "Such a marvelous opportunity to break from life's monotony, to dive off the hamster wheel into a snowy embankment and frolic in puffy jackets. I assume you've made the most of it?"

Sensing Phin was making fun of her again, Nicole sulked. "I would have if you hadn't shown up."

"Would you? Oh, do tell. What would you have done?"

Her cheer dwindled as she considered this. She would have spent the bulk of it on her phone, pumping up Brandi's fragile ego. Nicole no longer wanted anything more to do with that. If only she could go back to her life and do it better. If only she had Hannah to talk to again. And why had she allowed her relationship with Jay to deteriorate? Could she be upset with Jay for discarding her when she had effectively done the same to him years ago? How had she so completely lost touch with the essential people, those who truly loved her? *I wasted so much time and energy on shallow friends like Brandi.*

"You're thinking about Brandi, yes?" Phin raised his bulbous nose in the air as though to sniff out the scoop. "I believe you are, but it is difficult to tell. I get snippets here and there, always hazy and distant. In contrast to your brother—I can tell what Jay is thinking at any moment. He's a running commentary with his emotions floating on the surface, his thoughts as easy to skim as dead insects on a stagnant pond. But you, my dear Nicole, are unfathomable, submerged beneath the murky depths. You let no one get close except in brief spurts when you lower your guard."

Phin pressed his hands against his sides. As the finale hastened, he struggled to contain his excitement. "But Jay's choice was never really in doubt, only yours," he continued. "And even then, was it? When have you ever allowed Jay to get the better of you? What a shame you didn't know how Jay had selected before you made your decision. One might call it unfair." Phin paused to gauge her reaction. A grin tugged at his mouth. The seed planted, he gave it time to grow.

"Imagine if I came because you got angry at Jay? How absurd! If I visited every set of siblings who bickered, why, I'd have to visit them all! What a hassle. Not worth my time. Unlike this last hour." Phin kissed his fingertips and flicked open his hand as though a chef savoring his masterpiece. "Perfection. You did not disappoint. Oh, what a way to choose to spend your life's last hour! I must admit I did not think much of you when we met, but you've grown on me." A familiar reddish glow enveloped Nicole. "As mushrooms on a decaying log." A mist swirled up her legs. "The finest lies come home to roost."

Nicole gasped. She pressed close to the mirror, mouth open in terror. "No! This can't be the end. You showed me reflections of my past. You said there are as many of these as the future holds possibilities. So the future isn't fixed. That means I still have a chance!"

"Look at you," Phin positively purred. "Being observant. Paying attention. Who says you can't teach a new dog old tricks? Or however it goes. All terribly impressive, my dear."

"So the future has another possibility?"

"Possibility? I would call it an opportunity. Jay has chosen NicBot, as he likes to call her. He has discarded you for a new and improved sister, one who would never undermine him. Can you blame him? I couldn't. Maybe you could. But never fear, I have one last gift for you: the opportunity to amend your response. You didn't have all the information. You requested the full force of everything, and I failed to honor your wishes. We must rectify this injustice! As you know, I am exquisitely fair." Phin pressed his hands together and bent them towards her. "Please accept my sincerest apologies, my dear Nicole. I shall rescind your response and permit you to choose again. Do you pick Jay or the bot?"

A surge of excitement invigorated Nicole. She knew exactly how to take advantage of the opportunity. Except this time she wavered. *Why is this thrill so familiar?* She recognized her excitement as the same sensation that had lifted her when Gavin clued her in about how she could retaliate against Jay. After Gavin rejected her. The same thrill that had surged when she designed ways to push the other girls down to get ahead with Brandi. After Brandi made her feel awful. *I see the pattern. And I'm doing it again.* She noticed Phin's lips twitch to restrain his wicked grin.

Nicole knew what she needed to do.

"I've never felt in control," Nicole said. "Not just today, always. Other people take control, and

I react. You today, Brandi at school, Jay and my parents at home—I always do what I think people expect of me, what I've learned to expect of me. But never what *I* want." Nicole brushed her hair back. For the first time in a long time, she loved her wild curls.

"Watching myself from the portals, I kept wondering. Why would I do that? Why would I say that? And each time I remember: because I thought I had to. I did what others expected of me. Even when I knew it was wrong. Even when I knew I would regret it. But I am the thing I can control. I have free will. Not even you can take that away from me." She stepped closer to the mirror and spoke with a confidence that had eluded her for years. "I choose my brother."

Phin sighed the way pet lovers do after their dog entangles their lead around a shrub and whimpers. "Don't be daft."

"I choose my brother!"

A plume of smoke rose from Phin's hat. He appeared unaware, or at least unmoved. "You choose Jay even though he rejected you?"

She cringed. "That hurts, but I can't control Jay's actions, only my own. I know he cares about me. Even when he's a jerk, he still cares. And I care about him. I chose my brother."

The smoke thickened, blackening his hat. "You understand what this means. Jay will win, and you will lose."

"I think we both lost the moment we called

you, the moment we gave up on each other," Nicole said. "Those portals were a nightmare. I didn't like myself at all. I think I stopped liking myself a long time ago. I became this—" she searched for the right words "—other person. If I did what others expected of me, I no longer had to take responsibility for my actions. It would be everyone else's fault. But not really. I'm responsible for myself. My actions have consequences like you said."

Her tears flowed as Nicole accepted the consequences. "It may be too late to save myself, but it's not too late to like myself. I have to try. Whatever Jay has done is on him. I control what I do." Nicole wiped her tears and took a deep breath. Staring directly into his gleaming eyes, Nicole reveled in her newfound determination. "I want my brother back, faults and all. I choose Jay!"

Phin's hat exploded into flame. He looked up, finally noticing something amiss. Plucking a new hat from the air, he replaced the old with a swooping motion. Phin battered the scorched remains and flung it aside. His gleam fixed upon Nicole. "Do you believe I picked you two at random? Do you think I'm a rube, blundering blind, yielding to an arbitrary whim? Who do you think I am?"

Nicole didn't respond. She hadn't the slightest idea.

"I am the King of Kismet," Phin

proclaimed. He affected a regal pose. "Empires are specks of time I pick from my teeth. Worlds drop as pills of lint from my pocket. Yet you, young Nicole, dare to spurn your fate? What infinitesimal chance do you hold against the vast indifference of the universe?"

Nicole tried to back away, but a force cemented her feet to the floor. The air thickened. She pressed it with her fists. She expected to panic, but a calm swirled over her instead. "Maybe none," she answered. "Maybe it is hopeless. But I'm past worrying about what other people think or do. All it does is give them control. The best I can do is be the best version of myself. I choose Jay. That's me now."

"You now is the last waking moment of your entire life. With your last breath, will you allow Jay to beat you? Will you abandon your final opportunity to get him back? He replaces you, and you concede? Ludicrous. Not the Nicole I know."

"You didn't know me when I was a good person." She frowned. "I think I was, once. I've lost touch with what's important, but Jay has always looked out for me. It's time to step up, to be the person I want to be. So I choose Jay with all his faults. And I accept the consequences."

Like a gambler with a losing hand, Phin tipped his hat, magnanimous in defeat. "How refreshing. Such a shame the consequences are Jay winning and you having your atoms scattered throughout the cosmos. Might it be a tad late for scruples and ideals?"

"Jay said it's never too late."

"Ah, and wouldn't that be lovely? I'm afraid he was mistaken." The glow in his eyes deepened into a baneful crimson. "Everything ends, even wayward strands of time. And when judgment comes, as it does," Phin said, tapping his wrist, "your time is up."

The mist undulated the way a turbulent sea churns in a storm. Nicole swayed with the pull, her feet anchored to the floor.

"I'm scared," she said.

"You mustn't fear the end. You are born of stardust, and of stardust you shall become. So goes the great celestial dance." Phin bowed gracefully, maintaining his gaze. The roar of the waves intensified. "Farewell, Nicole," he shouted over the rising din. "I've enjoyed our time together." Phin pressed his face through the mirror. The glass fractured but held, amoeba-like, crackling as it stretched. When his lips reached her ear, he spoke his final words.

"You may be my favorite lost soul."

In a flash, Phin sprang back into the mirror, and the roar snapped into silence. A tingling flame blazed across Nicole's skin, popping connections atom by atom along the surface before plunging deep into her core. Nicole's breathing ceased and her heart quit beating.

An immense nothingness suffused the

air. Gravity abandoned its grasp. Nicole floated and spun, a stray satellite unmoored in the void, before compressing into a speck. Photons crystallized, emitting a kaleidoscope of color. The remaining matter vibrated and fragmented, entwining, dissolving, and ultimately collapsing into absolute darkness.

PART SIX

AFTERMATH

CHAPTER 33

*"Sometimes good people
do bad things."*

Once rematerialization had concluded its closing swoop, severed nerves conjoined to fire in unison. Nicole registered a piercing shock, forcing her eyes open. Reborn, she gasped for air. While her senses jelled, she labored to get her bearings. Blue cushions scrunched beneath her thighs. A familiar dog smell rose to her nostrils while she pinched fine dog hair shed atop the couch. The flat-screen TV loomed before her, mercifully black and silent.

Guess I'm not dead, Nicole thought. *That's odd*. But she didn't dwell on the subject for long. Nicole spied her phone—intact!—resting on the table and lunged for it.

The group text hailed her return with a notification of 271 messages. Familiar angst gripped her, rife as always with anxiety and self-doubt. Nicole fought the urge to follow her usual pattern, to dive back in and swallow the toxic emotional sludge. Instead, she swiped left and hit the trash button. Her phone, unconvinced, displayed an out: *Would you like to delete this conversation?* An inviting Cancel option offered one last opportunity to slide back. She tapped the Delete instead, banishing the group text. Relief washed away her dread.

But she had more to do. Much more! Nicole scrolled through her messages. Dates regressed. Her high school text record passed in a few flicks of her finger. She reached Hannah's name and hovered. *Here goes*, she thought.

Her last text to Hannah appeared, preserved for posterity: *Coming over now*, dated the day before Hannah's Bat Mitzvah. Following this was the last text from Hannah, dated two weeks later: *Are you really not going to talk to me?* Also preserved for posterity.

Nicole crumpled. She could do nothing to stop that devastating query from popping up once she texted Hannah. Nicole wished she could find a way to delete it off Hannah's phone. But no, Nicole was done with wishful thinking. She would have to own her past behavior. Honesty was her only way forward.

Nicole: I miss you so much and I'm so sorry about everything

Nicole: It's all is my fault
Nicole: Please forgive me

Nicole curbed her desire to add an emoji or two, remembering Hannah's baffling contempt for the cute cartoons. Nicole figured Hannah would take her time texting back, presuming she did. *However long it takes to repair the friendship*, Nicole pledged. She would not give up.

Her phone dinged, startling her, and she looked down.

Hannah: Who is this?

Nicole groaned. She knew she deserved it. *Time to eat crow and ask for seconds.*

Nicole: Your oldest and dearest friend who loves you
Nicole: The girl you once loved as a sister before she betrayed you
Nicole: Nic
Hannah: Where have you been?
Nicole: I fell down a rabbit hole
Nicole: Brandi Brandi Brandi Brandi Brandi Brandi
Nicole: but I'm back now
Nicole: if you'll have me
Hannah: I need time
Nicole: yeah
Nicole: as much as you need

Nicole: I'll be here

Nicole: BTW I also want to be friends with Keiko when you're ready

Nicole: She seems cool and you two make such a cute couple

Hannah: Nic?

Nicole: hi

Hannah: I missed you too

Hannah: still mad tho

Nicole: yeah

Nicole: don't blame you at all

Nicole: I've thought a lot about that day

Nicole: I could go on and on about how Brandi tricked me but you were my best friend and I should have trusted you and at least given you a chance to talk to me

Nicole: that's all on me

Nicole: I was so horrible I can't even

Nicole: so so so sorry about everything

Hannah: IDK how to respond

Hannah: Can I text you later?

Hannah: I have to process

Nicole: of course

Nicole: love you

Hannah: love you too

Nicole lit up at Hannah's last message and hugged her phone. A shaft of light had weaved its way through Hannah's impenetrable anger to warm Nicole's heart. At least until she became startled by a shuffling at the other end of the couch. Looking over, she saw Jay. Was it Jay? She couldn't be certain.

Nicole stood and stuffed her phone in her pocket. He also stood. She stepped closer, and he did the same. They stared at each other.

"Jay?" she asked.

"Hello, dear sister. How may I be of assistance?"

Nicole leaped back. "No! I want Jay! I said I wanted *Jay*! Phin, what have you—" Her panic melted into chagrin as Nicole recognized Jay's dopey gotcha smirk.

Jay chuckled. "Just messing with you. Wow, Nic, I had you going."

Nicole toggled between profound relief and the desire to smack him in the head. Before she could decide, Nicole had wrapped her arms around her brother. Then she pulled back and thumped him with both fists. "Jerk."

"It was funny."

"You had me going there," Nicole said. "Stupid Phin. Hey, how did you know I wasn't NicBot?"

"The way you snatched your phone off the table? No way."

"Fine. So you sat there the whole time waiting to pull off your little joke?"

"No," Jay said. "I sat there the whole time you texted and thought, *damn, has nothing changed?*"

"Everything's changed. I was texting

Hannah, not Brandi."

"Hannah?" Jay smiled. "I remember her. Good. I like Hannah."

"You like her?"

"Not like that. Anyway, I don't think Hannah is into boys."

Nicole drooped. "Why does everyone know this but me? I suck."

"Hey, don't insult my sister. Only *I* get to say how much she sucks." Jay leaned in. "You don't suck but you do need to pay better attention."

"I know. So, um, thanks for choosing me over NicBot. Phin told me you didn't."

"Yeah, Phin pulled that same garbage with me," Jay said. "When he told me you chose JayBot over me, I laughed in his face. I told Phin he was a lying twit and why don't you buy a tailored suit that actually fits you and ditch the old-timey hat and get a toupee if you want to cover your bald noodle. Then he gagged me with mist and shattered my atoms, and I'm like, *oops, I may have overplayed my hand*. But I suppose Phin has his morals, warped as they are, because he kept his word. I hate to admit it, but for a moment there I thought we were goners."

"I was sure of it."

"And yet here we are, still alive," Jay said. "So tell me, what did you say when Phin told you I picked NicBot? Did you tell him off?"

Mortified, Nicole forced out the truth. "No.

I believed him."

"What? Why? Everything he said was a lie."

"Not everything."

"Hold up. Who did you choose?

Nicole harrumphed. "You, you big jerk." Jay stared open-mouthed and Nicole huffed. "What? Say something. Right, I know. You think I'm stupid."

"No, I'm impressed. You thought I didn't choose you but you chose me anyway? Holy effing crap. That is some next-level absolution." Jay whistled. "I didn't know you had it in you."

"I don't think I did until today. The third option Phin gave me were holes, those portal things. That's how I connected with you but also how I connected with my past. The holes forced me to see all the ways I've hurt the people I love. But I learned how to control where they sent me, and I went to your past. I saw Gavin and Amaya and Jenna and you. The holes exposed all the lies I told myself, all the things I held true, or at least the things I wanted to believe. So yes, when Phin told me you chose NicBot, I believed him. Because I didn't blame you. I wouldn't have chosen me either. Jay, I'm so sorry."

"I know. Hey, don't cry. Sometimes good people do bad things. Dad said that. I think he's right. You can never change what you've done, but you can always be a better person."

"Yeah," Nicole agreed and wiped her eyes.

"That's why I chose you. I was devastated when I thought you tossed me aside, but I knew you didn't deserve the same fate. If I was going to die, I wanted to die being a good person."

Jay touched her shoulders, much the same way JayBot had earlier. "Wow. I have to say, Nic. You are my absolute favorite sister in the entire universe."

"I'm your only sister."

He dropped his hands. "Let's not ruin the moment."

"Fine. Jay, I'm—" Nicole turned away, ashamed. She forced herself to look Jay in the eye before continuing. "I'm sorry for what I did."

"Thanks. And I'm sorry I stopped wanting to talk to you."

"What I did was worse."

"Definitely," Jay agreed. "Way worse. Like, way *way* worse. But giving up on someone? Also pretty bad."

Nicole stuck her hand out. "I swear I will never intentionally hurt you again. And you swear to never give up on me."

"Deal," Jay said and shook her hand. "But that's not everything."

"No?"

"No. You also hurt Jenna."

Nicole dropped his hand and plopped down on the couch. "I know. I know I did. I feel terrible. Should I text her?"

Jay also sat. "I'd rather you didn't."

"What then, call her?"

"Don't be a psycho," Jay said, contorting his face.

"Then I don't know how—oh!" Nicole sat up. "Take a video."

"A video?"

"On your phone. You can send it when you think she's ready."

Jay considered it. "That's not a bad idea. Are you sure?"

"Yes. How has Jenna reacted so far?"

"You mean since yesterday?

"Obviously since yesterday." When Jay didn't respond, Nicole gasped. "Wait, you haven't texted her? Not since yesterday? Ugh, *boys*. So your plan is to ignore her?"

"I'm not ignoring her."

"How is she supposed to know? Don't be passive."

"I'm not passive."

"You have to do something!"

"I am doing something. I'm giving her time." Jay cringed when he realized what he had said. "Why am I quoting Dad? Oh, no!" The horror on Jay's face struck Nicole as grimly familiar. "I'm like Dad."

Nicole nodded. "Been there."

CHAPTER 34

*"I don't want to be
that girl anymore."*

"Are you sure Jenna even wants me to text her?"
Jay asked.

Nicole sighed. If her smart brother could be
this dense, what hope remained for the rest of
boy-kind?

"I mean," Jay continued, "I don't think you
know—"

"Don't know what, Jay? Girls? Romance? I
saw the way Jenna looked at you. She wants you
to win her back. The absolute worst thing you
can do now is to ignore her. It will confirm her
worst fears." She gripped his arm. "Jay, no one
wants you to give up on them. I'm an expert on
that."

"Yeah, all right. You've convinced me." Jay
pulled out his phone. "Let's record your video

first."

Nicole shifted on the couch. "Give me a sec." She considered what she could say to make things right. Was there anything? Hannah and Jay knew her for years, but who was Nicole to Jenna? A horrible mean girl. And meaner still if she didn't do something about it. Nicole smoothed her hair back. "Go ahead."

Jay started recording and pointed to her.

"Hi, Jenna. It's Nic. Um, I'm so sorry I—" Her voice trailed off. Nicole stared at the phone while tears streamed down her cheeks. After a prolonged silence, Jay asked her if she wanted to start over. She shook her head and wiped her eyes. "No, keep recording." After a few breaths, Nicole continued.

"When Gavin dropped me for a prettier friend, I was devastated. And when I found out Jay had something to do with it, I was furious. I wanted to get even. I didn't realize at the time how bad Gavin was or how he had tricked me." Nicole raised her hand. "But the truth is I wanted to hurt Jay and didn't care who else I hurt to do it. I didn't think about your feelings at all. I'm sorry, Jenna. I said terrible things." Nicole's voice caught. "I know what I said about you isn't true. And even if it was, I still shouldn't have said it. I don't want to be that girl anymore."

Nicole leaned closer to the phone. "What I said about Jay isn't true either. Jay is exactly who you think he is. He's honest and sweet. Well, *sometimes* he's sweet but he always looks out for me, even when I don't realize it. Your instincts were right, Jenna. You can trust yourself. Jay is for real. Please don't dump him because of me." A smile emerged. "Now, if you want to dump Jay, do it because he can be an arrogant know-it-all. That's a good reason."

"Nice."

"But please don't do it because of what I did or the stupid, hurtful things I said when I was angry. I can be horrible when I get angry. Insensitive and mean. Nasty. Hurtful. Vindictive." Nicole tugged on her hair. "Stop me any time, Jay."

"Nah. You're doing fine."

"See what I mean." Nicole laughed through her tears. "Jay's a big jerk, but I love him. I hope you accept my apology. If you're going to date him, you're going to see more of me. Because Jay and I are going to hang out more, right?"

"Definitely," Jay agreed.

"Do you mean it?"

"Yes." Nicole looked at Jay, tears glistening. "I'm stopping this," Jay said. He tapped the icon.

Nicole collapsed back on the couch. She pressed her hands against her face before dropping them to her sides. "I'm a mess."

"Matches your hair."

"Wow, really?"

Jay smiled. "I'm joking with you."

"Yeah, I know." Nicole smiled back. "So

we're going to hang out? What are we going to do together?"

"I don't know. We can play laser tag. I hear you're a good shot."

"Laser tag? Do you mean paintball?"

"No. *No* paintball."

"Chill, bro." Nicole moved next to Jay and pointed to his phone. "Text Jenna already and stop being such a lame boyfriend."

"I'll try, but I am pretty lame."

"Yeah, I noticed. Good thing you have me to help you."

Jay tapped his phone. "Yup."

Jay: Sorry it took me so long to reach out to you

Jay: Nic and I needed time to work stuff out
Jay: Are we good?

"We'll see how long it takes her to—oh, there she goes." Jay and Nicole watched the dot-dot-dot. Dot-dot-dot. Dot-dot-dot.

Jenna: Sorry I stormed off
Jenna: I believe you
Jenna: but I'm still scared once you get to know me better you won't want to be my friend
Jay: "Dear friend, whoever you are, here, take this kiss, I give it especially to you"
Jay: Walt Whitman

"That's so romantic!" Nicole gushed. "And pretty random."

"It's not random. Jenna and I talked about a different Whitman poem before. I told her about the time we went to the Walt Whitman House."

"Oh, yeah!" Nicole laughed. "I remember. The day we searched for four-leaf clovers. Me and my big brother." Her voice caught.

"Are you getting all sappy again?"

Nicole spoke through her tears, "I miss him so much."

"I am literally right here."

"No," Nicole said, waving him off. "I mean, I miss *us* so much."

Jay exhaled. "Yeah."

The dot-dot-dot appeared, soon to be replaced by three heart emojis.

Jenna: OMG did he actually write that?

Jenna: I'm crying again but mostly because you're not here and I want to hug you so much

Jenna: and do other things

Jenna: Are you going to come by again tomorrow?

Jay: You know I will

Jay: unless another snow day but then as soon as I can

Jay: It's the highlight of my day

Nicole covered her mouth. "I didn't know

you could be so romantic."

"Only with Jenna."

"You two are so sweet. I'm sorry, Jay. I thought—" Nicole squeezed her eyes shut. She flopped back on the couch and stared at the ceiling before looking back at Jay. "I was wrong about so many things."

"Speaking of which." Jay jiggled his phone. "Are you ready for me to send it?"

"Go ahead."

Jay: Nic asked me to send you this video apology

Jay: I'm also really sorry you got pulled into this

"And sent," Jay said, tapping the arrow.

Nicole sucked in air, her face twisting with apprehension. Knowing she had to wait to see how Jenna would respond filled her with anxiety. Nicole pulled out her phone but didn't turn it on. Holding it gave her comfort. She strained her neck to see Jay's phone. "Did she write anything yet?"

"Come on. Jenna has to watch the thing. And, you know, react to your very intense video."

"Ugh," Nicole said impatiently. She jammed her phone back into her pocket and stared at the blank TV screen. After a moment, her thoughts turned to Jay, and she snickered. "Who knew? My brother quotes poetry."

"Let it go."

"You've always had a thing for quotes."

"Absolutely," Jay agreed. "As much as anything, our quotes define us. And not just poets and famous people. Everybody, you and me. Take our conversation before lunch."

"I'd rather we forgot about that."

"No, hang on. When you said *you act like you're so superior*, I knew you were quoting Gavin because he is obsessed with winning. He has to beat everybody at any cost because he needs to believe he's better than everyone. And when you talked about dating Gavin and asked *when is it my turn?* I finally understood your resentment and your insecurity. Until then, I could not figure out why you'd want to get mixed up with Gavin. Do you see? Quotes give us insight into who we are and how we think. Meaningful quotes pop up all the time."

"Yeah," Nicole said. "I remember you saying *the truth is complicated*, and it stuck with me. It made me start to think that there might be more to what Amaya and Jenna went through with Gavin than I understood. And why you went to such extremes to keep Gavin away from me." Nicole nodded sharply. "Thank you, by the way."

"You're welcome."

"That was so disturbing." Nicole shuddered. "Especially the thing with Jenna. I mean, why would any boy want his girlfriend to do that?"

"They wouldn't, but Gavin is different. It's not about the sex with him. Gavin gets off on power and humiliation. He usually goes for more sexually innocent girls. Jenna is sex-positive so I guess he found a different way. I'm just relieved you're safe."

"*I* am but that's not enough!" Nicole's sudden outburst startled her brother. "Come on, Jay. I'm glad you helped *me*, but this isn't over. Why don't guys get it? If your sister doesn't deserve abuse from a guy like Gavin, why does any girl deserve it?"

"I mean—no, I get it."

"I know you don't like Brandi," Nicole said. "I'm also not a big fan of hers right now, but she doesn't deserve it either. No one does. And Gavin will keep doing horrible things if no one calls him out."

"I mean, yeah. But Amaya was scared if she said anything Gavin would hurt her even more, and Jenna is nowhere near emotionally ready."

"I didn't mean just them. It's not fair to put all the responsibility on the victims. This is on all of us. Everybody needs to speak out or nothing will change."

"Yeah, you're right," Jay said. "But what are you going to do?"

"I'll start by talking to Brandi."

Jay cringed. "I mean, really, Nic? Do you think Brandi's going to listen? Especially considering she thinks she stole him from you?"

"Doesn't matter," Nicole said. She sat up, energized. "Brandi needs to know Gavin's a sexual predator."

"Right, but how do you think it will go over? Brandi will be furious. She'll assume you're jealous, that you're trying to get in her way. Who knows what she might do to get you back."

"That might happen but I have to try." Nicole pressed her lips together. "It's the right thing to do. Whatever the consequences, I have to—why are you grinning?"

"You're going through exactly what I went through. The same conflict, the same worry. And you came to the same decision I did." Jay smiled. "You're like me."

Nicole smiled back. "I don't mind being like you. My brother is pretty awesome."

Jay's phone dinged. "Jenna responded."

"Oooh! What did she say?"

Jay held his phone so Nicole could see it. "Smiling face with tear emoji."

Nicole rested her head on her brother's shoulder. "Me too."

AUTHOR'S NOTE

When my children were little, they detested school assignments to write stories. Any effort to share my love of writing was summarily rejected. In their young minds, creative writing was a Draconian torture akin to getting your teeth drilled or losing Wi-Fi for an hour.

Clearly this required a diversionary tactic, so I created a flash fiction game. With the use of a writing prompt, we would each write a quick fifty-word first paragraph of a story and read our tale to the group for our mutual amusement. We used the same prompt and maintained absolute freedom to take our creation in whatever direction we fancied.

After a few months, my insidious plan triumphed. My children learned to enjoy writing. I didn't realize it until later, but this silly game would have the unexpected perk of forming the nidus of the novel you just read.

The writing prompt in question: CALL NOW

My oldest (then aged twelve) told the tale of Weird Old Man Bob, ignored by the townsfolk until hit by a train. This created a sinister force that would make the townsfolk pay "the ultimate price!" Andrew took great pleasure in writing himself into a corner, knowing full well he only had to write the first paragraph. Big brain!

My youngest (then aged ten) wrote a story about Joe McJoerson Jr., arctic explorer, who escaped on a spaceship moments before Russia nuked the earth five quadrillion times, becoming the world's last survivor. Approximately half of Maddie's stories ended in the destruction of the planet. Not sure if I should be worried about this. Moving on.

My paragraph involved a mysterious infomercial that offered an embittered girl the exciting opportunity to replace her annoying brother with a better one.

From the original fifty words, I expanded my story in both character and scope over many years of tinkering. When I began the process, my children had entered an implacable period of sibling rivalry. Were this a Hollywood production, I would describe the situation as Cain and Abel meet the Boleyn sisters. No joke. Well, yes, a bit of a joke, but my point remains. We're talking scary bad.

As the months turned to years with no armistice in sight, positions entrenched and siblicide looming on the horizon, my children inexplicably shifted from hating each other to tolerating each other's company to best buds for life. To this day, I have yet to decode the alchemy behind their relationship's rapid transmutation.

Or maybe it's a reflection of my superb parenting skills. Really, who's to say?

With the impetus for the book adrift, the idea languished until a new focus on forgiveness and redemption heralded me back into the world of Nic, Jay, and Phin. This is the powerful perk of independent authorship: free reign to type atop whatever shifting tectonic emotions compel me.

So here we are. After a mere seven years and almost as many iterations, my story coalesced into *The Finest Lies*. I hope you have enjoyed reading it as much as I have creating it.

ACKNOWLEDGEME NT

I wish to thank my children, Andrew and Maddie, whose familial love is an inspiration for siblings everywhere. And my dear sisters, Beverly and Heidi, who never argued or fought with me or each other to even the slightest degree during the entirety of our childhood. I'm almost positive that's accurate. I mean, no one can prove otherwise because back then we didn't document or record every aspect of our lives. Ah, the anonymity of the technologically embryonic past! Good times.

Thanks to Amy Betz for her insightful developmental editing and for pushing me to capture an authentic voice and elevate the story. Also thanks to Damonza for the striking cover art.

Special shout out to Walt Whitman, quoted twice in the book. Growing up, I went to Walt Whitman High School, shopped at the Walt Whitman Mall, and saw movies at the (now defunct) Whitman Theater. I'd like to think he'd be cool with me borrowing a couple of verses for my story. I mean, we practically grew up together. Whitman writes, "Take freely, Take without end--I offer them to you wherever your feet can carry you or your eyes reach." It's like he insists! Poetry is so delightfully ambiguous.

Thanks also to Mr. Phineas Taylor Barnum and his wonderful autobiography, *The Life of P. T. Barnum Written by Himself*. Searching for a charismatic but devious rascal in American history, I hardly needed to look any further than Mr. Barnum. His stunning breadth of peculiarities (or the ebullition of eccentricities, as my Phin would say) provided a rich chasm to mine. I suspect he would not object to a facsimile being brought back in print for a limited engagement.

Thanks as always to my readers, whose interest and support keep me going. Especially to those precious few who provide honest feedback in the form of reader reviews on Amazon, Goodreads, blogs, etc. Yes, I do read them. No, I don't take them personally. Have at it.

And as always to my wife, Joyce. No doubt there is some alternate universe bumping around the cosmos where we never meet, where I muddle through the protracted melancholy knowing that I am lacking in some essential factor. I feel sad for that me and always blessed that this me gets to share his life with you.

ABOUT THE AUTHOR

David J. Naiman

 David J. Naiman is a best-selling independent author of award-winning books for children, teens, and adults including JAKE, LUCID DREAMER, first place winner of the Purple Dragonfly Book Award and the Moonbeam Children's Book Awards in pre-teen fiction and DIDN'T GET FRAZZLED, humorous medical fiction written under the pen name David Z Hirsch. He is also a successful physician specializing in internal medicine and an unsuccessful speller specializing in vowels that sound identical to other vowels. He lives with his wife and two children in Maryland. Visit him at www.davidjnaiman.wordpress.com

BOOKS BY THIS AUTHOR

Jake, Lucid Dreamer

"A fantastical tale with a powerful message" raves SPR.

2018 Purple Dragonfly Book Award First Place winner for Middle Grade fiction
2018 Moonbeam Children's Book Awards Gold Medal Winner for Pre-teen fiction - Mature Issues
2018 International Book Award Silver Medal Winner Readers' Favorite for Coming of Age
2018 Finalist for The Wishing Shelf Book Awards and Quarter Finalist for the BookLife Prize

12-year-old Jake has been suppressing his heartbreak over the loss of his mother for the past four years. But his emotions have a way of haunting his dreams and bubbling to the surface when he least expects it. When Jake learns how to take control in his dreams, he becomes a lucid dreamer, and that's when the battle really heats up.

Using his wits to dodge bullies by day and a nefarious kangaroo hopping ever closer by night, Jake learns about loss, bravery, the power of love, and how you cannot fully heal until you face your greatest fear. This uncompromising novel is a magical yet honest exploration of emotional healing after a devastating loss.

Didn't Get Frazzled

"...the best fictional portrayal of med school since ER." – BlueInk Review (starred)

2017 International Book Award Bronze Medal Winner Readers' Favorite (Fiction - Humor/ Comedy)
2016 INDIES Book of the Year Award Finalist (Humor)

Medical student Seth Levine faces escalating stress and gallows humor as he struggles with the collapse of his romantic relationships and all preconceived notions of what it means to be a doctor. It doesn't take long before he realizes not getting frazzled is the least of his problems.

Seth encounters a med student so arrogant he boasts that he'll eat any cadaver part he can't name, an instructor so dedicated she tests the student's ability to perform a gynecological exam on herself, and a woman so captivating that Seth will do whatever it takes to make her laugh, including regale her with a story about a diagnostic squabble over an erection.

Didn't Get Frazzled captures with distressing accuracy the gauntlet idealistic medical students must face to secure an MD and, against the odds, come out of it a better human being.